The Hand Of God

A Homewold Novel

Eric S. Brown & Jason Cordova

SEVERED PRESS

The Hand Of God

www.severedpress.com

ISBN: 978-1-925225-75-4

Prologue

Saul had only wanted a drink.

Months passed between his visits to the spaceport at Caltus. He always told himself that he shouldn't be there, that he knew better than to come to the port. The port wasn't for his kind, but he needed to see people, to hear their inane banter and feel their overbearing presence to know that life continued on. It kept him sane, chased away the dark thoughts and memories of a life that he was desperately trying to forget.

He lived in the barren wastelands on New Mars that the terraformers of the Republic had failed to make fully compatible for human life. Sure, one could survive there in the heat and desert sands, but one could not actually *thrive* in such an environment. His home was nothing more than a simple shack by even the barest of modern standards, but was miles from the faintest edges of civilization, and more importantly, the headaches which came with it. His only neighbors were the random desert critters who had been imported from Earth long before, the winds, which blew constantly during the day, and the blistering cold of the desert night. It sucked the soul out of a man, leaving a void filled with bitterness and sorrow.

These reasons, along with the need for supplies, are what drove Saul to visit Caltus once every few months. He lived a solitaire life, boring, even if a small part of him secretly wished for the hectic, adventurous lifestyle of the Order. Back before everything had gone bad, before the Lord Protector had taken control and turned everything upside down. Before the power had corrupted everything which had been pure about the Order. Before his kind had become hunted and hated by all.

A clawed hand grabbed his shoulder, jarring him from his bleak memories. He sighed.

He had only wanted a drink.

Saul fingered the tiny cross, which hung from his neck and whispered a prayer for forgiveness, as well as one for the being touching him. The Darian repeated his comment, the cat-like alien hissing his syllables annoyingly in Saul's ear.

"I said, your kind isn't welcome here, priest."

The cat's companions yowled with laughter and jeered, egging their apparent leader on.

"Please unhand me," Saul said, his voice calm and flat. The grip on his shoulder tightened. Claws extended and pierced his thick coat, though not quite yet his skin. Saul tried again. "I don't want any trouble with you or your people. I want to sit here alone and have a drink in peace."

Saul felt the mood of the Darians change subtly and he moved, faster than expected. The Darian grasping his should howled in pain as his claws, still stuck in Saul's thick coat, were yanked hard. Saul's coat fell off, and spinning in his seat, he twisted the Darian's arm behind the cat's back. The cat, shocked, dropped to one knee as Saul applied pressure to the stuck claws. He pressed his knee into its back for leverage.

It had taken less than a second. Saul, still seated, grabbed his drink with his free hand and downed the rest of it. He had a feeling that the empty glass might come in handy, plus it would be remiss to waste good beer. He cocked an eyebrow and looked at the Darian's companions, who were now staring at him in shock and anger.

"I said I didn't want any trouble," Saul reiterated. One of the Darians hissed, exposing his needle-like fangs.

"I thought you priests didn't drink?" The cat growled at him. Saul shrugged.

"Whether you want trouble of not, priest, you're going to get it," the Darian that he held promised. "Get him!"

The Darians rushed him as a group, something that caught him by surprise for half of a moment. He reached out and slammed the edge of his hand into the throat of the Darian he was holding before shoving the cat towards its companions with his knee. The Darian stumbled into his friends, coughing and gasping, slowing their approach. It gave Saul precious seconds, seconds he used wisely.

He sprang out of his seat and used his temporary advantage, his foot lashing out and catching one of the Darians square in the privates. The cat's hackles rose along its neck and it dropped to the floor, mewling in pain. He barely dodged a swipe from the third Darian, the enhanced speed of the aliens on full display. Against a normal human being, the blow would have torn half their face off.

Saul, though, was far from normal.

He grabbed the Darian that had swung at him and spun him around, using the cat's momentum against him. The Darian was off-balance long enough for Saul to slam its face into his knee. The Darian staggered back, dizzy. Saul stepped inside the alien's reach and jabbed into the soft belly with a closed fist. He followed with another punch to the chest of the Darian, and then he smashed the back of his elbow into the temple of the cat. It dropped like a felled ox.

The last of the four went for its sword, which hung from a strap on its belt. As the razor sharp blade cleared the scabbard, Saul grabbed the leg of the stool he had been sitting on mere moments before. He whipped it across his body and slammed it against the Darian's head. The stool exploded upon impact, showering the bar with bit of debris and Darian blood. The alien staggered under the blow but stayed upright. Saul moved in, alternating jabs to the cat's face until the Darian fell, sword falling from the cat's grasp. Saul kicked it aside. He moved atop the creature and began to slam his heavy fists into its face, trying to drive them into the floor beneath them.

Sharp claws grabbed the back of his neck and drew blood. The first Darian, the one that had started the entire conflict, was back on his feet and livid. Saul had a half moment to curse himself for not watching his back before he felt the claws of the Darian dig deeper into his flesh. He swung Saul around like a doll and smashed him into the bar. Stunned, Saul reached out and grabbed the nearest object he could find. His hands closed around his empty glass. He pivoted and swung his fist, glass in hand. It connected with the lead Darian's face and shattered. The Darian stumbled back a step and Saul dropped into a crouch, the shattered remains of the glass still in his hand.

The loud ratcheting of a shotgun shell into the chamber interrupted their fight. The Darian, claws extended and mere inches from Saul's throat, paused. Saul, a single muscle twitch away from changing the sex of the Darian with his broken glass, stopped as well. He looked up and found himself staring down the absurdly long shotgun barrel that Willy, the bar's owner, usually kept hung over the bar on display. A smaller pistol was held in the proprietor's other hand and was pressed against the Darian's head.

"How'd you ratchet that round, Willy?" Saul asked, a slight quiver in his tone. It was the only indication of the adrenaline, which pumped furiously through his arteries, hormones raging as his heart struggled to keep up with the endorphins that now flooded his entire nervous system.

"Trade secret," the gruff old bartender growled. "That's enough out of you. Both of you. Hell, all of you."

"I'll slit your throat, human," the Darian promised, though its eyes were locked onto Willy.

"I believe in spaying and neutering your pets," Saul retorted.

Willy waggled his shotgun. Both combatants knew what the old barkeep meant.

Saul slowly withdrew his broken glass from the Darian's tender region, while the cat itself took a cautious step backwards, retracting its claws in the process. The Darian hissed at Willy, who cocked the lever of the flechette pistol back.

"Don't piss me off any more than I already am, kitty," Willy warned it. The Darian hissed again, its ears flattened against its skull, but it backed away further. "Now git. And take your friends with you."

The Darian nodded and backed away a few more feet. He began to help his gasping companions to their feet. Working together, they dragged their still-unconscious friend out the door of the bar and into the street.

Saul dropped the broken glass and slowly raised his hands. The barkeeper sighed and kicked the broken glass away from Saul.

"Saul, if you keep doing this, I'm going to have to ask you to not come back."

Saul's shoulders slumped slightly. "I didn't start it, Willy."

"You never do, Saul," Will reminded him. "That's not even the point."

"I'm good for the damages. You know I am," Saul tried to reassure the bar's owner.

"That doesn't matter, either," Willy said as he looked around his partially trashed bar. "Take a seat. I'll have one of the girls clean up."

Saul moved to one of the few surviving chairs and sat down, resting his elbows on the edge of the bar. He watched the mirror situated behind the bar but nobody approached.

Willy moved back behind the bar and slid the pistol beneath the counter. The shotgun went back to its resting place above the bar. Grabbing a bottle of something clear, Willy grabbed two shot glasses and set them down on the marble surface of the bar. He carefully poured two shots and slid one to Saul. Picking the other up, he offered a salute before downing the liquid in one quick swallow. Saul followed suit, gasping as the unfamiliar alcohol burned his throat. It rested lightly in his belly, the warmth spreading to his fingers almost immediately. He sighed contentedly.

"Look, I know that you're not a priest anymore," Willy began as he poured two more shots. "I also know that you're going through a bit of a rough patch right now, but I can't put up with this anymore. That cross of yours makes you a target to every heathen, die-hard patriot and alien that steps foot into this place. Anybody who has a grudge against the Order is going to have an issue with you. You know this, don't you?"

"I'm not in the Order anymore, Willy. Remember?"

"Hock! No matter what you claim in public, Saul, folks look at you and see only one thing. You've got God in your heart, and folk see that as a threat. The things the Order did before the Republic shut it down... they're unforgiveable sins, pal." Willy slid

5

the second shot over. They downed the alcohol in unison and set the glasses down.

"Salut," Saul grunted. "That was the evil in the hearts of men that made them do those things, Willy. Not the work of God."

"Don't matter much what it was that caused it, Saul. It's enough to keep bringing trouble into my bar," Willy paused before he reached for a cold bottle of beer. He grabbed it, popped the top and slid the bottle across the bar to Saul, who graciously accepted it. "I've known you for a long time now, a very long time. You've got your stuff mostly sorted, but you're gonna have to find another place to do the rest. I'm going to go bankrupt from your visits, and the constant brawls chase away my patrons."

Saul nodded in understanding. "I'm sorry, Willy. I'll miss your company. More importantly, your beer."

"Aw, hell," Willy shook his grizzled mane. "I'll give you one more shot. You owe me for the damages here today, though."

Saul took a swig from the beer. It was clean, refreshing. So very unlike the planet, he now called home. He gave Willy an apologetic look.

"I just wanted a drink."

Chapter One

As wars went, it was an odd way for one to begin.

The ERS *Serinus* drifted carefully through the outlying asteroid belt of the Retina system, hidden in the umbra created by the system's seventh planet. She was a lithe vessel, lightly armored with overpowered engines, designed to escape conflict and observe, not engage the enemy. Equipped with the latest sensor platform and stealth technology, she was perfectly designed for her current tasking.

Captain Darius Jaynes sat in his command chair, struggling to stay awake. He yawned, took a sip of his lukewarm coffee and grimaced as his stomach gurgled in protest. He knew he needed to cut back on the coffee, but since the Retina duty station was practically exile for Earth Republic Naval commanders, the medical orders of a man fifty thousand light-years away could be temporarily set aside for the sake of the mission. *Besides,* he thought as he downed another swallow of the brew, *it's vanilla flavored. That counts for something, right?*

He lifted his gaze back to the view screen, trying to make out Earth's sun amongst the billions of stars in the galaxy. He knew it was a futile gesture without the aid of the ship's navigational system, but he still liked to challenge himself. Except for his daily workout regimen in his quarters, he had little else to distract him from the tediousness of day to day life. His looked about the command bridge and took stock of his crew.

Ensign Emelio Thomas was at the helm controls in front of his position, and Lieutenant Lara Alison was tasked to the comm station on his right. Both young, but both very good at their jobs. He saw that Thomas was manually plotting the next course change while running a simulated scenario confirming his math. Jaynes nodded, impressed. *That kid's going places*, he thought with no small amount of pride. Rarely was a recon ship blessed with a mathematical prodigy, and the ensign was humble about it to boot.

Alison was bored, Jaynes could tell from how she was slumped over her console. Only so many times could one recycle the relays of the comm station before it became an exercise in redundancy. He watched her surreptitiously switch back to the small game of mahjong she was playing against the computer. He thought about saying something but stopped, hiding a small smile. He remembered his own days at the comm station and knew that morale, already low, could break if he cracked down on his bridge crew. *That's Detrik's job, in any case.*

Detrik Ryshnova. Jaynes shook his head at the thought of his brand new State Security Officer. Every Earth Republic ship had one to ensure that the technological secrets of the republic stayed safe, as well as the loyalty of the crew remained firm. Disliked by the rest of the crew of the *Serinus*, Detrik kept to himself and did his duty, which was precisely the way Jaynes had always envisioned how an SSO to be. He was somewhere on the ship, lurking, being his usual anti-social self. Detrik didn't play favorites among the crew, unlike other any other SSO Jaynes had dealt with in the past, so his presence was tolerated by the ship's CO. It still did not mean that Jaynes had to like the diminutive man, though.

The sensor station was unmanned, as was weapons. Chief Pulliman had called Ensign Malik Clark away to engineering a few hours before to help with the realignment of the ship's cloaking system, while Lieutenant Xia was off duty. The weapons system was not very important on a recon ship, so periodically, the controls were slaved to the ship's programming while the weapon's officer was away from their station, set to automatically respond once the ship was actually attacked. The sensor station was vital though, so Clark had transferred control to the captain's chair before he had left for engineering.

The *Serinus* had been drifting in the system for weeks without sign of any of the Republic's many enemies, which was to be expected by any captain assigned to the distant posting. While there was the slim chance that the Ra'tids could try to sneak into the Republic's backdoor via the Retina system, they still had to cross Gener space to do so. Despite all their bluster at the latest round of diplomatic talks, the rock-like aliens featured a navy that was barely half the size of the Republic's, and their technology wasn't much better. Compared to the mysterious alien Geners, the Ra'tids were still in rocket-propelled capsules armed with slingshots. Nobody thought that the Rocks would risk war with the Geners just to attack the Republic.

Still, their claims of coming aggression against their own system, coupled with how the war between the Coalition and the Earth Republic had gone, even the densest politician could see that the Rocks were nervous. Nervous enemies made for paranoid bureaucrats, and paranoid bureaucrats made life miserable for the Admiralty. Jaynes mentally grumbled as he looked back at the sensor display *"Since crap rolls downhill..."* but he left that thought unfinished. The war with the Coalition had already cost them much, and vowing to never be caught unprepared again, the Republic was taking the sudden Ra'tid threat seriously.

Even if the best ship the Rocks could throw at the Republic was an armed junker with FTL capabilities and a small nuke.

Jaynes thought back to the recent past, one that he – like his fellow senior Navy officers – was trying to come to grips with. Countless millions had died during the final battle for Earth. Jaynes had been serving aboard the ERS *Phoenix*, a *Shoshone*-class destroyer, which had been assigned to protect Earth at all costs. It had been the largest naval battle ever fought by humanity, by sea or space. It had left both fleets shattered and broken, with barely enough personnel to keep the surviving ships in geosynchronous orbit afterwards. As bad as the space battle had been though, Jaynes knew that it had been nothing when compared to the carnage wrought upon the surface of mankind's birthplace.

The veteran Republic army had been off world, out in the distant frontier attacking the Coalition. The attack on Earth had been a surprise, a move that had shocked and stunned the

Republic, as the maneuver was far different from the usual smash mouth tactics favored by the Coalition. They had taken Mars almost without resistance, and instead of consolidating their victory on the red planet, rapidly pushed for Earth, which was hideously unprepared.

Green troopers, straight out of boot with their uniforms still ironed and fresh, had formed up into squads and promptly died as soon as they entered combat. Men and women who were beyond the normal age of duty had fought tooth and nail to protect their homes and families from the invaders, only to be dragged from their homes by Coalition troops and executed like criminals. Veteran officers, recalled from the front and desperately plugged into command positions in the line, had struggled to form defensive positions with their new recruits and paid the ultimate price.

Jaynes remember well the screams and chaos, which had flooded the *Phoenix*'s comm channels that day. He dreamt of their voices, imagined their faces. If preventing something like that from happening again meant sitting in the middle of nowhere in a tiny ship with little to do but watch the stars, then Jaynes was more than willing to do that. He felt a distinct honor in it, even if the Retina system was far away from the rest of the Republic Navy.

The sensors chirped suddenly, but then quieted down almost as quickly. Puzzled, Jaynes reached over and punched a few buttons on his chair. The sensor data rolled up on his view screen, the stars fading as the information began to trickle down. He read the data and waited a moment for the computer to spit out what had triggered the sensor.

Gravitational Anomaly Detected

Jaynes blinked. *What the hell is a gravitational anomaly?* He punched another button on his chair.

"Clark," Jaynes called through the intercom.

"Sir?" Clark responded back almost immediately.

"Report to the bridge. Tell the Chief to hurry up with that realignment."

"Problems, Captain?" Clark asked, his voice tinged with worry.

"I don't think so," Jaynes paused, his brow furrowed as he

stared at the sensor display. "But... I want you to double-check something for me. Sensor's wonky, and I need you to take a look at it."

"Cloak's back online in any case, Captain," Clark reported. "Be there in five."

"Good. Captain out."

Minutes later, Clark was back on the bridge, in his customary position at the sensor station. The young Ensign began to run a diagnostic program. His deft fingers flew across the board with practiced ease. A few seconds later, he clucked his tongue in annoyance.

"Problem?" Jaynes asked. He had been watching Clark work, the small gnawing feeling in his gut unrelated to his coffee. Something was wrong, but damned if he could put his finger on it.

"Stupid program is picking up the gravity wells of the larger asteroids in the belt, sir," Clark explained. Jaynes exhaled softly.

"Programming issue?" He asked.

"Looks that way, sir."

"Fix it."

"Yes sir," Clark replied. He cocked his head, as more data streamed own his screen. He frowned before looking back over his shoulder. "Captain, I–"

Something slammed into the ship, cutting the ensign off and throwing everyone sideways. Belted into his chair, Jaynes was protected from the kinetic energy of whatever had hit them. Lieutenant Alison, however, was not so lucky. Caught unprepared and not belted into her seat, she was vaulted across the bridge and slammed violently into the bulkhead. Her body landed in a crumpled heap on the deck, her blood smeared down the bulkhead and pooling beneath her rapidly cooling body. Jaynes didn't need a corpsman to tell him that his comm officer was already dead.

Impact alarms began to blare.

"Report!" He shouted.

"Something hit us, sir!" Clark replied.

"I figured that part out on my own, Ensign! *What* hit us?"

"No idea, sir!"

"Damage control? Chief?" Jaynes called into the comm. He slapped the alarm silent so he could hear the chief down in the depths of the ship, where engineering lay.

"Venting air in the starboard C-frame, Captain," his chief engineer called back seconds later. "I had one life sign in there, but it's gone now. I think it was Lieutenant Xia."

"Damn," Jaynes swore softly. "What about the SSO?"

"That bastard Detrik? No idea, sir."

"Find out if he's dead. Seal off the C-frame before we vent too much air. We have a casualty up here as well."

"Damnation, I'll get on it, Captain. Engineering out."

Jaynes grunted and killed the comm. He refused to look at the still form of Lieutenant Alison, instead focusing his anger and shock on trying to figure out just what had happened.

"Moving us out of the Belt, sir," Thomas said as he began to activate the ship's drive.

"Belay that, Ensign!" Jaynes ordered.

"Sir?"

"I want to know what that was before I run home to the barn," Jaynes said as he took over the weapons station from his chair. "Clark, give me something."

"Nothing, sir," Clark's frustration was evident in his tone. "There's nothing there– wait."

"What is it?" Jaynes asked.

"Sir, the computer is picking up another one of those gravitational anomalies again," Clark grunted. "Could be that the larger asteroids are getting close to us."

"Impossible, sir," Thomas interjected hotly. "I ran those numbers multiple times. We weren't scheduled for a course alteration for another eight hours."

"Well, *something* happened!" Clark shot back. "There's nothing on the sensors–"

The *Serinus* shuddered as pieces of a larger asteroid nearby bounced off the hull. Jaynes brought up the sensor screen on his chair and frowned as he glanced over what Ensign Clark was looking at.

"Damn it, we can't see anything," Jaynes nearly shouted in frustration. "Bring up the view screen."

The sensor data disappeared for a moment from the view screen. Jaynes watched as the space around them was displayed on the screen. Blood drained from his face as he saw what sat a mere hundred thousand kilometers from their position.

"What the hell...?" he whispered, horrified. "Magnify."

The Ra'tid ship – it could only be a Ra'tid, with the rocky outcroppings on the design, creating a misshapen form – was larger than the largest of the Republic's super dreadnaughts. The view screen zoomed in on the ship and Jaynes felt his hand tremble as he punched in a few buttons. The small box beneath his seat whirred to life, recording all information that the ship was now seeing upon the screen.

The bow of the giant vessel was pointed, though angled poorly, and was diamond shaped. The composite nature of the Ra'tid and their technology made designing a ship difficult for them, and the beast before the *Serinus* was something that the Republic had thought the aliens were incapable of. It was angular and ugly, but deadly in shape and form. Small holes on the port and starboard side of the bow indicated tubes for missiles, while Jaynes could only guess what sort of beam weapons the ship featured. The aft of the Ra'tid ship glowed brightly in space, the engines running hot. It was approaching the system's star, which meant that their next destination would be the Weligo Terminus.

It was not alone. Four more ships, identical in design and size, flanked the vessel.

"Is our cloak still up?" Jaynes whispered. Without waiting for a reply, he glanced at the data readout. He saw that it was up and functioning at 90% efficiency, which meant that the ship was supposed to be virtually undetectable. To the universe, they were nothing more than a black hole.

Then how did they know we're here?

Jaynes knew, as every captain of a recon ship did, that a fight was the last thing they wanted. Armed with only four CKs – capital killers – and no beam weaponry, they would not last long against any ship larger than a cruiser. The Ra'tid ship's *engines* were bigger than a cruiser, so Jaynes knew that even a lucky shot from his CKs would be for naught.

Instinct screamed for him to run, but years of training told him to stay. The Ra'tids might not know where the *Serinus* was exactly. A lucky shot had could have struck them, or perhaps they had simply started shooting at the asteroid belt.

Target practice? Jaynes frowned, but knew that the idea wasn't too farfetched. Earth Republic ships had done the same thing in the past.

"Sensor's still have nothing, sir," Clark told him. His voice cracked as he broke the oppressive silence on the bridge. "The computer insists that nothing is out there."

"If the eyes lied," Jaynes said in a soft voice, "then I'd believe it, but my eyes do not lie. Do yours, Ensign?"

"No sir. Picking up another gravitational anomaly warning, sir," Clark announced. His eyes left the sensor screen as he looked back up at the view screen. A bright flash erupted from one of the holes near the bow of the Ra'tid ship, and a missile streaked out from ship. Jaynes looked back at his sensors.

Nothing. The computers continued to say that there was nothing out there. No ships, no missiles, no threat. His hands shook harder as icy tendrils of fear clutched at his heart. He knew what this meant for him, for the Republic. The Ra'tids had, somehow, figured out stealth technology and crossed Gener space. They had built ships more powerful than Earth Republic super dreadnaughts. They were coming for the Republic, and there was nobody in position to stop them.

"Thomas, map out a trajectory course for that missile," Jaynes ordered.

"Sir, the computers can't see it," Thomas protested.

"Use that big brain of yours then," Jaynes growled dangerously. Thomas swallowed nervously and nodded. He punched in numbers into the computer, eyes flicking rapidly between the view screen and the smaller screen at his station.

"Got a guesstimate, sir," Thomas announced four seconds later. "It's not targeting us."

"Asteroids?" Jaynes asked as he breathed a small sigh of relief.

"No sir," Thomas dashed their hopes. "Looks to be headed about four thousand kilometers from the asteroid belt, fourteen degrees above zero plane. Not sure, but... sir, are we alone out here?"

"Why do you–" Jaynes started to ask but stopped as a massive explosion lit up the bridge. Something flickered into view and the sensors of the *Serinus* suddenly went nuts as another Republic recon ship appeared. He stared at the ship as it broke apart, the damage from the Ra'tid missile obvious even from the distance. A few fires flared out from escaping oxygen of the hull, and the engines of the recon ship began to fire randomly. Jaynes knew what was next, and he the gnawing fear he had felt earlier in his stomach and his heart was now crystallized into form.

The fuel cells within the other recon ship breached, sending a bright blue light across space as the fuel reached critical mass. The explosion scattered the remnants of the new recon ship across the system. The resulting shockwave that followed was mild compared to the earlier damage the *Serinus* had been hit with. Nevertheless, it was enough to remind Jaynes that seven fellow sailors had just lost their lives. It washed over them, rocking the ship slightly but causing no further damage.

"Another recon ship?" Thomas asked, shocked as he watched the dying light of the now-dead recon ship. He glanced back at his computer. "IFF says it's the *Coronus*. Was. Oh God."

"Makes sense to have more than one recon ship out here," Jaynes murmured, his eyes still locked onto the screen. "Thomas, plot a course out of this asteroid belt and away from the Weligo Terminus."

"*Away*, sir?" Thomas asked.

"Yes, Ensign. Away," Jaynes responded. "Preparing a Final Dispatch now. You... you boys want to send messages out to your families?"

"Orphan, sir," Thomas replied instantly. Jaynes looked at Clark, who shook his head.

"Thomas, prepare to fire main thrusters," Jaynes said. "On my mark. Clark, keep an eye on the view screen. I doubt the computers are going to be able to identify anything inbound at this point."

"How're the Rocks doing it, sir?" Clark asked.

"Best guess? They're using organic warheads, or some low-density material. Maybe silicon? True stealth? Hard to say. Ready on my mark?"

"Ready, sir," Thomas replied.

"Full thrusters in three, two, one, mark!"

The *Serinus* roared to life, accelerating out of the asteroid belt and into open space. The lead Ra'tid vessel turned, matching their angle and trying to cut off their retreat. Jaynes chewed on his lip as the ship accelerated rapidly.

"One minute to void space, Captain," Thomas announced, hope in his voice. "We might make it out yet."

"Multiple launches from the lead Rock ship, sir," Clark said as he continued to watch the enemy ship onscreen. "I'm counting a dozen– no, two dozen. Wait, no. I've got fifty, now... crap. Sir, I can't keep track of all these missiles."

"ETA til impact?"

"I can't do it all at once, sir!" Thomas screamed in protest, sweat dripping down his face as he frantically punched numbers into the computer. "Forty seconds to void space. Missiles... I just don't know!"

"We're not going to make it," Jaynes whispered as he watched the streaking missiles cut the corner and fly to intercept his escape trajectory. He punched in a command into his chair console. "Firing off the Final Dispatch now." The ship shuddered slightly as the dispatch probe shot out of the hull and into space, angling towards the Weligo Terminus. It disappeared into void space immediately after. Jaynes sighed. At least somebody would now know what had happened to them, and to the *Coronus*. He leaned back in his chair and watched the screen. "Gentlemen, it's been an honor to serve with you."

"Godspeed, sir," Clark said as the first missile tore into the metallic hull of the *Serinus*. Five more of the Ra'tid missiles impacted milliseconds later, tearing the once-proud Republic ship apart at the seams.

Captain Darius Jaynes' last thought was that he had failed his crew, his ship, and his Republic.

*****

Lieutenant Robert Paige was the midwatch officer aboard the Weligo Terminus, the massive space station situated near the Haldus system. He loved the midnight to eight watch, and made a point to request the shift whenever possible. His skills at traffic control and direction were above average for an officer of his rank, and he prided himself that for his time in service, he was already more skilled at his duty than most others. He knew that he was destined for more, but with the new commanding officer still settling in and his yearly evaluation incomplete before the death of the terminus' previous CO, he was forced to wait for his advancement. He had no other options.

Captain Wightman's death had come as a surprise to all. He had been only fifty-six standard years old, a young man to die so suddenly, the stroke cutting short a promising life far too early. Medical science could have saved him had he received medical assistance immediately, but the stroke had caught him in bed, asleep. It had been a quick and painless death, the Chief Medical Officer had insisted.

The change in command had been swift due to logistics. Lacking a warship CO in the immediate vicinity, the Admiralty decided to move a grounded Naval officer to the terminus as a temporary solution. Commander Lionel Berkman had been the next ranking officer on the terminus, but was too inexperienced for the job, having just transferred in himself. Lieutenant Paige didn't know why the new CO had been grounded, or why she was still there after the battle for Earth, since senior officers were in short supply now, but was thankful that his new commanding officer mostly listened to his suggestions.

Captain Hsi Stoko was adjusting to the frantic pace of life aboard the terminus, but she was only human. The Weligo Terminus handled all hypervoid travel for the entire Sigma sector, and dumping an unprepared Naval officer into the chaotic surroundings of life on a terminus was almost unfair. Especially when the officer was merely a quick fix and not a permanent solution to a long-term problem. Dozens of military and commercial vessels required passage through hypervoid space, which required diligent, organized guidance. In addition to the problems of being a terminus, Weligo was *huge*, requiring a crew the same size of a Republic super dreadnaught. Even on the best of days, Weligo Terminus was a challenging and nigh impossible duty station. Lieutenant Paige used the chaos to his advantage.

The midwatch was much slower paced than the regular shifts. Only high priority vessels, such as warships or emergency responders, were allowed to transit the terminus after the midwatch began. A skeleton crew, under Lieutenant Paige's command most times, ran the midwatch from Central Control, located near the center of the terminus. Oftentimes, it was nearly deserted and the Officer of the Watch had absolute authority on the terminus. Which gave Lieutenant Paige almost as much power as the new CO, and as luck would have it, the night was already shaping up to be a nice one.

No vessels needed immediate passage through the Terminus, content on waiting for the following day to transit the wormhole. This left Central almost abandoned, save for the lieutenant and a few bored souls. Paige was leaning back in his comfortable chair and daydreaming of sandy beaches, scantily clad women and ice-cold margaritas. He had many plans for his next shore leave, most of which included random women and much alcohol consumed. He had saved the past six months of his pay up, and hadn't used any of his accrued leave in over two years, and he planned on hitting the white beaches of Senga and blowing all his cash in one fell swoop. It would be the greatest time of his young life.

So caught up in his daydreams (oh, how amazing that cold margarita would taste upon his lips!) that he almost missed the Priority One message that suddenly appeared on the comm screen. He scowled and looked around; hoping someone else would answer it. His hopes were realized when one of the sensor technicians, Wataski, checked the screens and began to input commands into his terminal. Paige closed his eyes and leaned back, visions of bikinis dancing in his head.

"Sir, I have a Priority One FLASH message," the sensor tech interrupted his daydreams. Paige grumbled and straightened his chair, letting his feet rest on the metal desk of the Central Command once more.

"Damn skiffs," he grumbled. It was probably some rich playboy with daddy's yacht lost in an asteroid belt who needed rescuing, which would require him to file paperwork. Reams of paperwork, as well as a full SITREP for his relief, who was due in approximately two hours. In addition, explaining to the Admiralty how a pricey yacht ended up at the wrong end of the wormhole. He hated extra paperwork, feared the heavy hand of the Admiralty, and for a moment, he almost considered passing the buck off to the next shift.

No, he decided. *I want to get promoted. This'll look good on my record, a rescue op of some sort.*

"Whadya got, Wataski?" Paige leaned forward and brought up the message on his screen.

"Emergency message pod, sir," the tech replied instantly. "Blasting on all encrypted frequencies, coming in hot. ETA through wormhole is ten seconds."

Paige whistled. That was *fast*, even for an emergency pod. The only pods that traversed the wormhole at those speeds were–

"Oh hell," Paige muttered under his breath. "Wataski, lock down that pod. As soon as it's through, shut down the general broadcast and bring it in. *Nobody* else hears this thing but us. Got it?"

"Uh, yes sir," Wataski was confused but knew how to follow orders. Paige stood up and began to pace along the command deck, waiting for the pod to drop out of voidspace. The tech looked back at him. "Coming through now, sir."

"Channel it through our systems, route the message through to my station and nobody else's," Paige ordered as the pod blinked into existence. The tech did as he was told and Paige sat back down in his seat. He began to read the message. His face paled as blood drained from it. *Impossible*, he thought as he read it a second time.

"Sir?" Wataski asked. Paige held up a hand, telling the tech to wait as he read the message again.

"It's a Final Dispatch," the lieutenant whispered, unable to believe what he had just read. "From the *Serinus*."

"Captain Jaynes' ship?" the tech asked, recalling the vessel instantly. It wasn't often that a recon ship passed through the Terminus while cloaked, which had caused some good natured humor on the command deck when the stealth ship had been forced to decloak momentarily to transit.

"Oh, my God..." Paige looked at the vid that had been part of the Final Dispatch. Streaming vid, plus stills of giant... were those ships?

"Sir?"

"What navy ships are waiting for daytime transit?"

"Uh, one moment, sir," Wataski said as he flipped through his logs. "I've got the *Poe* and the *Ticonderoga*, both heavy cruisers, and the *Potemkin*, a battleship. All part of the Eighth Fleet, sir.

"Set Condition One throughout the station," Paige instructed him. "On standby for now. Get on the horn with the CO of the battle group. Tell him we're setting Condition One throughout the Terminus. Relay the message from the *Serinus* to him and wait for a reply. I'll wake the Captain."

"Yes sir," Wataski responded instantly. He switched the comm for the entire Terminus over to his station, where every man and woman would be able to hear. "General Quarters, General Quarters! All hands, man your battle stations. Set Condition One-Zebra throughout the station. This is not a drill. I repeat, General Quarters, General Quarters! Set Condition One-Zebra."

"What the hell are you doing, Lieutenant?" an angry voice demanded. Lieutenant Dera, the Communications Officer of the Terminus, stalked onto the bridge. Her hair was pulled back in a tight ponytail, giving her angular features a rather severe effect, and her uniform was immaculate. Once more, he wondered if the witch ever slept. Dera gave him a pointed look. "One-Zebra? Imminent attack? What the hell is going on here? Did you fall asleep again and have a bad dream?"

"A Ra'tid battle fleet just popped into the Retina system and destroyed two recon ships," he responded, temper flaring as he turned and stared down his fellow officer. "The *Serinus* and the *Coronus*. They may or may not be moving for Earth, which means they could be moving in for *us*. I've got to wake the Captain. Since you're here, Lieutenant, you have the deck."

"I have the deck, aye," she affirmed, surprise evident upon her face as she followed the order. Paige whirled and quickly exited the command deck, pleased. *That'll put the fear of God into her*, he thought grimly. His thoughts turned back to the potential Ra'tid attack. *The Rocks must be feeling pretty cocky to think about open warfare with us.*

A groggy and disorientated Captain Stoko stumbled from the

lift and onto the command deck, her uniform disheveled. Paige recognized the confusion, exhaustion and simmering anger on her normally placid features. She saw his approach and directed her fury towards the Officer of the Watch. He swallowed nervously and stopped in his tracks, bracing himself to attention. "What the hell is going on, Lieutenant? Sitrep?"

"A Ra'tid fleet entered the Retina system, ma'am, approximately ninety standard minutes ago, according to the Final Dispatch we received from the *Serinus*. The Ra'tid fleet hit her and the *Coronus*, destroying both vessels. It's unclear how they spotted the recon ships at this time, or how they even managed to sneak up on them in the first place," Paige reported in a hurried rush. He took a deep breath and continued. "I placed the Terminus on Condition One, but on standby for the moment. We have three ships on their way to rejoin the Eighth Fleet waiting for the morning transit. I've notified them of the situation and warned them of imminent action."

"Holy Mother of God!" Stoko gasped. She rubbed her eyes and nodded at the younger man. "Good work, Lieutenant. Fire off a pod through the Terminus to Earth with a copy of all the data we received. Leave nothing out. Request fleet support ASAP. In the meantime, let's set up a comm call with the CO of that battle group out there, along with his captains. If the Ra'tids come before our support arrives, we'll most definitely need to be on the same defense plan."

"Yes ma'am," Paige acknowledged her order and went to work, doing his best to make them happen. His perfectly boring night had just turned into something far more exciting that he had anticipated, and for the first time, he regretted his request for the midwatch.

Chapter Two

President Alexander Ryan followed his military escort into the oversized briefing room. A large table dominated the otherwise plain room, with chairs lining both sides. His escorts split into two groups, with two of the guards on each side of the room. They stopped and turned on their heels, facing towards the table. The only other men in the room stood to greet their commander in chief. The President eyed his two most senior military commanders in the room as he walked around to the head of the table. His Secretary of Defense, Mikhail Gustav, followed close behind. They waited for the President to sit before they followed suit.

Ryan's gaze drifted over all of the men and women in the room, a casual laziness that fooled none of the men in the room. He was a shrewd poker player, and his features almost never wavered, no matter what the news. It had fooled his opponents during the past election, allowing him to glide into the presidency as the others tore one another apart. He used it now, even knowing that it did not fool all of the men in the room. One did not awaken the President of the Earth Republic over trivial matters, however, and he could feel the tension and nervous energy in the room.

High Fleet Admiral Cho Hien's face was flushed with a combination of anger, anxiety and fear. The President had seen that look on many of his opponents when they were forced to deal with the unexpected. Already wary from the sudden and unexpected interruption of his sleep, he could nearly hear the alarm bells screaming in his head. His opposite, General Joel Soltas, was a stoic man with a darker complexion. It was difficult for Ryan to judge the highest ranking general in the Earth Republic Army on his best day, and sleep deprived, the President was not off to a good start.

"Gentlemen," he began, his elbows resting on the edge of the table. "Ladies. What, may I ask is so urgent that you had the Presidential Guard drag me out of my bed, force my SecDef to fly in from out of town, and not even bring me any coffee at this ungodly hour?"

Admiral Hien's face had changed again, the President noticed. It was now a mask of burning hatred, nothing hidden, his soul bared for all to see. Ryan sincerely hoped that the anger was not directed at him. He would hate to lose such a quality officer to suicide by Presidential Guard.

"Around twenty-one hundred hours yesterday, local time, a Ra'tid battle fleet invaded the Retina system," Hien said, his voice low and dangerous. Ryan nodded, encouraging his senior admiral to continue. "They engaged two recon ships we had in-system: the *Serinus*, and the *Coronus*. All hands on both ships were lost. Neither ship managed to get a shot off with the CKs. Not that it would have mattered, judging from the dispatch."

"I'm sorry, you said around twenty-one hundred hours, correct? Why the rough estimate? Did we not get a Final Dispatch from either ship?" Ryan asked as his mind raced, figuring the implications – militarily and politically – of the Ra'tid attack. With the Retina system compromised, it meant that the Weligo Terminus would be next. From there, it was a short hop to Earth, with nothing to stand in the way. The Mars defense network was still shattered from the Coalition's attack, and the Republic Navy was still limping along, picking up the scattered and broken pieces. His own party was suffering from being caught unawares by the invasion from the Coalition, and he was aware of the ugly rumors of impeachment. The War Powers Act, though, mitigated most of the damage until the conflict was at an end. The rumors still made him wary, though. Other than impeachment, the word a President feared most was coup. The air in the room suddenly felt stifling to the man who had carried the last election in a landslide.

"The *Serinus* fired off her Final Dispatch, sir," General Soltas said. "The Admiral has to guess, however, because it appears that the Navy somehow missed their entry into the system."

"The captain of the *Serinus* did not 'miss' it, damn it!" Hien exploded, slamming a fist down against the table. A few Navy officers jumped at their boss' sudden outburst. "They were never on their sensors. The *Serinus* had no idea they were there for some reason!"

"Lord help us," Ryan breathed. "Are you suggesting they have stealth tech?"

"It gets better, sir," Soltas grunted. He looked at Hien. "Tell him."

"The Rocks were able to see the recon ships, Mister President," Hien said, his anger bottled now but still simmering. Ryan's face paled.

"Do we know how?" he asked. *Impossible*, he thought. *We can't even find the damned recon ships. It's why we stole the tech from the Coalition in the first place!*

"Not at this time, sir, no," Hien admitted. "Sir, what we thought might happen is happening. The Ra'tids are taking advantage of our recent war, and with our navy barely at twenty percent of our normal operational capacity, are making a move for the Retina system."

"Why?" Ryan asked, but he already knew.

The Ra'tids hated the Darians. It was a long-standing feud spanning centuries, a conflict which had been red-hot before mankind had reached for the stars. It had only intensified during the split between the Republic and the Coalition, though it had cooled somewhat since the Coalition's push for Earth. Now, though, with the Republic allied with the Darians, whose borders practically surrounded the Rocks, it drove the Ra'tids into threatening their most hated enemy's new ally.

"Our new policy of lending military support to assist the Darians with border security in exchange for their assistance in reclaiming Earth from the Coalition was the last straw," Soltas stated, confirming what Ryan had already guessed. "They've never been happy with how fast and far we've spread throughout the galaxy. Humanity, sir, not just the Republic. Xenophobic little bastards. If you want my opinion, Mister President, it's amazing they even waited this long before making a move."

"I concur, sir," his Secretary of Defense said as he rubbed his face in his hands. "I wish Marty were here. State Department is up on the situation better than we are. They understand the Rocks, sort of. A little. Maybe less than that. Sorry."

"The only thing that kept them from doing this sooner was our sheer numbers, sir," Hien said as he motioned for a junior officer – a Captain, the president noted – to slide his data pad down to him. Hien punched in a few keys before handing the device over to the president. Ryan glanced down and watched the star map of the Republic appear on the screen. A second later, it lifted off the screen and hovered above the pad, fully three dimensional. Hien jabbed a finger at a small cluster of stars near the edge of Republic space. "That's Retina, sir." He dragged a finger across the tinted space, which marked the Republic boundaries. Inside the line, an occasional blue blip appeared, signifying a Republic Navy battlegroup. Ryan immediately recognized the problem, but Hien explained anyway. "As you can see, sir, we're already stretched pretty thin as is. We barely have enough ships to patrol our borders against the Coalition, much less supply the Darians with enough vessels to hold up our end of the deal. Yeah, okay, the Coalition suffered as much as we did during the Battle of Earth, possibly more. But was it enough? Is it going to take them as long as us to rebuild? We have no indication or suggestion that it will."

"However, the Ra'tids haven't had a major naval engagement in fifteen months, and that was a mop-up operation against an old Darian outpost. Their ships are in top shape, and if these new designs are as dangerous as they appeared in Retina–"

"Wait," the President interrupted. "What do you mean? What new design?"

"I'm sorry, Mister President," Soltas said, bobbing his head. "Forgot about that last bit. The Rocks have a new ship, five of them actually, possibly more, all as large as or bigger than a super dreadnaught. Not only do these new ships not show up on sensors, their missiles don't either."

"Beam weapons?" he asked. Blank looks from around the

table were more than a reply. The president sighed and looked back over at his oldest friend. "Mikhail, talk to me. How did they get this tech?"

"You've got me, sir. Could the Coalition have sold it to them?" the Secretary asked. Admiral Hien shook his head.

"The Rocks distrust the Coalition," the admiral reminded him. "They may hate us, but to them, humanity as a whole is not to be trusted." Hien reached over and tapped the screen of the pad. It switched over to the vid recordings and images the *Serinus* had captured before it had been obliterated from existence. The room fell quiet as the jagged monstrosities appeared above the table.

"Jesus..." the President swore under his breath. Angular, rocky and with little symmetry, the hulking Ra'tid ships appeared to be the same length as a super dreadnaught. However, Ryan immediately spotted something that terrified him more. He jabbed a finger at the lead Ra'tid ship. "It looks like the same length as a super dreadnaught, correct?"

"Yes sir," Soltas nodded.

"It looks like its mass is double though."

"NAVINT thinks so, too," Hien admitted, thinking back to his own briefing from a disheveled Naval Intelligence officer twenty minutes before. "Which means that it can take a pounding, assuming we can even shoot at the damned thing. It'll close on our ships, sir. Get in knife fighting range and rip us to shreds. No more skulking about for the Ra'tids. They're for real now."

President Ryan nodded slowly, his mind screaming in protest even as he stared at the Ra'tid ship. "Do we know if the Rocks just got clever and copied our super dreadnaught design, or did anyone else have a hand in this?"

"We can cross off the Coalition from the list of suspects," Hien said as he frowned. "Once the Rocks are done with us and the Darians, the Coalition is probably their next target. That said, though, the Coalition has not been known to think long-term in their planning. They could have assisted the Rocks with their 'Great Leap Forward', tech wise. If the Ra'tids used up these new ships in a war against us and the Darians, then the Geners would be the only resistance to Coalition control of all explored space." Hien stopped and cocked his head. "I must admit, I'd pay a little bit of money to see that fight."

Something about that comment tickled the back of President Ryan's mind. "I see," he said. He didn't see, not really, but he knew he had to appear that he understood. He was a politician, like his father before him. He knew exactly how the game was played. He could only pretend to grasp all the military implications of what the admiral had said.

"We've dispatched a squadron from First Fleet, all we can spare, to support the forces at the Weligo Terminus. Captain Hsi Stoko is in command of the Terminus, and Captain Mike Wellington of the ERS *Buchanan* will be her second for Order of Battle," Hien told the assembled body. "Captain Stoko has a good head on her shoulders, despite past events. The primary goal of the battle group will be to hold the Terminus at all costs. The success of their mission, I'm afraid to say, rests mostly on whether this new Ra'tid super dreadnaught can dish out enough punishment. In the meantime, Mister President, Military Command requests that the Senate declare a state of war with the Ra'tid Empire, and that we begin preparing a counterstrike against Ra Prime."

"You want to hit their home world like the Coalition did with us?" Ryan asked.

"Unlike the other powers in the known universe, the Ra'tids don't have a true star empire," General Soltus interjected. "They possess a few scattered planets and industrial outposts. If Ra Prime fell, their ability to fight any sort of sustained war falls off dramatically. Granted, I also want contingency plans prepared, just in case."

"Can we, though?" the defense secretary asked. "I thought you said that we barely had enough ships to patrol our own borders."

"These new super dreadnaughts aside, Mister Secretary, their fleet is small. Dangerous under the right circumstances, yes, but still small. They simply don't have the resources to bulk up their numbers, nor do they have the population to do so either," Admiral Hien reminded the group. "We can, more than likely, overwhelm them with sheer numbers, if we're willing to take that risk. It's better than sitting back and letting them come into Republic territory, forcing us into a defensive stance. For once, sir, I'd like to hit back. Hard."

"The only issue is that we don't have the manpower to actually *hold* Ra Prime, Mister President," Soltus said. "Admiral Hien is correct, though. We could destroy it."

"You're talking about genocide, General," Ryan pointed out. "The destruction of an entire alien race."

"Us or them, sir," the Defense Secretary reminded him. "If we let them continue to attack us with impunity on their terms, then we are sending a loud message to our enemies and allies alike. If those super dreadnaughts of theirs get into Earth space, there'll be nothing but a molten, ruined rock left after they're done with us. Billions dead, sir. *Billions*. Do you want that on your conscience?"

"Plus, with the way our fleet is spread out, the likelihood of them doing just that is higher than even I want to think about, Mister President," Hien lowered his head. He continued in a voice barely above a whisper. "The Republic isn't the military giant we were before the Coalition claimed their independence and turned on us."

"I'll need some time to consider all options," Ryan said.

"We don't have enough time for that, Mister President," Soltus shook his head. "That's why we called this emergency meeting. We need to know if we have your approval, so we can mobilize in preparation for when Senate approves your *casus belli* and votes for war. If the Rocks take Weligo Terminus, we've pretty much lost the war before it begins. It's the only launching point close enough to Ra Prime to mount an operation of the size and magnitude which we're proposing."

Ryan rubbed his chin, then his unshaven cheeks. After a moment of contemplation, he nodded. "The War Powers Act gives me authorization for limited operations in a military capacity without seeking a declaration of war from the Senate. I'll have Marty draft a resolution and present it at an emergency session of Senate in two hours. Meanwhile, I'm authorizing the battle group you've assembled at the Terminus to strike back at the Rocks at Retina, Admiral. General, put together something and have it ready for me to sign off on as soon as the Senate votes in favor. I'll strong arm this through if I have to, but I doubt there'll be a need for that."

"Thank you, sir," Hien smiled, visions of a glorious victory gleaming in his eyes.

*****

As General Soltas exited the briefing, a young lieutenant sidled up next to him, her uniform impeccably creased and pressed. She had a severe look upon her, which Soltas had come to recognize as her "thinking face". Her hair was pulled back tightly against her scalp and it was tied in a ponytail. Even when she left it down, it was still well within regulation-length. A long, thin scar ran down the side of her face, accentuating her jaw line. She took a respectful position less than two feet behind General Soltas and to his left, her usual post whenever he was out and about. Soltas glanced at her and half-smiled before his eyes drifted back down the corridor.

He returned the salute of a passing colonel and stepped into a smaller office off the corridor, where two more of his security detail awaited him. They braced to attention and Soltas nodded, allowing them to go about their dangerous task of standing around in his office, waiting for a deranged lunatic to try to take a shot at the commanding officer of the Earth Republic Army.

As soon as the outer door was closed, the young lieutenant spoke up.

"Sir, I want to lead the team to Ra Prime," she announced. Soltas sat down behind his desk and began to flip through his small console.

"Assuming that such a mission is being prepped," he murmured as his eyes locked onto an interesting tidbit out of New Mars. He made a mental note to do a little more digging as soon as he could into the matter. "Why in the world do you think I would let you lead your team out there, Dinah?"

"Sir, my team is the best prepared to handle an infiltration right now," the young woman insisted. "Ever since we got out of Titan, you've let one of my team run off into some godforsaken meat grinder mission–"

"Lancaster's World was not your mission to be had, Dinah," Soltas gently reminded her. "And Drake was never a part of 'your team.' Drake is a soldier and does what all good soldiers do. He

29

goes where he is told. Plus, he's more of a solo act. You know that."

"With all due respect, sir," Dinah began, her jaw clenched tightly in anger. Soltas interrupted her, recognizing the anger for exactly what it was.

"I'm not suggesting that you are incapable in any way, Lieutenant," he said, as he looked her in the eye. "Turning Drake to our side helped save Earth. The entire Republic owes you for that, and for the insane stand on Earth, you helped him lead. Why do you think I allowed your request into the Special Operations Directive despite your limited combat experience? We need smart operators as well as tough ones. And yes, your team performed admirably on Titan, even *if* it got pinned down and needed extraction by another team. But why, Dinah? Why should I let you lead a theoretical team out on some harebrained mission to Ra Prime? What sort of mission could a small team accomplish against the entire Ra'tid hierarchy? Do you even *know* how their rank structure works within their people?"

"Sir?"

"You heard me," Soltas said, his voice calm. "You're an intelligent officer, smarter than I am, most likely. Do you know the Ra'tid?"

"I know the Coalition, sir," she admitted, her unhappiness obvious to both of them.

"And how well do you know the Coalition, Lieutenant?"

"I know their entire rank-and-file, sir," she said. "Drake talked, I listened. I know their operating patterns, their shock troop dispositions, their Navy and Army. I speak their slang, know their habits, and their mentality when it comes to training their shock troops. I've studied their tactics, their theories, their practices, their politics. I even read over their stupid Principality Declaration, which seemed to me to be nothing more than a political scribe's self-congratulatory masturbation material."

"Which means, Dinah, you and team seven are in a better position to extract a high-level target from the Coalition," Soltas said as he passed over the small console to the young officer. "And trust me, if there was a mission to Ra Prime, you'd almost be my first choice."

"Almost, sir?" Dinah looked up.

"But then there's the Janus Option..." Soltas continued, his voice trailing off as he looked at her. She cocked her head, interested. He carefully hid a smile and pressed on. "What can you tell me about Janus, Lieutenant?"

"The Roman god, sir? Or the planet?"

"Amuse me."

"Well, sir, Janus is the god of beginnings," Dinah said, her eyes drifting away as she thought of everything she could remember from her parent's book collection back home. "And transitions. He usually associated with doorways, gateways, and stuff like that. The two-faced god, since he's looking both forward and back. The future and the past. The month of January was named after him, sir."

"And the world?"

"The home to the Coalition's Naval Academy," she responded immediately. "Protected by their Eleventh Fleet, it houses roughly fifteen thousand potential Navy officers. A full battalion of their Rapier Commandos are stationed there as well. It's also one of the few Terminus locations that the Coalition controls outright, and it jumps to the Praxum Ceti system. It is also the suspected location of their Fleet HQ, including their top brass, though with the war they may have moved them. There is also a fully-armed mobile battle station protecting the planet, as well as two differing defense grids which are interlocked by the planet's two moons. It is the second-most important planet to the Coalition, sir."

"Very good, Lieutenant," Soltas nodded. "Now tell me again why I'm not sending you on some insane and never-going-to-happen mission to Ra Prime?"

"Sir, it's because you need me and my team for an op on Janus," she said, her eyes widening in realization.

"I told you that you were smart," Soltas said and smiled. "Read that information over and get back with me. I want you to know everything you can about the habits of that man in the portfolio."

"High Lord Admiral Joseph Eidos? Never heard of him, sir," she admitted as she peered at the console pad.

"I'll give you fourteen hours to correct that," he said and

stood. She followed suit, with pad in hand. "I'll be in touch. Let your team know."

"Yes sir!"

"And Dinah?"

"Sir?"

"Leave Drake out of this one."

"I don't even know where the man is, sir," she said.

Soltas nodded. "Good."

*****

Ambassador Xarn, the Darian representative to the Earth Republic, looked up from the numerous reports he had been weeding through as the human burst into his office, uninvited. Years of training and a close proximity to typical human brashness kept him from ripping the Admiral's throat out instinctively. Instead, he calmly inspected the intruder and smiled, human-like. Xarn knew that Admiral Hien would not be bothered with the simple fact that Xarn was busy. Especially, the Darian noted as he twitched an ear, when the Admiral appeared to be on a mission.

"Custom and protocol on your world suggests that someone knock upon the door before entering," Xarn stated wryly, his fangs showing slightly in his smile. "Darians who burst into a room uninvited are seeking to establish dominance over the resident and one of two things happen. The resident acquiesces to the demands of the dominant individual, or a battle of honor is begun."

"Spare me the sociology lecture, Ambassador," Hien grunted and plopped himself down in the chair opposite of Xarn's desk. He leaned back, crossed a leg over his knee, and looked at the ambassador. "Ra'tid ship. Large. Bigger than anything we've ever seen before. As big as a super dreadnaught. Ring any bells?"

Xarn felt his anger begin to rise. Darians did not like being ordered around by anyone, especially honorless individuals like Hien. Demands led to duels, which led to blood. Xarn checked his fury and twitched another ear. "What gives you any idea I know anything about them, Admiral?"

"Your race and the Rocks have been warring with one another for a very long time," Hien observed. "It makes reasonable sense that they would have tested these new ships out against you.

32

Especially since you two have been at a semi-constant state of war for the past six hundred years."

Xarn laughed, which was an odd sound for a cat to make, but yet another habit that the ambassador had picked up from his time amongst the humans. "Your navy is much weaker than ours, and your weaponry is not as advanced. You have yet to implement shielding technology fully, and your beam weaponry is rudimentary at best. What makes you think they would test their newest ships out on us, their most powerful and dangerous enemy?"

Hien scowled. "You never know."

"You've run up against something new, then?" the ambassador asked rhetorically. "No, wait, let me think. I haven't heard of any Ra'tid activity near our borders, so... Retina. They somehow crossed Gener space and attacked Retina."

"They've got some sort of super dreadnaught," Hien informed the ambassador, confirming the Darian's suppositions. "It destroyed two of our ships and is readying to move against the Weligo Terminus."

"I see," Xarn said after a moment. "Thank you for this information. I shall pass it along to my leadership shortly."

"Wait, that's it? You really expect me to believe that you knew *nothing* about the damned ships?" Hien asked, his tone incredulous. "I know you better than that, Xarn."

"What is the real purpose of your visit here today, Admiral," Xarn asked, stacking the papers neatly with his claws and marking his place. He shifted both ears forward. "I am pressed for time and have an immense amount of work to complete."

"In fifteen minutes, an emergency session of Senate will open," Hien stated, a smug smile on his face.

"Is that all? Is it to impose new trade tariffs upon my people's goods?" Xarn asked, toying with the admiral. "You might just start a trade war if you keep taxing us."

"The President of the Earth Republic is going to show that he has just cause for declaring war against the Ra'tid menace," Hien said, annoyed that the cat not was taking the news as he had expected. "I'm here to see if our Darian allies are interested in a joint venture against their oldest and most ancient enemy."

Xarn's fangs became fully exposed for a moment before he was able to conceal his sudden outburst of emotion. "My people suffered greatly at the hands of the Coalition, taking great losses in securing your home world for you. The Ra'tids are a great threat to us all, and we look forward to the day when that threat is finally extinguished from this galaxy. However, at this time, the Darian Empire is unable to offer any form of assistance. We are simply too weak to fight a two-front war."

"The President is asking for war, but you may want to hear the battle plan before shunning the idea so quickly," Hien prodded some more. "General Soltus is planning on destroying Ra Prime and the Ra'tids for good. Completely, in a single stroke."

Xarn's whiskers bristled and the hackles on the back of his neck stood upright at the news. He took one, two breaths before he allowed himself to speak again. "That is a most intriguing proposition. I must confess, though, that I do not see how it changes to situation. The Darian Empire must regrettably decline your invitation to join your just and noble war."

Hien cocked his head, unsure at the diplomat's language for a moment before charging ahead. "If we eliminate the Ra'tids together, Xarn, the borders of the Darian Empire will no longer need such stringent protection."

"Incorrect," Xarn snapped. "We are now open enemies of the Coalition of Outer Planets because of our past assistance to your Republic. They will eventually come for us to retaliate, and to hurt us as they hurt you. If you believe otherwise, then I am compelled to point out to you your fallacious beliefs."

"You're wrong, Xarn," Hien argued. "The Coalition is hurting, too. Their move against Earth cost them just as many ships – if not more – than it did us."

"If this is the case, then why hasn't your impressive navy taken the battle to them, as you are proposing to do against the Ra'tids? The Coalition left your planet in ruin, your fleets are decimated, and you have been unable or unwilling to keep your end of the agreement you made with my government to attain our assistance. You brashly predict a quick war against an enemy my people have not been able to eradicate, yet cower at the thought of finishing off your own hated enemy– no, no, don't say anything yet. My Emperor – Glory unto Him – understands this, but do not believe that He will send you more warriors to die in the Republic's name until you provide us with what you promised."

Hien countered quickly. "We gave you back the systems we promised you, Xarn. All that we took during our first contact war is back in your claws once more. I'm not asking your warriors die for Earth, Ambassador. I – in essence, my president – is asking your military to assist in eliminating an enemy that has plagued your people for time immemorial, and will continue to be the aggressor against your innocent civilians and colonists until they are stopped. This is a much better offer than simply lending a few frigates and destroyers for picket duty, no?"

Perhaps," Xarn admitted after a moment of silence. "Perhaps it is a better offer. However, it is not my decision to make. I will take your president's request to my Emperor."

"Thank you, my friend," Hien said as he stood. He let himself out the door, closing it behind him.

As soon as he was gone, a second cat that Admiral Hien had not seen standing in the corner emerged from the darkened shadows. Xarn twitched an ear at the other, who quickly sat down in the recently vacated seat.

"Thoughts?" Xarn asked his chief intelligence officer, whose cover in the embassy was Xarn's personal assistant. In reality, the agent was second only to Xarn himself.

"They're scared," Korl replied. "They bluster, as always, but the Ra'tids have them scared. These new ships are no lie, or else seem real enough for the humans to believe it so. We picked up stray message traffic, which suggests that the ships are real enough. The real question is, can the battle group the humans are assembling be enough to stop these new Ra'tid ships?"

Xarn nodded slowly. "What do you think? Can they stop them?"

"Depends on too many variables to predict at this time, *Shalassai*," Korl said as he dipped his head apologetically. "I am sorry. I will check my network and see if any of the humans know anything else."

Good," Xarn said as he began to read his reports once more. He flipped through the pages until he found his mark. "Get back to me as soon as you have solid information. I must contact the Emperor for instructions."

Korl bowed his head and stood, leaving the room rapidly. Xarn looked back down at the papers and continued to read.

*****

Lieutenant Paige watched quietly as Captain Stoko spoke with the captains of the warships she had drafted into helping prepare the Terminus for attack. Three others had joined them a mere hour before, bolstering the battle group which was not prepared to guard the Weligo Terminus from the potential Ra'tid threat. Two heavy cruisers, three of the massive battleships and a destroyer were now under Captain Stoko's command to use as she saw fit.

The current meeting was far different from the frantic one from the previous night in multiple ways. First, they were meeting in person, gathered in the War Room of the Terminus. Secondly, the mood had shifted from panic to anxiousness as the expected Ra'tid attack never came. The best guess was that the Rocks were waiting for the Earth Republic to come to them, though Paige couldn't understand why. Lastly, the gathered captains had an expectant aura about them, a sense of pride and readiness to go to war, which had not been evident the night before.

Plus the SSO is here now, Paige thought sourly as he looked over Manny Herrera. No rank, no insignia, no uniform but a plain gray suit, yet the sight of the man gave Paige chills. He hoped that the senior State Security Officer of the Terminus kept his eyes off of him, and paid more attention to the gathered officers.

The lieutenant was seated directly to Captain Stoko's right, which surprised him a bit. Usually the XO of the Terminus sat there but, with Commander Burkman up at Central Command, he figured that he was next in line. Stoko seemed to think highly of him, and in any rate, he had been the one who was the Officer of the Watch when the message came through. The Condition One the Terminus was currently under was because of his quick thinking as well, which was another good mark in his file.

"People," Captain Stoko began as she looked over the assembled captains. "The Ra'tid fleet seems to be content in staying on the other side for the time being. This leaves us with two options. We can hold here, using the Terminus as a defensive wall to lash out at the Rocks with as we wait for more ships to arrive. Or we can use what ships we currently have here and go hunting. Thoughts?"

Captain Wellington, a big, beefy man who did not share Stoko's belief that a fleet officer should keep their body as sharp and toned as the mind, grunted. "I would like to think that our course of action is quite clear. The Terminus is too important to the Republic's long term plans for this sector of space for us to even consider risking it all in hope of driving the Ra'tids away. The defenses of this Terminus are formidable, and I would recommend using this to support our ships for when the Ra'tids come out of the wormhole. I would like to keep the *Buchanan* in close to the Terminus to use our combined firepower to greet the intruders when – and if – they come."

The captain of the *Kamehameha*, Germaine Washington, laughed loudly at his fellow officer. "Playing it safe never won any wars, Wellington. Your namesake would be ashamed."

Washington was a young captain, barely twenty five standard years old, according to the file that Paige had read before their arrival. A file he had no reason to be reading and yet, thanks to Captain Stoko, had found its way into his hands. Youthful exuberance was to be expected of any new captain, and one that was five years younger than Paige himself and already the CO of a destroyer lent credence to the captain's cockiness. He was talented, smart and daring.

That doesn't make him right, though, Paige thought. He himself had mixed feelings about going on the offensive, especially after seeing the carnage the new Ra'tid ships were capable of for himself.

"I agree with Captain Washington," an Asian woman with battle-hardened eyes and tight lips spoke up. Paige knew that Captain Hikia was a veteran of many space battles, and that she ran a tight ship. The battleship *Potemkin* was one of the more deadly pieces of human ingenuity ever to fight in a war, and the captain was right to be proud of her ship and her crew. "We should hit them. Hit them as hard as we can. The *Serinus*'s report suggested that while there were five of them, their rate of fire was pathetically slow for such a large vessel, and their fire control was spotty at best. They were barely able to cycle five missiles per second! The *Potemkin* alone can cycle fifty."

"Plus, we have three battleships with support," Washington added, his tone and posture eager. "We've taken out a Ra'tid fleet before with just one battleship!"

An extremely lucky event, Paige recalled. The Rocks hadn't even known that the battleship was there until six hundred missiles were en route. With that many missiles flying in undetected, it had been a wonder the Republic had been able to find any alien technology worth salvaging afterwards.

The lieutenant looked back at his captain, whose eyes were moving about the room at a rapid pace. They lingered, just for a moment, on the SSO before moving on to the elderly captain at the other end of the table. While not the ranking officer in the room, Captain Louis Phillips and the *Buckler* had seen more action than all the other captains combined had. His opinion would matter the most, and everyone in the room knew it.

"It *is* a gamble," Phillips began, his eyes meeting Stoko's. "Handled correctly, I believe that it's on with odds in our favor. No offense, Lieutenant Paige, but I have never heard of a Ra'tid ship that could stand toe to toe with a fleet of Republic battleships. I know that the Final Dispatch of the *Serinus* claimed much, but how much of that is the fact that the recon ship was damaged before they even spotted the Rocks? There's always the possibility that the readings weren't there because the ship had been damaged."

Paige's cheeks flushed angrily. The other captains looked at him expectantly. "Sir, the Dispatch was complete. With all due respect, you need to be an utter fool to discount the threat that these new Ra'tid ships pose to us. If it weren't a serious threat, would you be here?"

"On your word, Lieutenant," Phillips reminded him. "Politicians back home are elected to say the right things during a crisis, to react, to show that they are 'doing something'. *Our* job, Mister Paige, is to protect and defend the people and the Republic. We have to use *facts* in our decision making, not guesses and suppositions. Do I make myself clear?"

"Yes sir," Paige acknowledged, his cheeks burning brightly.

"The Weligo Terminus has a sophisticated defense grid, overlapping all exit points of the wormhole," Captain Jan Howard pointed out. "It can take on small fleet by itself if the attack into Retina fails. I would love to get a crack at those Rocks with the *Ticonderoga*, to be honest with you."

Captain Stoko nodded. "It's decided then. The *Buchanan* will carry the flag, and I'm designating this battle group Task Force Weligo, Captain Wellington commanding. The *Potemkin*, *Buckler*, *Ticonderoga* and *Kamehameha* will escort. The *Poe* will remain on standby here at the Terminus, ready to assist us, or the task force as needed. Any questions?"

"A bold decision, ma'am," the SSO spoke for the first time. Smiles and nods of agreement could be seen around the table.

Paige kept his mouth shut, though something about the plan was bothering him. *It's a big mistake*, he wanted to scream. He had seen what the Ra'tids were capable of with their new ships, and had felt the hopelessness of the men who had died aboard the *Serinus. But they're captains, and I'm a lieutenant waiting for promotion to lieutenant commander.*

Who was he to correct a room full of captains? Surely, with their vast experience and knowledge, they knew what they were doing.

Didn't they?

*****

"You mind telling me how you were able to fight off those Darians, Saul?" Willy asked, thoroughly drunk as he poured them each another shot. Saul gladly accepted the alcohol and took a sip.

"It's all about training," Saul said, his mind still sharp despite the nearly empty bottle of high-quality vodka which sat between them. He took a sip and nodded. "Each muscle and tendon is connected to another. The body's one large piece of it all. If you know how the muscles work, and how the body is positioned, you can narrow down the possibilities of what they are going to do."

"So you have to see them coming?" Willy nodded and

finished his shot. He looked at the bottle with bloodshot eyes and sighed. "That was good hooch. I should do this more often."

"You'd be out of business in a month," Saul reminded him. "No, you don't *have* to see them, but it helps. Once you get a feel for hand-to-hand fighting, you start to sense what your opponent will do. I guess you could say that your senses get sharper when the adrenaline is pumping. You can feel the air."

"Hock," the bartender grumbled. "Sounds like mystical voodoo crap to me."

"It's not easy to explain, Willy."

"They teach that at the Order?"

"Kind of," Saul allowed, dredging up memories he had struggled for so long to forget. "We were bringing the light to the people, Willy. That's what I signed up for. Going into the darkest of pits and showing them the glory and light of God. Somewhere along the way, I was recruited for something else because I showed an...aptitude for violence. I didn't shun it like most of the brethren. I wasn't a messenger anymore. I became–"

"A Templar," Willy nodded, his tongue thick with alcohol. "Heard of them. Scary bastards."

"Scary indeed," Saul agreed. "I'm not proud of what we did. I'm ashamed of what I became. I let myself be lied to. I *knew* the Lord Protector was lying us to, but there was a part of me that didn't care anymore. We could preach and preach the Word but, at the end of the day, it was direct action that got their attention. That made me feel like I was doing something more."

"Done that before," Willy nodded sagely. "Told myself the woman loved me and not my bank account. Knew better. Still went through with it. Ran off with my piano player. Tempestuous bitch."

"But those cats..." Saul shook his head as he pushed darker thoughts aside. "They weren't even Initiates yet. They were nothing but a bunch of teens jacked up on hormones and ego."

"Initiates?"

"You know anything about the Darians, Willy?"

"I know they don't like being called pussies."

"Well, okay," Saul snorted with laughter. "But anything about their religion? Their beliefs?"

"I don't really do religion that much," Willy admitted.

"That'll make this easy, then. They have circles in their society," Saul began, unconsciously slipping into the role of instructor. "Nine, to be precise. Yes, I think it's ironic that the Darians have nine circles. But they're like rings, surrounding one another. Ninth, eighth, so on and so forth. It's all honor based, so the more honor you've accrued, the better circle you are. Ninth circles are younger cats; eighth slightly older and more mature... you get the picture."

"You called them Initiates," Willy reminded him.

"No, I said they weren't even Initiates yet," Saul corrected him. "In order to be in the circles and start accruing honor, you have to be an Initiate. None of them had dyed whiskers, which meant that they had yet to be chosen. None of them wore the right clothes, either. Plus, they attacked in a group. Honor demands that the combat be singular, one on one. They didn't do that. No honor gained. So, not even Initiates."

"Darians fight massive space battles all the time," Willy commented. "That's not solo combat."

"It's not hand to hand," Saul pointed out. "No honor to be lost there. These... kids, for lack of a better term, had never been taught the fine art of *ka-nan*, their form of karate. That only begins once you're an Initiate."

A squad of Republic troopers entered the bar suddenly, fanning out and covering all exit points. Saul looked them over before finishing his drink. Their weapons were drawn but angled at the floor, setting off all sorts of alarms in Saul's head. These were professionals, veteran troops, Saul recognized. Wally glanced at the digital clock on the wall and snorted as a colonel in full dress uniform walked in the door behind them, his hat perched jauntily upon his head. He walked past his guard and stopped near Saul and Willy.

"Thirty hours, eighteen minutes," Willy grunted. "Slowest 'disturbing the peace' response ever."

"Willy..." Saul warned as he looked over the colonel.

"Templar Saul Derring of the Order?" the officer asked.

"*Formerly* of the Order," Saul corrected, keeping his voice light as he looked over the rest of the guard. Their body language screamed many things to the trained former operative, and he was not happy with what they were saying. "Not sure if you heard, but they've been outlawed."

"I'm going to need you to come with us," the colonel stated. Saul's eyes narrowed slightly.

"And if I refuse?" His voice dropped a few degrees in temperature.

"I can detain you for... what did the old coot say? 'Disturbing the peace'? Yes, I can do that."

"Who you callin' an old coot?" Willy demanded.

"I'm a free citizen of New Mars. I have rights," Saul argued. "What if I choose not to come with you?"

"Things will go badly for all of us," the officer stated. He motioned with his hand at the armed men and women behind him. "Please, Templar. We need you to come with us."

Saul sighed. He didn't want to risk anything happening to his old friend. "Keep a beer in the fridge for me, Willy. I'm going to see what this gentleman wants."

Saul clucked his tongue. "For you, I'll save two."

"I appreciate it."

Ten minutes later, Saul found himself in a darkened room at the bottom of an official government building. He was pushed into a seat opposite a man in grey cloth and silver trim, which he identified immediately as a man of justice. The guards who had escorted him left, save for four, who moved to positions behind him. The colonel remained standing nearby.

"Saul Derring, are you aware of your rights as a Republic citizen?" the man across the desk asked as he looked over the former Templar. Beside him, the colonel rested comfortably in a chair. Four armed guards stood behind Saul, all watching him, wary of any sudden movement. Saul knew that they were on edge, and did not want to give them any reason to kill him on the spot. So he stayed as still as possible, keeping his breathing slow and measured.

"I am aware of my rights," Saul nodded.

"And you are aware of the charges against you?" the man continued.

Saul shook his head. "What charges? Are you really going to

charge me with disturbing the peace?"

"I'm referring to more... serious charges," the man continued. "As Magistrate, it is my duty to inform you that you are being charge twenty-three counts of murder in the first degree. Also, are fourteen counts of involuntary manslaughter, seventy-six counts of possession of stolen firearms, one hundred and seventeen counts of crimes against humanity, four hundred and eight counts of willful destruction of government property…and one count of disturbing the peace."

"Disturbing the peace..." Saul chuckled softly. "The Bryan Act pardoned all surviving members of the Order, if I recall. So please, will you tell me what this is really all about?"

"The Bryan Act does not apply here, Mister Derring," the Magistrate said, his voice tight. "The Marines you murdered at the Tangiyia spaceport here on New Mars took place well after the official surrender of the Order."

"New Mars was a warzone at the time. Things were as bad, if not worse, than Earth is right now, trying to pick up the pieces after the Coalition's attacks," Saul said, his voice still calm. His mind, however, was racing, trying to figure out what the two men were really there for. "Fighting continued on both sides for weeks after the word to stand down came through."

"Be that as it may," the Magistrate glanced at the data pad in his hand. "The charges still stand. How do you plead?"

"If I plead guilty, will you tell me why the State Department has a man dressed up as a colonel in the Republic Army and a general is pretending to be a Magistrate?" Saul asked.

"I'm sorry?" the colonel behind him asked.

"You're with the State Department," Saul explained. "Don't deny it. Your shoes were too nice to be a Republic Army officer, and your hands are too soft. That screams government paper pusher, but you're used to being in charge, so a high level paper pusher. You also didn't remove your cover when you entered Willy's, and your dictation is perfect. So you don't really know military decorum, and you're an educated man. That leaves Justice or State where you could get that high without military training or experience. You're not comfortable with a firearm on your hip, which eliminated Justice. So I guessed State."

"And the Magistrate?" the man in the uniform asked.

"That was easy," Saul said as he tapped his ring finger. He looked at the seated Magistrate. "West Point class ring. Too old to be a colonel, too fit to be a Magistrate. Bearing is all wrong, too. Your posture is perfect. A Magistrate signs papers all day, so they have more of a hunch when they sit down. Plus, I recognized you, sir. How are things, General Soltus?"

The officer behind Saul walked around and slid a chair next to the seated "Magistrate". He pulled a small bill from his wallet and handed it over to the General. Without a word, the General pocketed the bill. The officer sat down next to the General.

"Could be better, Saul," General Soltus said as he straightened the tunic. "I told Tim here that you'd see right through this, but he thought a strong arm tactic might work. What he told you was true, however. We need you."

"I appreciate the frankness, General," Saul said. "But I don't see how I can help you."

"Did you know that there were stories about you, Templar?" Soltus asked as he stood, walking around the desk. "Late at night, when the moon was dark and the cold chill of the air was the absolute worst, the Marines would whisper about the Templar. Not the Templars as a whole, but *the* Templar. Their boogeyman, so to speak. The Templar who would slip in at night, slit the throat of the highest ranking officer, and escape into the night once more, disturbing nobody else, never triggering an alarm, not even disturbing the man sleeping near him. The Hand of God, they called you. As you can see from the Marines around you, they are still afraid of you. Still their boogeyman."

"I was just a humble servant of God, sir," Saul said as he bowed his head. His fingers reached for the cross dangling from his neck.

"You do yourself an injustice, Templar," Soltus said. "You fought in skirmishes with the Ra'tids, defeated them quite handily, if I recall. You even led a group of Templars deep into a Ra'tid vessel and captured it. It was the first time any Ra'tid vessel had been able to fall into the Republic's hands. We learned much from your victory. A servant and nothing more, you argue? You were more than that. You were a soldier, dedicated to your cause and your belief. I don't fault you for following the orders of that madman. But you have to forgive yourself eventually."

Saul ignored the fact that the men who had been with him successful mission after mission had been executed by order of the very Republic who was now singing his praise. Men and women who had remained loyal to him, to the Order, to the Lord Protector when their world was coming down around them in flames. He remembered every one of their names, recalled every detail of their faces. They had been his soldiers, all secure in their belief that the Order was right. He could still see their eyes when even that was taken from them as the firing squads had lined up.

"You need me for something..." Saul's voice trailed off as his mind kicked back into gear. "War with the Ra'tids has finally come?"

Soltus nodded. "We all knew it was coming, sooner or later."

"Twenty hours ago, a Ra'tid fleet entered the Retina system, destroying two recon ships. They are now less than three hypervoid jumps to Earth," the State Department official stated. "They've ignored our calls for a cease-fire, as well as any overtures to a peaceful resolution."

"Currently a task force is at the Weligo Terminus," Soltus said. "We aren't certain yet if the Ra'tids are waiting for the task force, or vice versa."

"I still don't see what you need me for, General."

"I'm getting to that, Templar," Soltus explained. "The Republic Navy is currently scrambling to assemble every single possible ship, including some destined for scrap, to launch an all-out attack on Ra Prime. Cut the snake off at the head..."

"And it grows two more, General," Saul corrected. Seeing the man's confused face, he sighed. "In ancient mythology, if one cut off the head of a hydra, two more takes its place. That's how most civilizations work. The five major players in the universe are all spread out. Even if Earth fell, there are still options. The Ra'tids are the same way, sir. Unless you're talking complete and utter genocide..." he crossed himself at the thought.

"Fleet Admiral Hien believes that the attack on their home world will work. Me? I'm a pragmatic man who doesn't like to put all his eggs into one basket. I have quite a few things in the works, and – I hope – you're one of those things."

"The Ra'tids have a new ship, a ship nobody's ever seen before," the other man said. "Tim Kelsey, by the way."

Saul nodded but said nothing, shifting his gaze back to the general.

"Tim's right. There's a new Ra'tid ship out there, and she's a beast. Worst part about it is, they have at least five," Soltus said. "Naval Intelligence believes that they only have five, but again, I'm paid to be paranoid. I want to know more. I *need* to know more."

"What about the Darians, sir?" Saul asked.

"Surprisingly reticent about helping us," Tim said. "Given that this is their sworn enemy we're talking about here."

"They usually jump at the chance to beat up on the Rocks, but not this time," the general agreed. "They took a pounding during the Battle of Earth, though, so it's reasonable that they want to fall back and lick their wounds a bit before rejoining battle. That's against their usual *modus operandi*, but other than them playing political games with us – and State can't figure out why they would do that – they must be really hurting. They never turn down a chance to show just how superior they are to everyone else."

"Sir, would you *please* tell me what you want me for."

"Infiltration," Saul stated. "I don't think that these five ships are their only ones. It wouldn't make sense to risk all of your new ships in one combat. We need to know more about these ships. Weaponry, armor, point defense, command structure, engines, everything. How they built them, and most importantly of all, who helped them build the ships."

"You think they had help?" Saul asked.

"I think they may have had some influence from someone," the general allowed. "This all smells too pat to me."

"You think the Navy is being led into a trap of some sort?"

"I'm not looking past the possibility. I would like to know if anybody like, say, the Coalition is secretly helping the Rocks in their military endeavors. Or if there's a new player in the game, and unknown factor we're unaware of."

"There's only five galactic powers in the explored universe," Saul reminded him.

"I'm well aware of this fact," Soltus said. "I also have some suspicions, so humor me. I can't go around pointing fingers until I have confirmation. And since I can see you are interested in getting to the bottom of this mystery as I am..."

"I never said that, sir," Saul argued. He paused for a second before a slight grin spread onto his face. "Though I'm not saying no."

"Then go to Ra Prime," Soltus said. "And help me find out what's going on."

Chapter Three

Captain Mike Wellington was a practical man when it came to commanding his battleship, the *Buchanan*. Certain Navy regulations, such as no fraternization aboard military vessels, were followed to the letter. Others, such as smoking on any Republic Navy vessel, many captains overlooked for the good of their bridge crews. In this case, the captain was not the exception. Even his SSO partook occasionally, albeit in his private quarters and not in front of the crew of the *Buchanan*.

He stubbed out his cigarette in the archaic ashtray resting on the arm of his command chair and gazed at his instruments. He knew that the air scrubbers were more than adequate to handle the smoke without risking the integrity of the ship. He pulled out a fresh cigarette and lit it, taking a long drag. The nicotine flooded his system and he sighed, letting smoke waft out of his mouth. He figured it was his body, and he could do with it as he pleased. *Plus, nicotine is great for the concentration and focus*, he reasoned.

The Retina system was merely a half hour hop through voice space from the Terminus. The ships of the task force has already reached the system and were now awaiting his order to enter normal space. They had been waiting for four minutes now as Wellington contemplated the tactical situation. On the face of it, things did not look good.

He knew that the Rocks had to be waiting for him to drop out of void space to engage. It was Tactics 101 – wait for the enemy to move, and then counter. Their own sensors would be blind for the first few seconds after returning to normal space, which left them vulnerable to any incoming fire. If he dropped the entire fleet out of void space simultaneously, it would present the Ra'tids with an optimal attack. It also made for more targets, which often helped confuse the technologically inferior aliens. The captain had not survived the Battle of Earth by being predictable and stupid, though. He nodded to his communications officer.

"Send the message, Doug," the captain ordered.

"Aye sir, sending now," Commander Doug Burbey replied. He patted a sensor tech on the shoulder, who fired off the prerecorded message to the *Kamehameha* and waited for acknowledgement. The wait for a response was not a long one. Burbey turned to look back at his captain. "*Kamehameha* shows green, sir, and entering normal space now."

For a few tense moments, Wellington sat motionless, cigarette smoldering in his hand as he waited for one of two things to happen. Either, the *Kamehameha* would be destroyed and they would pick up its Final Dispatch, allowing the rest of the fleet to escape, or it would be able to relay sensor readings to the rest of the task force. It was risky, leaving one ship out as glorified bait, but Wellington knew that losing a destroyer was a far better proposition than losing an entire task force.

"*Kamehameha* reports nothing on sensors, sir," Burbey announced. "Shall I engage the Snapdragon, Captain?"

Wellington considered his options. Engaging the Snapdragon symbiotic program would slave all the ships together at once, allowing them to share data instantaneously, without any sort of hampering. The downside was that as long as the Snapdragon was engaged, the *Kamehameha* would be blind until the rest of the task force entered real space, and be at real risk.

Nonetheless, the benefits outweighed the potential costs. Wellington nodded.

"Attention crew, activation of Snapdragon will commence in five seconds," the comm officer announced over the general comm. "Entering real space simultaneously. Engaging in five, four, three, two, one, activate!"

The universe around them twisted as the ship dropped out of

void space. Breaths were held as they waited as the first vulnerable seconds of being in real space, blind and ignorant to the potential dangers around them slowly ticked by. Wellington took another drag off his cigarette, trying to exude an air of calm about him to show the crew that he was unconcerned and prepared to face whatever the universe would throw at them. Inside, however, he was a coiled bundle of nervous energy.

"We're in," Burbey breathed. Wellington didn't sigh with relief – it would have been unprofessional – but he could not help to smile a little.

"Drop our towed array system," the captain ordered. "Move the *Kamehameha* to the rear of the formation and have the *Potemkin* and *Buckler* move to our port and starboard, respectively. Order the *Ticonderoga* to take point. Let's form a nice, tight diamond."

The bridge crew exploded into activity as each man and woman went about their tasks, the Snapdragon relaying the orders instantly. The massive battleships accelerated to come alongside the *Buchanan*, their towed array sensors falling behind them to sniff out any potential threats from the rear. The *Ticonderoga* moved past the flagship to take point on the task force.

Wellington nodded, satisfied. Though the task force had been created a mere two hours before, it was already operating at an efficiency that would please the strictest of evaluators. He glanced over at Commander Burbey.

"Anything yet, Doug?"

"No sign of any Ra'tid ships, Captain," the comm officer replied instantly.

"I doubt that they just up and left the system after destroying two recon ships, Comm," Wellington observed. He stubbed out his cigarette and pulled out another. "Find them."

"Yes sir," Burbey said.

"Picking up some strange surges in gravity, Captain," a sensor tech called out suddenly. "Reading off of the *Kamehameha's* towed array. Range, one hundred thousand kilometers."

"Gravity surge?"

"Yes sir," the tech responded back immediately. "Computer's saying it's a gravitational anomaly of some sort."

"Strange..." Wellington breathed as he tried to recall why that seemed important.

"Captain," Burbey called out, a slight tremor in his voice. "I watched the Final Dispatch from the *Serinus*, sir. They reported something similar right before the Rocks attacked."

"Order the *Kamehameha* to axial about!" Wellington roared and stood, his face twisted in surprise and anger as he realized just where the Ra'tids were hiding. "It's a trap!"

The small destroyer whipped around, continuing to follow the task force but now with both her missile tubes and beam weaponry facing towards the rear. Wellington slammed his hand on the arm of his seat, bringing the view screen up. He was now looking at the *Kamehameha* and beyond, where the task force had dropped out of void space minutes earlier. Behind the small destroyer, he could faintly see what appeared to be asteroids at first glance. He magnified the view and suddenly the massive Ra'tid super dreadnaughts filled his entire screen. They were just as big as he remembered, only now they seemed much more dangerous, far deadlier than the Dispatch had made them seem. The *Kamehameha* was barely a third of the size of the lead Ra'tid vessel. His unlit cigarette fell from his fingers, forgotten.

"I don't have them on sensors, sir!" the sensor tech shouted. "I've got– wait! I picked up a missile launch. Holy crap! Vampire, vampire! I count one-eight-zero missiles coming in from the lead Ra'tid vessel, designating Thrall-One. Designating the other ships Thrall-Two, Three, Four and Five on the view screen now. Task force point defenses coming up now, sir. ECMs are up and running."

"Now we wait," Wellington said as he sat back down in his chair. He punched a button on his chair. "XO, what do you make of it?"

His executive officer, buried away near the belly of the giant *Buchanan's* auxiliary command deck, replied almost at once.

"Same old diamond missiles, sir," came the reply. "Maybe the damage to the *Serinus* made them blind?"

"Not picking up the Ra'tids on sensors," the captain reminded him. "With Snapdragon up and running, though, things will be different for us that it was for the poor *Serinus*. Bridge out." The captain looked up at his bridge crew, his smile feral. "Triangulate the positions of those ships using view screens. It'll be rough but we can pound them some."

"Eighty seconds until missiles impact," the sensor tech called out. "I count sixty of them targeting the *Kamehameha* alone, and twenty are targeting us. The other ships have not been targeted."

"God help those poor, unlucky bastards," Wellington muttered. "Bring up the white noise on those ECMs, Techie. Make them earn it."

"Aye, sir," the sensor tech said as he dialed up the strength of the electronic counter measures. Power thrummed throughout the system as the task force all responded simultaneously. He watched as the countermeasures went to work, confusing the alien missiles with noise, false signatures and misleading information. Ra'tid missile after missile veered off or prematurely exploded, defeated by the superior ECM of the Republic.

"They know which ship to shoot at," Burbey called out over his shoulder.

"This isn't their first rodeo, Comms."

"Target lock. I have target lock."

"Weapons, do you have a firing solution for our missiles yet?" Wellington asked.

"We have a solution, sir," the weapons officer replied. "Permission to engage?"

"Match bearings and fire at will. Concentrate *Buchanan*'s fire on the lead Ra'tid ship. Order the other battleships to focus on Thrall-Two and Thrall-Three. Bring the *Ticonderoga* up to cover the topside plane, and have her blast the Rocks so hard with ECM that there's going to be a sterile generation." The *Buchanan* shuddered gently as five hundred missiles poured forth, the small engines burning brightly as they accelerated. On either side of the Buchanan, the *Potemkin* and *Buckler* poured their own missiles out in space. Wellington watched them for a moment on his personal screen, fifteen hundred missiles targeting Ra'tid ships. "Go kill me some Rocks, little devils."

"Damn!" the sensor tech suddenly yelled. "I just saw the other four fire off missiles visually, but sensors have been spoofed somehow. Looks like the *Serinus* was right, Captain. They got some sort of stealth tech on those missiles. Doing a manual count... shit. Too many to count, sir!"

"Sir, the *Kamehameha*'s been hit!" Commander Burbey suddenly called out. "Five direct impacts on her forward missile bay. Port beam weaponry is gone. Damage control is reporting that they have nineteen dead, forty-six wounded and eight MIA. Hull has been compromised, structural integrity is still sound. The spine is solid."

"Sir, Captain Washington is requesting permission to close on the lead Ra'tid ship," a comm technician stated. "He wants to him them with beam weaponry."

"Request is denied," Wellington said in a flat voice. "There will be no martyrs today, PO. Just some damn war heroes."

"Sir, we've got two vampires inside our point defenses! Domes are engaging... miss. We have two inbound, ETA four seconds!"

The *Buchanan* shuddered as the two missiles burrowed into the thick steel hull of the ship, pausing for a millisecond before detonating. The diamond-tipped missiles cut through the protective bulkheads, circuitry, and men as the concussive blast opened up a small hole to space. Oxygen screamed out the hole, venting into deep space. Men shouted in alarm as klaxons blared loudly, deafening them. A second, similar hole erupted near engine three, but the massive engines were designed to take a pounding. A damage control crew reached the first breach in less than a minute and immediately began to seal the hole, drilling a heavy steel plate into place. An arc welder appeared and the sealant began to be applied. A second later, they reported in, the Snapdragon dutifully relaying the message to all ships.

"I'm done pussyfooting around," Wellington growled. "Guns, go full-auto. Give 'em hell."

"Aye, sir!" the weapons officer replied. "Missiles are hot! Flood tubes and launch all birds. Repeat, launch all birds! Target designee Thrall-One. Prepare beam weaponry for point contact. I want varying solutions on those Ra'tid ships, stat."

"I have a solution, sir. Relaying to you now."

"Launching birds now," the weapons officer announced, his voice cool as more missiles streaked out from the forward missile tubes.

"Sir! *Kamehameha*'s been hit again!"

"Jesus," Wellington whispered as a white flash blinded the view screen briefly. He glanced at his display and felt a growing horror in the pit of his belly as he watched the proud destroyer break apart, the screen focusing on the small ship. Spine broken, the *Kamehameha* began to drift apart, two large sections leaking oxygen and debris. He zoomed in and saw, for a fleeting second, a body drifting amongst the debris. He quickly zoomed back out as his entire body broke into a cold sweat.

"Sir, the Snapdragon says that *Kamehameha* showed hot birds in her tubes," Burbey announced, an edge to his voice. "Her magazine is primed–"

Secondary explosions tore through the fallen destroyer, a familiar blue-tinged shockwave rippling out as the nuclear missiles went active. Detonation after detonation tore through wreckage, the bright flashes, causing Wellington to see white spots in his vision. He rubbed his eyes and looked back, the spots fading. Where once a proud Earth Republic vessel had once sailed, nothing more than a few pieces of scrap metal remained. The bridge crew suddenly fell silent as they realized that every single man and woman aboard the *Kamehameha* had been lost. Two thousand brave souls, gone in the blink of an eye.

"Thrall-One has no point defense system up!" a sensor tech cried out, breaking the deathly silence on the bridge. "All our birds have a lock on that big old bitch! Time to impact, fifteen seconds."

Wellington leaned back and watched his screen, where over fifteen hundred missiles began to close on the front three Ra'tid vessels that the sensors continued to insist were not there. The missiles silently clawed through space, intent on their imaginary targets. Just as Wellington expected the missiles to pass through empty space, the first impacted the hull of the massive Ra'tid ship. A second later, the rest of its brethren joined it, the kinetic energy of the missiles driving deep into the rocky hull of the ship before exploding.

A few of the missiles were duds, shattering upon impact and floating lazily across the hull of the super dreadnaught. A bare few, however. Over four hundred and eighty from the *Buchanan* alone were active and ripped through the outer hull of the ship. The detonations shook the massive vessel, forcing a course change as it struggled to adapt to the sudden barrage. Explosion after explosion rocked the alien ship, the impact reports cluttering up the screens of the *Buchanan*, overloading the Snapdragon for a moment. That, too, soon passed.

After the dust settled, Wellington's jaw dropped to the ground. *Impossible*, he thought. He could see the missile craters from where the hundreds of missiles had struck, but other than scorch marks across the surface and the craters themselves, the Ra'tid ships appeared to be undamaged. He swore under his breath as the implications of what he had just seen struck home.

"Multiple vampires inbound! ECM blocked some, sir, but point defense didn't even engage," the sensor tech called. He turned in his chair and looked up at his captain, fear evident across his youthful face. "Didn't even see them until just now! ETA in three seconds! Sir, I'm sorry–"

Chaos erupted on the bridge as the first of four hundred enemy missiles tore into the *Buchanan's* tough hull, their specially shaped heads easily defeating the metal. The secondary explosions wiped out the entire bridge, the heat incinerating any and all organic material that it could find.

*****

Aboard the *Potemkin*, Captain Hikia looked up from her display. Thus far, the Ra'tid fleet had been primarily focused on the *Kamehameha* and the *Buchanan*, but now she was certain that the Rocks would turn their attention to the mostly undamaged ships of the task force. A small symbol appeared on her screen and she frowned. Her dark eyes looked around.

"PO Khandry, is this correct?" she asked, eyes boring into her comm technician.

"Yes ma'am," she responded immediately. "Snapdragon has transferred the flag to us."

"The *Buchanan* looks fine though," she protested.

"She took over three dozen direct hits, ma'am," her comm officer reminded her.

"So tell me, James," she asked as she shifted her gaze to her officer. "How many missiles does it normally take to cripple a battleship enough to force it to relinquish command to another ship?"

"Uh," he paused before his eyes snapped open as his brain did the math. "A helluva lot more than that, ma'am."

"Precisely, Lieutenant," she tapped a finger on her chair as she thought it over. She had seen something like this before, long ago when she was commanding a light cruiser, the *Renegade*. During her time of hunting members of the Order. But *what* was she seeing now? Was it the same? She didn't think so, but it was eerily similar. "Replay that missile strike." She waited for a moment before pausing the feedback. "Look, right there. Look what those missiles did."

"They followed each other in," the sensor tech muttered. She pursed her lips. "Ma'am, *can* missiles do that?"

"Apparently they can," Hikia stated. "Ignore what they did for a second, chief. Look at where they *went*."

"Center spine, armored... they went directly to the command deck!"

"Right," Hikia nodded. "And this second group here? Coming up the belly?"

"The auxiliary command deck! Jesus, ma'am... they knew exactly where to go!"

"We have multiple inbounds, Captain! Vampire, vampire! Thrall-Three has volleyed. Two-zero-zero missiles inbounds, countermeasures engaging," another sensor tech shouted. "These are the ones we can see, ma'am. Thank God."

"Now they're targeting us," Hikia whispered. Her mind raced as she thought about what had happened to the *Buchanan*. She looked at her sensors, the pattern right before her, and she made her decision. "Disengage countermeasures!"

"What the hell?"

"Window dressing, Lieutenant," Hikia told him. "They engage first with the old standard missiles, we blast them away with our ECM and point defense. They then attack with these new missiles, and they don't even show up on our sensors. Why would they do that?"

"Inbound missiles have acquired us, ma'am! Hard lock! ETA is seven-five seconds."

"Come about, Helm, heading zero-five-eight, flank speed," Hikia ordered.

"Are you out of your mind, Captain?" the comm officer asked. "We're *running* away?"

"We can be out of maneuvering range of those missiles in thirty seconds, Lieutenant. Those missiles only have enough range for four hundred thousand kilometers."

"You *are* running away! You damned coward! Get us back there and fight!"

"You are relieved, Lieutenant," Hikia said. "PO Khandry, you are acting comm officer until otherwise noted."

"I'm filing a formal protest, ma'am!" her former comm officer stated. Hikia nodded.

"I wouldn't expect otherwise. Master at arms, escort the Lieutenant from the bridge. You are confined to quarters until otherwise noted."

"Ma'am, course laid in. Heading is zero-five-eight, flank speed," her helmsman announced as the former comm officer was led from the bridge.

"Captain, the *Buckler* and the *Ticonderoga* have not matched course, ma'am. Captain Phillips requests a SITREP," Khandry said. Hikia grunted and silently cursed the stubbornness of crotchety old men.

"Tell them that the Ra'tids are specifically targeting the command decks of the ships, and they know precisely where they are," Hikia told her. "Show them on the Snapdragon."

"Captain... the Rocks just launched missiles at the other ships," her sensor tech announced. "Not picking them up on anything. Towed array has nothing."

Hikia looked at Khandry. "See?"

A minute passed, then two. Khandry noted that the missiles that had been perusing them were no longer actively engaged. She looked over the Snapdragon and watched as the other ships were still pounding the Ra'tid fleet. She wished them luck.

"Oh my..." the younger woman's voice trailed off as first the *Ticonderoga*, then the *Buckler*, went silent on the Snapdragon. She looked back at her captain.

"Kill Snapdragon, Khandry," Hikia ordered quietly. "Helm, let's go to void space."

"Back to the Terminus, ma'am? The Rocks are blocking our way back to the wormhole."

"No," she thought for a second. She brought up a star chart onto the view screen. "There's only Gener space beyond here. We'll hide out... here, in the Felix Cluster. The Rocks will never think to look there."

"Ma'am, the radiation levels of the cluster..."

"That's why the Rocks won't think to look there. It'll be a nice little hiding spot for a few days before we need to move on."

"ETA to the cluster, ma'am, is ninety hours."

"Did any of the ships manage to fire off a Final Dispatch?" Hikia asked.

"Yes Captain. Both the *Buckler* and the *Ticonderoga* did."

"But not the *Buchanan*?"

"No ma'am."

"Very well then," Hikia sighed. "Make the jump."

"Ma'am, if I may...?" Khandry tentatively asked.

"The Rocks knew exactly how to hit us," Hikia explained, already guessing as to the question. "That means they know the interior design of our ships. Those missiles were programmed to go directly for the head of the snake, so to speak. Now, how do you think the Rocks figured this out? Through ingenuity and guesswork? Or...?"

"They had help," Khandry nodded. "And somebody needs to tell the Admiralty."

"Precisely. There's only one other galactic power out there who designs their ships like us, and we happen to be at war with them right now."

"They gave them stealth tech, missile tech, information..." Khandry's voice faltered. "In exchange for what?"

"To attack us, of course," Hikia pointed out. "To give the Coalition time to breathe, and to regroup. It's pretty simple, if you think about it."

"They'd risk the entire galaxy just to hurt us?"

"They'd do a lot more than that, Khandry," Hikia said as the universe around the *Potemkin* twisted, the ship hurtling into void space.

No ships followed them through.

*****

"This, people, is High Lord Admiral Joseph Eidos," Dinah began as her team began to look over their personal data pads. Information scrolled down their screens as she transferred her screen to the overhead display. "He's a graduate of Annapolis, class of '23, and was a Distinguished Graduate at that. He's their number three in their rank structure for the Navy and has access to all sorts of classified information we want to have. He's also the least protected, individually, than the other High Lords. He's shown to have an exceptional aptitude in theoretical tactics, and he had two degrees in Engineering and Physics."

"So he's as smart as you, ma'am?" Specialist Ricky Ervin asked, his grin wide and bright against his dark face. Dinah rolled her eyes and tried not to kill her technical specialist.

"Smarter, actually," she said. "I'm smart. He's genius."

"Ah, so not necessarily a good soldier then," Ervin decided.

Dinah gave the older man a look. "Would you say I'm a bad soldier, troop?"

"Uh, no ma'am," Ervin apologized hurriedly.

"Good." She flipped to the next screen. "Janus is protected by the Eleventh Fleet, which is, as you may know, not a mothball fleet in any way, shape or form. It has sixteen battleships, eight dreadnaughts and four super dreadnaughts, not counting the smaller destroyers, cruisers and corvettes. The total tonnage of said fleet is enough to give our Navy pause, though you'd never hear the Admiralty admit to that. Janus was deemed one of the off-limits worlds after the initial Bornstein Offensive, given our losses trying to *get* to the damned planet in the first place.

"The planet itself has a dual modulation defense grid, always running in geosynchronous orbit with the two moons of the world. There is a mobile platform station protecting it as well, and over one thousand Rapier Commandos on Academy grounds. This is possibly as well defended as Earth was before the Coalition's attack.

"This mission is going to be a grab and bag, people," she announced as she brought up the schematics for the flagship of the Eleventh Fleet. "Latest intelligence has Admiral Eidos on board the *Dadaejin*, a super dreadnaught of some impressive reputation. This ship went toe to toe with the *Enterprise* during the Bornstein Offensive and walked away. That ship is one impressive beast."

"And there's three more like it," Sergeant Mike Masters reminded them. The grizzled veteran looked around the room. "Seems like this is some sort of desperation ploy, ma'am. Kidnapping some admiral."

"I agree," she stated. "However, it's what General Soltas has ordered for us to do, though. And we have a window of opportunity coming up."

"Ma'am?" Ervin asked.

"The admiral is transferring back to the Naval Academy on Janus," she said as she brought up a third display. "Not sure why, but there are hints at some sort of political shakeup in the Coalition itself since we beat them back at Earth. Our window is small, people, so we're going to need to move quickly. We have the *Solitude* at our disposal, and her usual crew. The op plans are on your pads, so go over them. We'll do workups en route, and go over the final extraction plan."

"Lieutenant..."

"Corporal?"

"Is Drake coming with us?" Corporal Zhin asked.

"Negative, Corporal," Dinah shook her head. "Just the seven of us."

"Is Drake even still alive?" the corporal pressed.

"Zhin, if I knew anything, I'd share it with you guys," she replied instead. After a moment, she relented. "I've never met a harder man to kill. I'm sure that Drake is alive, somewhere. Alright? The General says this our op. Gear up. Our shuttle leaves in an hour."

*****

Aboard the Weligo Terminus, Captain Stoko lay silently in

her bed, staring up at the gray ceiling of her private quarters. She couldn't sleep, not now, perhaps not ever again. The guilt she felt over sending the task force to Retina weighed heavily upon her damaged psyche. Realizing that people often died in wars, and being the one responsible for their deaths were far different things. Before being assigned to the Terminus, the majority of her career had been spent behind a desk, shore side on Earth. Her lone posting aboard a ship years before had resulted in an adequate grading from Admiralty, which was a career-killer if one wanted to command any sort of ship or battle group later on down the line. Relegated to administration, Stoko there had found her calling.

In a time of peace, she recognized that the Weligo Station needed such a captain as herself. Tactics and strategy were not her strong points though, which meant that her talents while aboard the Terminus were sorely underutilized. Even with the war against the Coalition raging, the Weligo Terminus had been so far from the front lines that there had been little danger of her seeing any combat.

That illusion of safety and security was no more. That became evident to her that afternoon upon the bridge as first the *Ticonderoga*, then *Buckler's* Final Dispatch had come through the wormhole. She didn't know what had happened to the rest of the task force but since none of them had returned in the sixteen hours since the Dispatches had arrived, she assumed the worst. The Republic was officially at war with the Ra'tids, and she was the front line defense.

The thought terrified her.

Rolling over onto her side, Stoko realized that she had given up on any hope of sleep. She shoved back the covers and placed her feet on the metal floor. The chill of the cold shot through her. She shivered and wrapped her arms around herself, and seated there on the edge of her bed, felt the overpowering wave of guilt wash over her. She couldn't hide from it, not anymore. She needed help if she was going to live up to her rank, and get the job done as she had been ordered to do. If the Ra'tid fleet had easily dispatched three battleships, a destroyer and a heavy cruiser, she knew that the Terminus would not fare much better. Especially with the Terminus lacking any sort of maneuverability.

Once more, she felt that the Admiralty's faith in her abilities were sorely misplaced. She was not cut out to be a line officer.

She stood and shrugged on her robe, covering her naked, goose bump-covered body as she considered where to find the help and relief she so desperately craved. Her XO was a bumbling, simpering moronic fool of a man, and could not help her. She could see why the Admiralty had passed on him when command of the Terminus had opened up. No, she needed non-Naval personnel, but on a space station under the auspices of the Republic Navy, such an individual was hard to find.

Unless one thought outside the box, that is.

She stabbed the comm on her desk with a finger, opening a channel to Central Command. Ensign Dotson was on watch, thankfully. She couldn't begin to think about how Lieutenant Paige would have responded had she reached him. The Lieutenant was too sharp for his own good sometimes.

Dotson nodded, his tanned, leathery face filling her view screen.

"Evening, Captain," the ensign said. "How can I help you tonight?"

"Comm Mister Herrera for me," the captain said. "I need his assistance with a matter of utmost urgency."

"The SSO, ma'am?" the ensign's face twisted with worry. Stoko sighed.

"Personnel reports haven't been filed yet, Ensign," she tried to soothe him. "That's all. Just some performance evals he never signed off on."

"Oh, okay ma'am," Dotson rubbed his forehead, his relief obvious. "I'll send him your way."

"Thank you, Ensign." she killed the comm and looked around her quarters. For half a moment, she was tempted to pick up but decided that there was no need. The SSO wouldn't care about the state of her quarters.

Minutes later, her door chimed quietly.

"Come," she said. She was still in her robe, and quickly checked to make sure it was still tightly around her waist before the State Security Officer entered her room.

"You needed me to sign off on some forms, Captain?" he

asked. His dark features were calm, stoic, something she needed at that moment. The fire in his eyes though, and the way he made her feel during their meetings, was something she wanted.

"Eventually," she replied. She took a tentative step towards him, then another.

The SSO looked at her robe, then her unmade bed. His eyes met hers and he shifted, uncomfortable. It was the face of a mouse who had been cornered by the cat.

"Captain, I..."

"You're obviously straight, Manny," she said as her fingers deftly untied the knot holding her robe closed. She allowed the smooth fabric to slide off her shoulders and to the ground. "You don't wear a ring, so I assume you're single. You look at me during the meetings like a man who hasn't had his needs fulfilled in a very long time."

She slid into his arms and kissed his stubbly chin, tracing his jaw with her fingertip before moving up to his lips. She slid her leg up his thigh and felt him shiver. She kissed his lips, grasping the back of his neck with her hand. He responded, his strong hands pulling her close, his heart quickening, his breathing ragged.

She leaned away slightly, a coy smile on her lips. "Some people smoke, Manny. Others drink. Me? I have a whole other means to keeping it together when my stress gets too high. I need you, Manny. I need... all of you. I need you for this, and for the battle that is to come. Tell me... can I count on you by my side in the heat of the battle?"

Manny turned her around and buried his face into her neck, smelling her scent. She purred as his hand reached up to her throat. She arched her back into him more. His free hand caressed her hip. She reached back and began to unbutton the fly of his trousers. He groaned softly.

It was not rational. There wasn't a shred of rationality to be had. But at that moment, it was precisely what she needed before the Ra'tids made their next move.

*****

Dinah hooked her sled to the undercarriage of the *Solitude* and watched as the rest of her team followed suit. She focused on the metallic hull of the small stealth ship, her magnetic clips tethering her securely in place. Beyond the edge of the sled lay near-space, the thin region of the planet's atmosphere. The *Solitude* had slipped in at a crawl two hours earlier, going as slowly as possible so the ship would not disturb the air. Being stealthy had its advantages, but physics sometimes negated them.

Even dampened, the plated hull of the *Solitude* was still a metallic substance, subject to the varying degrees of heat and cold. To prevent any sort of visible trail, the *Solitude* would have to enter the atmosphere at a slow enough rate to keep the outer hull of the ship from heating, which could potentially create a large enough source of heat to be tracked by any anti-aircraft warning systems.

The slow speed would enable the *Solitude* to stay invisible on both infrared and electronic scanners. The downside was that the insertion process took nearly three hours after reaching the upper limits of the Janus' atmosphere.

She checked her seals a third time. In the vacuum of space, the smallest of holes in her suit could mean a quick and painful death. Even in the upper atmosphere, a breach would be deadly. The small electromagnetic field around her suit helped keep the microscopic particles of space dust from shredding her to pieces, as well as provide a small buffer for the trapped molecules of oxygen and nitrogen, which managed to leak out of the suit. They would be recycled back through the system, but it cost quite a bit of energy to use the process continually. As a result, the system tended to fluctuate as needed to conserve power, all the while keeping her alive. It was terrifyingly efficient.

"True atmosphere in five minutes," Captain Adim Heravi announced over the comm. He and his copilot were old hands at working with Dinah and her team. "Dinah, you're team ready back there?"

"Ready," she replied.

"Got some spotty AA fire off the starboard bow, range fifteen klicks," the *Solitude's* copilot informed them. "Exospheric shots. Looks like they're shooting at meteors or something. Adjusting course now."

"Captain, set us up for a LALO," she decided after consulting the coordinates and the direction of the shooting from near the base. "LZ could be hot."

"Negative," Heravi argued. "HALO jump only, LT. AA is just a bunch of high-altitude shots. Nothing to be worried about."

"I don't want to risk it, Captain," Dinah said. "Go low, about one thousand meters. We'll drop from there."

"You won't have any time for your reserve packs to kick in if the sleds fail, Dinah," Heravi reminded her. "Those sleds aren't rated to crash in these types of speeds."

"We best not crash, then."

"Dinah..."

"I'm away of the risks, Captain," Dinah stated. "This is my decision to make, and I've made it. Let's do the low altitude jump."

"Prepare for drop," Heravi said with a sigh as the nose of the *Solitude* angled sharply down. G-forces pushed Dinah deeper into her sled, the sudden increase in gravity causing her head to grow dizzy. She clenched her stomach and forced the blood to continue to circulate, allowing her to stay awake. She blinked her eyes and struggled to focus on something, anything other than the sensation of sleep. Dimly in the distance, she could hear Heravi counting down. "Three. Two. One. Drop drop drop!"

The *Solitude* jerked up and away she hurtled out of the back of the small stealth craft, the wind immediately grabbing her metallic chute and slowing her. The parachute slowed her down for an instant as the shuttlecock effect dragged the nose of the sled down and pointing towards the darkness below. Dinah smacked her head on the interior of the sled as her momentum was halted.

The parachute suddenly broke apart and fell back as the weight of the sled pushed her onwards. She was in free-fall, and only the thin layer of plastic around the sled was protecting her. She opened her mouth to scream but didn't have a chance as her sled plowed through the branches of a tall, thick tree.

Her head snapped to the left as the sled shattered, her protective shell gone. A branch emerged out of the darkness and slammed against her chest, knocking the wind out of her. She flopped limply against another tree branch and fell to the ground, her entire body wracked in pain. She heaved, struggling to get her breath back as more parts of her body informed her that she had been injured.

As she lay there on the soggy ground, her eyes staring up into the night sky, she wondered for the first time if black ops was really the career she wanted.

She sat up and groaned as new parts of her began to hurt. Her right elbow, she saw, was a bloody mess. Parts of her battle armor had been torn away during her uncontrolled descent, and the results weren't pretty. A small twig, no thicker than her finger, protruded from above the injured elbow. She bit her lip and looked down at the rest of her armor. There were no more holes, nor could she see any other signs of blood. She rubbed her ribs and groaned softly.

She was bruised and battered, but she was alive. That had to count for something.

She lifted her damaged arm and cursed as a fresh wave of pain washed over her. She yanked the small branch that had broken her armor and cursed as more pain exploded from the wound. She grabbed an injector from her pouch and slammed it into her arm. The injection flooded her arm with localized pain medication and the throbbing began to ebb. She looked at the bloody elbow and scowled. It hurt far worse than it looked, though aside from the blood, it didn't appear to be that bad at all. Even the branch that had stuck her had left a small, neat hole.

"Team, check in," she ordered as she disposed of the injector. She struggled to her feet and spotted the wrecked remains of her sled. She limped over to it and began searching for her gear.

"Ervin... Shoulder's dinged and I think I broke my wrist, but other than that, I'm good."

"Masters here. Busted ankle but I can walk."

"Zhin. No injuries."

"Anybody else? Kriyana? Mencia?" Dinah asked. Silence answered. In one fell swoop, she had lost half of her team to a fluke circumstance. She rubbed her elbow and checked the chamber of her combat rifle. Satisfied, she powered up the link between her rifle and her helmet. A small display window popped up in the corner of her eye, showing her exactly what her rifle was currently targeting. She tested the sight, lining up the old iron sights on a tree. Seeing that the link was solid, she looked around at her surroundings.

They had landed somewhere in a small swamp, which was nowhere near the original drop point that they had intended land in. The moons above were bright and made the swamp well lit, and the insects and animals in the area had fallen quiet. *Probably due to our disturbing them*, she decided. Vines clung to the trees and the ground felt soft underfoot. The air smelled of decaying animals and flowers. She tried not to gag but it was difficult, the pungent smell nearly overpowering. Intellectually, she knew that the Janus Academy rested near a swamp, but had not looked it over extensively. Nor had she given the thought of being stuck in a swamp much thought. One more mistake on a list that was rapidly growing longer by the minute. Dinah swallowed nervously and brought up their coordinates.

"Okay, we landed five miles off course. We need to swing east and get through the swamp. Ervin, you take point."

"Got it."

"Zhin? What's the status on the *Solitude*? Anything?"

Her comm tech responded immediately. "Gone, ma'am. That AA fire brought 'er down. Captain Heravi didn't fire off a distress beacon."

"Damn it," she grumbled. Her mood grew darker. "There goes our ride home."

"If I may, ma'am?" Zhin asked. Not waiting for a response, he pushed on. "We can always steal a ride home afterwards. Let's complete the mission, LT."

Dinah nodded. Zhin was right. She needed to stay on task if they had any hope of accomplishing their mission. Getting home, right now, should be the last thing on her mind. Finding Admiral Eidos and removing him from the picture was primary.

"Right. Let's move."

Chapter Four

When Dinah had gone to the Special Operations Command Survival School at Fort MacDill, she had been certain that there was no other place like it in the universe. The Florida heat and humidity was punishing enough, but when combined with the murky swamp, which surrounded the base it became the most inhospitable place, she could imagine. The swamp water smelled horribly, the air was thick with gnats and other bugs she shouldn't have breathed in, and the snakes were larger than the alligators. It was a purposefully designed hell to push the limits of human endurance.

It still was paradise when compared to the swamp that she currently found herself in.

The mud sucked at her armor, leeching through the miniscule cracks she didn't even realize were there, the ooze sliding down inside and chafing. Mosquitoes larger than birds screamed through the air on suicide missions, trying to suck the life out of them. Strange animals cried out in the dark, their howls promising a quick and particularly bloody death to anything they meet. All of these pales in comparison, however, to the life-sucking cold that enveloped the remnants of the Special Forces team.

Janus' southern hemisphere, where the Navy Academy lay, was in the midst of one of their harshest winters on record. However, because of the axial tilt of the planet, weather patterns prevented most forms of snowfall. Extreme weather patterns formed, with wind shear driving storms across the surface at rates only seen on Jupiter. Pushed by the wind, water turned to sluice and ice, so cold that even the battle-tested armor was barely able to withstand it.

Dinah's teeth chattered as she slid through the waist-high bog, the mud beneath her feet creating more resistance with each passing step. Her whole body was shaking slightly from the cold, and her hands felt like ice inside the insulated gloves. She didn't even want to try to guess how bad the frostbite would have been had she not had the gloves on. She held her rifle high above her head, keeping the chamber as dry as she could manage. The close combat rifle was designed to resist all elements, but she knew from long experience that keeping it dry and ooze-free meant that it would last longer and fire better.

"F-f-f-f-f..." she tried to swear but failed. Her lips were numb, and she was almost certain that her nose had fallen off somewhere behind her. She spotted the edge of the bog, and the dry land beyond it, and almost wet herself in relief. Atop the bank stood Ervin, his rifle up but not aimed anywhere in particular. His normally cheerful face was scowling.

"Damn swamp," he growled and extended a hand. Dinah willingly accepted the helped, and she quickly was out of the bog and on solid land. A cold breeze blew past, sending another chill up her spine. "Zhin and Masters are right behind you, ma'am."

"Right," she said and shouldered her rifle. She turned and reached out for Zhin, who grasped her proffered hand and used her to pull himself up and out of the water. He fell to the ground and sighed, resting for a moment. Masters arrived last, his bulky, swearing form completely covered with the tar-like mud of the swamp. He spat back at the bog as soon as he was on dry land.

"That was some bullshit right there," he grumbled. "I've got mud in places I'd rather not talk about."

"Good news," Dinah said as they all huddled close, partly for companionship, mostly for warmth. She pointed northerly through the underbrush. "Target's residence is five hundred feet through those bushes."

"Their Rapier Commandos train in this crap?" Zhin asked and shook his head. "I'm impressed."

"Don't be," Dinah countered. "Drake said that they only spend three days in the muck. How long did you spend in the swamp at

MacDill?"

"Yeah, but at least there it was warm," the young corporal argued. "Very warm."

"Come on," she urged them. "Dawn's five hours away. I want to be off-planet long before then."

Zhin set out first again, shaking his leg every few steps to break loose the last of the muck. Dinah and Ervin waited for him to separate from the group before following, with Masters on rear guard, still muttering and cursing under his breath.

They slowed their pace as they moved through the rapidly thinning forest, their weapons up and ready. Dinah spotted Zhin lying prone next to a small bush, his rifle pointed towards the target house. She got Ervin's attention and signaled for him to follow her. He nodded and they moved to the left, her rifle coming off her shoulder. She knelt down and pulled out a small tool she had used sparingly during her sniper-training course back on Earth.

Two sentries were posted outside the admiral's house, Dinah saw as she spotted them through her laser viewfinder. Next to her, Ervin was peering at the two guards through his scope. The long barrel of his rifle was trained on the left guard, while fifteen feet away, Masters and Zhin were targeting the guard on the right. Both men waited patiently for Dinah to give the word.

"Execute," she sub vocalized, her tone lower than a whisper. Two flechette rounds lanced out and dropped both Coalition guards. They slumped to the ground, dead, each with a neat hole right where their hearts had been being the only sign of any wound.

Dinah was on her feet and heading towards the house before the guards had fallen to the ground. She barely spared them a glance as she leapt up the porch stairs. She stopped, looked at the electronic lock affixed to the front door, and pulled out her lock picking kit. She set the magnetic disruptor next to the digital readout. A moment later, the lock clicked as the strong magnetic device scrambled the hard drive inside the lock. The door *clicked* and swung open. She exhaled in relief. They were in.

She carefully pushed the door open and peeked inside. The entry parlor was dark and silent. She lowered the filter over her visor to scan for any signs of a laser alarm. There was none in the parlor, so she motioned for Ervin to move in. Zhin and Masters came in right behind him, leaving her to turn and sweep the front yard one final time. Nothing moved.

Dinah stepped inside and motioned upstairs. Ervin went first, his rifle aimed up the stairs as he quickly ascended the stairs, Zhin right behind him. She pointed for Masters to remain where he was, received a confirmation nod, and followed the duo upstairs, every sense in her body tingling with excitement and adrenaline.

Having spotted Masters and Zhin waiting for her outside the master suite, Dinah kept moving. She saw the two fingers that Zhin held up and slowed down, annoyed. Her mind flicked back over the intelligence briefing in her brain, but nothing about a wife or mistress came to mind. *Perhaps the old coot is sleeping with his protection detail*, she thought. She gently touched Zhin's shoulder and leaned past him, looking inside. Two dark shapes lay still on the bed, sound asleep.

She chewed her bottom lip for a moment as she considered taking both of them. If the second person was someone that the admiral cared about, then they could potentially use that as leverage during the debriefing process. On the other hand, she wasn't sure if she could manage two prisoners, since she had already lost half her team during the insertion process. Tasking Zhin and Ervin to babysit the two prisoners meant that only her and Masters would be fully combat capable.

She looked back at Zhin, who nodded and slipped into the room. Staying in the shadows, Zhin moved to the left side of the bed, while she took the right. She brought her weapon up as she drew closer, her eyes fixated on the tuft of silvery hair she could see on the pillow. The other occupant had dark hair, she saw. Intelligence reports had the admiral having silver hair. Zhin had the mystery occupant, while she had the admiral.

She made a small chopping motion at Zhin, and then pointed to his target. He nodded and pulled out a small hypodermic needle from his belt pouch. Carefully, he checked the liquid inside before sliding the tip of the needle into the other person's arm. He injected the contents and gave Dinah a thumbs-up sign. She began to count to five, slowly, in her head.

"Get up!" she suddenly screamed into the ear of Admiral Eidos. She jerked back his blankets and roughly pulled him from the bed. Dazed, the elderly military officer stumbled to the floor and fell to his knees. His eyes were wide with fear as he looked up and at Dinah, who pointed the barrel of her weapon at his face. "Admiral Joseph Eidos?"

"What?" the man stuttered, confused.

"Shut up," Dinah ordered and smacked him across the back of his head. She had to keep him confused, disorientated, so that he would not offer much resistance. "Bind his hands."

"What's going on?" Eidos repeated, his voice filled with terror. "What'd you do to Moira?"

Dinah struck him again. The admiral yelped as Dinah's heavy blow drew blood. Zhin moved behind the admiral and bound his hands, securing them with zip ties. He grabbed the admiral by his elbow and hauled him to his feet.

"Gag him," Dinah said. Zhin nodded and slapped a piece of duct tape across the admiral's mouth. She glanced over at the still-sleeping form of the woman the admiral had identified. "Leave her."

"How we looking, Masters?" she asked in the comm.

"Golden, ma'am," came the reply. "I've hacked their local network and found a bunch of potentials for our exit strategy. An old airfield used to train pilots is about half klick down the road. There might be something we can use there."

"Good plan," she said.

"No noise about the *Solitude* yet either."

"That's... good, I guess," she shook her head. "Would have thought the net would be buzzing with the news."

"Counting our blessings, ma'am."

"I agree. Let's bug out and find this airbase. We're coming down now." She pushed the admiral against the wall and leaned close to his ear. "I can keep you alive and in constant pain, or I keep you alive and without it. I'd recommend without. Don't resist, don't fight, and this will all be over shortly. Understand, admiral?"

The admiral nodded. Dinah smiled.

"Let's move."

*****

The old training field was easy to find. Zhin immediately set out to locate and commandeer a ride for the group and their hostage.

Dinah guided Admiral Eidos to a small crate, where she forced him to sit and rest. She grabbed the duct tape, which secured his mouth and ripped it off quickly. The admiral gasped and began to work his jaw loose, which had grown stiff from the tape. Dinah withdrew a small bottle of water and offered him some. He turned his head away. She frowned.

"Drin it," she ordered. "I need you alive. I don't need your teeth, however. You don't drink. I'll break them and force the water down your throat."

"Barbaric," Eidos muttered but took the water.

"There aren't many women in special operations," she said as she rested her gun across her knee. "Do you know how hard it is to accomplish what I have? You can try to downplay my accomplishments all you want but, in the end, I've succeeded where countless have failed. You think of me as barbaric? Pal, you have no idea just how barbaric I can be."

"Succeeded how, exactly?" Eidos asked as she took the water bottle away. "You are Lieutenant Dinah Elisbeth Ridge, age twenty-seven, of the Earth Republic. Oh, don't be surprised. We know who all of the black ops operatives are these days. It's hard not to, what with the war on. Let me see... ah, yes. You are the daughter of Reginald Ridge, one of the so-called 'Piper's Dozen' who made their ill-fated stand against the Coalition back when we were nothing more than a few hundred desperate, starving rebels. So brave of him to die after slaughtering us by the hundreds, wouldn't you agree? Granted a battlefield commission after actions during the Battle for Earth. Correct me if I'm wrong, but later you were tested to see if you were a Gener upon your conscription into the Army, right? Your own people don't trust you. All your so-called accomplishments, and they still don't trust you. You passed their tests, and then you passed more tests. Tested more frequently than others. That doesn't show a high degree of trust on their part."

"They trust me enough," she said and raised her gun. She aimed directly at his chest.

"Look at yourself," Eidos said, his voice calm despite the gun which was trained on him. "You're brilliant, young, but not quite the ideal physical specimen. Yet you're struggling to be something more, fighting against the rising feeling of ineptitude. You've failed, and that stings you worse than anything. You know that the criticisms are true."

"It means nothing," she growled. "I've dealt with a ton of criticism. They're just words. Empty words and stupid whispers." Eidos clucked his tongue.

"Poor girl," he said. "This is your parents doing, you know?"

"You need to shut up. Now."

"They taught you that you can be whatever you want, be whoever you wish to be," Eidos' voice grew softer. "But that's false. Nature has led you to be an inferior being physically, to be designed to be intelligent, to break the mold when it comes to your brain. Nature has done this to you, yet your parents nurturing has tried to break what was intended for you to be. You idealized your father's exploits, his heroics, and his sacrifice, and you wanted to be like him. Your mother, foolish woman, allowed you to become deluded in your pursuit of greatness, to believe that you can be something that nature did not intend for you to be."

"I could choose to put a bullet in your head right now," Dinah said. "So quit talking."

"You could, yes," Eidos dipped his head. "But you won't. Would you like to know why?"

"Humor me."

"You could never put your emotions aside. You could never be... Drake."

Her eyes widened. "How...?"

"We knew who betrayed us to the Republic when the counterattack began," Eidos explained, his voice smug. "It wasn't hard to figure it out. A Rapier Commando goes missing, and then all of a sudden the tide of battle completely turns? War doesn't happen so neatly, girl. War is messy, and the sort of this that makes a person wish they could never look upon it again. So you were promoted from a common conscripted soldier to an officer, given a choice assignment... and for what? For spreading your legs and asking a traitor to join your ranks? You didn't earn anything on merit, girl. You didn't prove anything. They don't follow you because of what you've accomplished, oh no. They don't see you as a warrior, a heroine. They follow you because they are told to."

"I'm three seconds away from blowing your brains out," Dinah threatened.

"You already promised that a minute ago," Eidos reminded her. "Sad, really."

"What?"

"You."

"What do you mean?"

The admiral stayed silent, however. Dinah looked away as Zhin entered the small bay.

"Ma'am, I think we found us a bus," the corporal said. He looked over at the admiral. "How's the turkey?"

"Nothing I couldn't handle," she said, managing to keep the bristling rage she felt in her gut from exploding outwards. "What's the ride?"

"I found an old Mercury transport, ma'am," Zhin answered. "Engines look good, and Masters thinks he can rig the transponder."

"A civilian transport?" Dinah asked, surprised. "Can it pull the speed in Void space that we need to escape when the alert – and there will be an alert – goes out?"

"It better," Zhin shook his head. "Or this'll be the shortest hostile extraction in the history of the Republic."

"LT, this is Masters," a voice came over the comm. Dinah turned away from the admiral.

"Go ahead, Mike."

"Our bus looks good to go, ma'am," he said. "We're ready to liftoff in ten."

"Got it. Eyes on target," she said. "Be there in five. Out," she killed the comm and looked at Zhin. "Grab the turkey. We're ready to roll."

"Yes ma'am." Zhin smiled. He pulled out a fresh strip of duct tape. "Finally, something is going right for a change."

****

"Yeah, that's the throttle," Masters muttered as he looked over the instrument panel. He pushed it full, but the engines continued to cough and howl in protest. He scratched his chin. "Well, that didn't work. Flaps? No, this thing doesn't have flaps. Maybe there's some sort of parking brake?"

"Well? Can you fly this damned thing or not?" Dinah screamed into Masters' ear.

"I don't know, ma'am!" the old soldier yelled back. "I keep pushing the thrust, but the damned ship ain't moving!"

"Ma'am?" Zhin tried to interject.

"Well, figure it out!" Dinah shouted back, ignoring the diminutive corporal. "If we can't get enough speed to break gravity, then we're stuck on this godforsaken muddy hell!"

"If I knew what was stopping us from exiting orbit, ma'am, I'd fix it," Masters stated.

"I think I might know..." Zhin tried again.

"Have you checked the relay from the thrusters to the control panel?" Dinah asked.

"Twice," Masters replied.

"And the systems show green?"

"Yes ma'am."

"And the throttles are maxed?"

"Of course."

"Then what the hell is going on here?"

Zhin pushed past the two and slapped an instrument on the console. The engines suddenly ceased their choppy howling and settled into a smooth purr. The vessel began to increase speed, and within moments, they were in the planet's upper atmosphere.

Dinah and Masters looked at Zhin, dumbfounded. The corporal shrugged.

"You left the choke on," he explained. "Older combustible engines like these use a choke to help it start. Once the engine is running, you turn off the choke. It won't run well with the choke, because too much fuel is being dumped into the engines. You were flooding the engines."

"Maybe we should let you fly..." Dinah murmured as she

looked around the cockpit. "Is there some sort of manual or anything?"

"How hard can it be?" Masters asked as he guided the ship into space.

"We couldn't even figure out why the engines were making that sound," Dinah reminded him.

"Details."

"Ma'am?" Zhin interrupted again. This time Dinah let him speak. "Let me fly this thing. I'm rated for small cutter vessels, and this thing isn't much bigger than them."

Dinah blinked. "Why didn't you say so earlier?"

"I *tried*, ma'am."

"Okay, fine," Dinah tried to keep the frustration out of her tone. "Take the helm. Masters, help him."

"What about you, ma'am?" Masters asked.

"I'm going to check on Ervin and the prisoner."

****

Dinah writhed in pain as the dark energy folded around her, black tendrils wrapped around her midsection. Pain manifested from every pore in her skin, down to the cellular level. She tried to break free but the pain was too much to bear. She opened her mouth to scream, but nothing came out. The air in her lungs burned from the energy, sucking every bit of willpower from her soul. Whatever it was, it had hit her the second she walked into the section of the ship where Eidos was. She could see him through the haze of pain and terror, moving towards her.

"What the hell. . ." she moaned, knowing that it was useless to cry for help. The others would never hear her in the forward section as the door had sealed itself behind her as she had entered.

"Oh, that? That's something we found years ago," Eidos explained as he walked around Dinah's twitching form, his soft footsteps echoing inside Dinah's ears. "It harnesses the electromagnetic energy surrounding a human being, and well, I suppose you would say that it eats that energy. The problem, we've found, is that the energy around a human being is very important to staying alive."

He looked at her and clucked his tongue. "Poor Dinah. Poor, poor Dinah. You should have been one of us. You would have enjoyed using your brain to unlock the puzzles in the universe. Your delusions of grandeur would have passed when you realized that your brain was needed for the greater good. Such a waste."

Dinah managed to groan in pain. Eidos nodded, impressed.

"You're a tough one, I'll give you that."

"How?" She grounded out.

"Ships we have plenty of. More than you could possibly imagine girl. We needed more troops however," Eidos explained, his tone gentle as he touched her cheek. The contact made the hairs on the back of Dinah's neck stand up. "Our losses were so severe that we were in danger of losing all we had fought for. The Republic continued to grind at us, to wear us down until one day we wouldn't have any more men to fight. Then we'd be under their yoke once more, ruled instead of free. So we started looking into alternative... methods."

"Clones," she hissed as the dark energy wavered for a moment. She tried to pull herself up but the energy came back quickly, crushing her to the floor.

"Again you impress me," he said. "I never thought that one person could continue to surprise me. Yes, dear girl. Clones. We needed fully capable soldiers, and we needed them quickly. Each person in the Coalition is the proud genetic parent of one thousand cloned soldiers, and our numbers are growing. Our ranks are filling. Meanwhile, the Republic continues to have unsustainable losses. We *will* win, Lieutenant. All we have to do is keep applying pressure."

He knelt beside her twitching form. "Your genetic diversification will help us win this war, Dinah. I should thank you."

"But. . ." Dinah thrashed about as another wave of pain washed over her, struggling to get out the words, "Where did you get the tech?"

Dinah wasn't a scientist but even she knew viable clones were way outside of either Republic or Coalition tech. There was only star power who possessed the means to create that sort the sort of army Eidos was bragging about. It also explained how the Ra'tids had gotten the new ships that everyone back home was scared to death about.

Eidos merely smiled but Dinah saw her guess at who was behind it all confirmed in his eyes and it horrified her. If it were true, it would change everything about the war between the Republic and the Coalition. It would change the entire balance of power in known space too. She had to get away. Get word to the General.

Dark energy lanced out again, enveloping her. She screamed in a combination of pain, fury, and fear, as her flesh began to melt away from her bones. Her skin sloughed off her body by the handfuls. Her tears evaporating as they formed. Dinah tried to scream but all that came out was a sickening gargling noise. The energy continued to lash at her long after she had blacked out and her lungs had shutdown. The last thing she saw before death claimed her was Eidos heading out to deal with the remainder of her squad. There would be no escape for them either.

****

Masters was at the helm, taking over for Zihn who turned to meet Dinah he heard as the door behind them opening.

"How's the prisoner?" Zihn started but Eidos shot him point blank in the face with a pistol he'd lifted off one of the other troopers' bodies.

Fragments of bone from Zihn's skull struck the screen near Masters as Zihn's blood splashed over him.

Eidos fired at Masters but he was fast and lucky enough to duck the bullet streaking towards his head. It hit the ship's controls sending a shower of sparks flying.

Masters lunged at Eidos, tackling him like an old Earth football player before the Coalition officer could get off a second shot. Eidos's gun was flung from his grasp. It bounced across the floor of the pilot compartment as Eidos and Masters crashed into the wall. Eidos took the brunt of the impact, his breath being knocked from his lungs.

Seizing the moment, Masters lashed out, swinging a fist at Eidos but the older man was faster than he looked. He caught

Masters' arm, twisting it until the snapping sound of breaking bone echoed in the compartment.

Masters cried out more in surprise than pain. He was used to pain. It came with the job. As Eidos released him, he staggered backwards, regaining his balance. His broken arm hung limply at his side as Master eyed Eidos, searching for an opening.

A new eruption of sparks burst from the controls of the ship as the damage from Eidos bullet finally became too much for the emergency autopilot system to deal with. The ship lurched in the air, sending both Eidos and Masters bouncing about the compartment.

"It doesn't matter if I die here," Eidos was laughing. "Your precious Republic is doomed!"

Eidos had landed on the other side of the compartment from where he came down. Master drew his sidearm with his good hand and put a bullet into the Coalition officer. Eidos's head snapped back as the round entered his brain and reduced it to pulp inside his skull.

Masters leaped to his feet, racing for the damage controls. As he did so, he saw the ground coming up at him fast, too fast. Then there was only fire and followed by darkness.

****

General Soltus was in his office, attending the day's accumulated paperwork when he got the word. Not only had Dinah and her team failed in their mission, but also if the reports were to believed, they were all dead. He knew there would be Hell to pay when Drake found out about Dinah but he had bigger things to deal with right now than even the former Coalition savior of Earth did. Templar Saul's mission was getting underway and there was much to be done. Unlike the one he'd sent Dinah on, Soltus very much doubted the Republic would survive if the former Templar failed as the young lieutenant had.

Chapter Five

Thierry Hunter was righteously ticked off.

Having his ship, the *Caliban*, drafted into the Republic's service was bad enough, but knowing that the mission he and his crew had been assigned to assist with was an Army black op, well, that was just fragging *wrong*. He yanked the data pad containing his orders from the hands of the Lieutenant who had delivered them and threw it against the metal of *Caliban's* airlock. It smashed into pieces on impact, showering the deck with now-useless bits of electronic hardware.

"This? *This* is what you draft us into doing?" Hunter shouted, jabbing a finger at the broken data pad. "How dare you uptight, boneheaded snake eaters come in here and tell me that I have to help with a black op when all I agreed to was supply and support!"

The stunned Lieutenant took a step back from Hunter. "I don't write the orders, sir. I just deliver them. I'm nothing but some low-paid flunky like yourself."

"Excuse me?"

The Lieutenant paled. He was saved when a statuesque, raven-headed beauty stuck her head in through the partially open airlock. She slid into the room and placed a hand on her boss' shoulder, trying to soothe him.

"Easy, boss," she murmured. "Ain't worth it."

Hunter paused. Mizi was right, as always. Damn it. The Lieutenant was eyeballing Mizi now, his eyes freely exploring what there was to be had. He beamed a smile at her.

"Morning, ma'am."

"You lack the proper parts to make my morning good," she said, her tone as cold as void space itself. "It's time for you to leave."

The Lieutenant's grin slipped off his face. He looked from Mizi back to Hunter, and decided that it was in his best interests to heed her advice. He whirled, and almost running, escaped from the docking passage of the *Caliban*, out the airlock and back to the courier ship he had been tasked to.

Mizi dogged the hatch behind him and checked the airlock. As it cycled to green, the *Caliban* shuddered slightly as the courier ship disengaged. The air tube retracted and once more was the small ship alone in space.

Hunter was shaking his head as Mizi looked at her longtime boss. "I don't like it, Mizi. Not one bit. Orders so secret that they're hand delivered, in person, for a black ops mission that's too secret to even mention in the hand delivered message? That, dear girl, is never a good sign."

"Who says you have to like it, boss?" Mizi laughed softly. She followed Hunter as he headed for the *Caliban's* bridge.

The *Caliban* was a small ship, as far as civilian vessels went. Most, at casual glance, often mistook her for a simple courier ship, like the one that had just departed. That was often a dangerous mistake, since the *Caliban* was so much more than that. A prototype that had been developed by the Republic Navy during the early months of the Coalition War was designed to be an all-purpose infiltration operations boat. Just over eighteen hundred feet long, she could easily house a small platoon of power armored soldiers, or a large black ops unit, with room for a land vehicle, should the need arise. Bristling with armament, the former Republic prototype had been sold to Hunter by an acquaintance during the chaotic aftermath of the Battle of Earth. Deemed unsuitable by NAVINT for sustained warfare, the ship design was set aside for larger naval units.

Black ops. The ugly underbelly of modern warfare. *Caliban* had been designed perfectly for this task, to carry out the secret, and oftentimes, illegal operations of a military unit. In Hunter's entrepreneurial hands, it was a perfect ship for smuggling. The acquaintance who had sold Hunter the *Caliban* had known precisely what Hunter had intended for it, and Hunter had paid him more than a small fortune to get his hands on the dangerous little ship. She had been worth every penny then, though now Hunter was regretting leaving his contact information with his acquaintance. He had not expected the Republic to come calling for help, no matter how good the pay was.

The pay is damn good, though, he allowed.

"Blast it," Hunter muttered. Mizi watched him pace through the *Caliban's* narrow corridors.

"You gonna tell me what our orders are, boss, or am I guessing here?"

"Let's just say that it's going to involve a little bit of what this ship was designed for, as well as going deeper into explored space than any human being has gone with some uninvited guests. That kind of says it all, doesn't it?"

Mizi whistled. "Gener or Ra'tid?"

"Who's been threatening war?"

"That *is* some bad mojo. I take it this is all on the unofficial side of things, too. No support?"

"Blacker than your hair, darling," Hunter spat. "So take a gander."

"I figured as much, judging from how you were acting," Mizi grinned. "So where are we picking up our *guests*?"

"Oh, you're going to love it. You sure you want me to spoil the surprise?"

"You always spoil the surprise. Tell me anyway."

"That big gathering of Republic warships we keep here about on our side of the Weligo Terminus? Well, that's where they're supposed to be. We're to drop into normal space outside the fleet's sensor range, pick our guests up from a transport that's malfunctioning, slip *through* the Terminus undetected and go from there."

"Great!" Mizi laughed. "It's so simple, isn't it? I know how much you love hanging out with the Navy. Should be fun. It's not like we're an illegally owned and operated mercenary warship or anything. I'm sure they'll welcome our presence with open arms and kittens if they spot us."

They reached the bridge. Mizi flopped into her co-pilot's chair and looked at her boss expectantly.

"That's one of the things I love about you, Mizi," Hunter retorted as he climbed into the captain's chair. "You are ever the optimist."

The helmsman spun his chair around, glowering at the two. "Did I just hear you two right?" Alves asked.

"Eavesdropping again?" Mizi chuckled. "Don't you have anything else to do, Alves?"

"Hey! I can't help it when you guys talk so loud," Alves glanced over at his boss.

"Don't get your panties all in a wad, Alves." Hunter started calling up data on his chair's arm viewer. "This ain't nothing we haven't done before."

"Really? I can't recall us ever trying to sneak in under the noses of an entire battle fleet on high alert at the edge of a war zone," Alves grumbled.

"The *Caliban* can handle it," Hunter said, pride evident in his voice. "You just keep her powered down to civilian freighter levels and her other systems will do the rest. We'll pick up our guests and be through the Terminus before they even know we're there."

Alves cocked his head to the side, shooting Hunter a *whatever you say* look, then spun his chair back to face the helm. "Laying in course," he said as the data Hunter had uploaded began to cycle through the computer systems, charting the most optimal route to their rendezvous point with the black ops team. "ETA, two hours."

True to Alves' word, the *Caliban* slipped into the system undetected precisely two hours later, which made Hunter happy. He knew his ship. When she performed as well or better than he often bragged about, it made his day. Of course, the damaged freighter they had recovered the black ops team from had nearly rammed into the *Caliban* as it tried to adjust its course. Nevertheless, Alves, for all his worrying and troubles, was a skilled enough helmsman to avoid the freighter. The *Caliban* had left the freighter behind as fast as possible, letting the vessel drift in space. Hunter knew that in about eight hours, the freighter would be rescued by its parent company, and promptly towed back to their home port of Perth Prime. Hopefully, no one would be the wiser.

He looked up at his readings as they slipped into the space around the Weligo Terminus. The station remained on high alert, he saw as his scanners picked up every single sensor that was both active and passive emanating from the powerful station. The station probably had them on sensor but, with any luck, the sensor techs wouldn't know what they were looking at.

He rubbed his eyes. He just hoped the bastards in the back weren't going to give him any trouble.

*****

Saul sat in the cargo hole of the *Caliban*, separate from the seven elite Republic shock operatives. They mostly sat around, talking quietly amongst themselves. One paced continuously, muttering under his breath the entire time. He hadn't had time to get to know any of them yet, though he had read a little bit of their files. General Soltus had thrown the entire team together so quickly that Saul hadn't even had time to truly delve into their personnel files. While he had faith that they were the best at what they did, or else they wouldn't be there, doctrine reminded him of one very important saying before combat.

"In God we trust; all others, we verify," he whispered the unofficial mantra of the Templar. He looked at the nearest operative. He needed to know the men and women who were dropping with him. When one was behind enemy lines, all they had were each other. He wanted to know what kind of people had his back. He motioned at the young operative. "Hey, what's your name?"

She looked up from cleaning her rifle, though her hands continued to field strip and clean the firing mechanism. He could see a lean and toned figure beneath the combat armor, and the familiar ease in which she cleaned her weapon told him much. She was a confident woman, late twenties, and was very familiar with the wet work side of the military. She finished cleaning her weapon before she slapped it back together, her hands nearly a blur. Locking the barrel into place, she met his eyes.

"Specialist Hera Gunter, sir."

"Nice to meet you, Gunter. I'm Saul. Please don't call me sir," he added, his voice slightly louder than hers. He wanted to ensure that anyone listening in could hear. "I'm not military, not really."

Gunter gave him an appraising look. "Could have fooled me, sir."

"What do you mean?" he asked, curious.

"You have what we call the thousand yard stare, sir. You've been in the fire, seen the blood."

Saul shrugged. "I suppose I have at that, once upon a time."

"I'm your comms geek, sir," Gunter stated, answering the unasked question. "I'm also doubling as your backup medic."

"Everyone's cross trained?" Saul asked, surprised. He had thought that only Templars thought that way.

"Something the brass learned firsthand when fighting the Order, sir," Gunter said. "The Order troopers cross trained so much that there was always someone else to pick up the slack when they lost a troop. Good idea that we took and ran with."

"And him?" Saul jerked a thumb at the biggest operative in the group, who had not stopped pacing since he first set foot in the *Caliban*.

"Him? That's Staff Sergeant Booker Sheffield, sir. We call him Sarge Zombie. He's our cobblesmith, our, uh, tinkerer I guess. He has some sort of background in xenobiologic technology, which means he gets to play with alien toys a bunch. He's also our sniper's backup spotter, should it all hit the fan. He also backs me up on comms"

"Zombie?" Saul asked.

"Long story, one that he should tell, not me, sir," Gunter said. "It's a good one, but he insists upon getting the honor. He gets sensitive about it if someone else gets to tell it. Hey, Zombie!"

The large operative stopped pacing and locked onto Gunter, his ice blue eyes unblinking for long moments before he turned towards them. He slowly walked to where Saul and Gunter were seated. Gunter smirked and motioned for the man to come closer. He stopped and stood at parade rest, his hands clasped behind his back, his feet precisely shoulder-width apart.

"Why do we call you Sarge Zombie?" Gunter asked the giant. "Saul here wants to know."

"I've been dead, sir. Three times, officially now," Zombie

replied, his voice metallic and hollow, the artificial voice box lodged where his Adam's apple should have been. "First time was at New Mars. Training exercise where our transport crashed. An accident, but an avoidable one. We were integrating Gener tech with our stuff. Nobody knew then about the fail-safe that they'd built into their tech yet. Second time was, pardon the expression, a total clusterfuck of a mission. We'd gone in to extract a force recon team that had gotten cut off by the Coalition. They had anti-aircraft. We were unarmored. Intel never passed on the message, so we went in without any sort of air support. Got the hell blown out of us, lost most of my squad. Third time was my fault. Electrocuted myself while pissing on a fence one night while on a drinking spree on my way up the old Eagle's Nest fortress back on Earth. Brass keeps saving me, though. I'm more cloned tissue and cybernetics than true human now. I like to think that my skills are too valuable to waste. I suspect, though, that the brass just doesn't know what to do with my corpse, so they keep bringing me back. I must have an endearing personality when dead."

Gunter was quiet for a moment, and then asked "Are we really going to Ra'tid Prime, sir?"

Saul gave her a funny look. "You weren't briefed on what we're doing beforehand?"

"No sir," Gunter confirmed. "OPSEC. Scuttlebutt suggested Ra'tid because of the *Serinus*. None of us were briefed on the actual mission, though, just that you were in command and follow your orders."

"Seriously, stop it with the sir stuff," Saul rose from where he sat. He glanced at Zombie and saw that the massive operative was as big as advertised. "General Soltus needs intel. We're going to provide it, and perhaps leave the Ra'tids a little gift when we extract."

"Good to know, sir... uh... Saul," Gunter's smiled grew feral. "I just like to know who I'm about to kill is all."

Saul laughed. "Rocks aren't easy to kill. Not by a long shot."

"Never thought otherwise," Gunter continued to grin. "Guess I'll need to practice on them. A lot."

Saul left her sitting on the piles of boxes as the cargo bay door dilated open. The *Caliban's* captain entered, looking every inch his name. Saul had yet to introduce himself to the captain of their ride.

"Captain Hunter," Saul extended his hand as he approached. "I'm Saul."

Hunter ignored the offered hand. "Let's get a few things straight from the get-go, Mister Saul. The *Caliban* is *my* ship. I don't care what sort of authorization and power you've been given. While you're onboard my ship, I'm in command, not you. Our lives depend on this understanding. We *will* get you to Ra'tid Prime and fate willing, off again, assuming you don't miss the rendezvous at the pre-designated time. That is *all* we are gonna do, though. My crew stays with the ship at all times. It's not our job to help you with whatever it is that you'll be doing while not on my ship. The *Caliban* is your ride. Is that understood?"

"Understood," Saul said, taken aback by Hunter's sudden hostility.

"Good. Anything you need, my crew will bring to you here. Your troops are confined to the cargo hold and the aft berthing area. I don't want them moving about my ship and mucking stuff up. Just call for one of us if you need something," Hunter stated before turning on his heel and left, leaving a surprised Saul in his wake.

"Thank you?" Saul tried. The door to the hold closed shut. Zombie began to laugh, metallic echoes emanating from deep within his chest.

"Nice sort of fellow, now ain't he?"

*****

Fleet Admiral Hien stood on the bridge of the *Behemoth*, which he had made his personal flagship after taking command of the combined Darian/Republic fleet. Being aboard the super dreadnaught made him feel at home once more, and reminded him of how he had made his way up the ranks so very long before. His eyes swept across the bridge meticulously, looking over every detail with a critical eye. While the *Behemoth* was officially Captain Banner's command, Hien felt that he would be remiss in his duty not to double-check everything that the captain did.

While no captain liked having their ship commandeered out

from underneath them, there was always the added career benefit of being captain of the flagship of a fleet. Not only did it make a man privy to all the inside dirt on the Admiralty, it also looked excellent on a review folder when the promotional boards came up. Any officer desiring a flag ranking wanted to be the captain of a fleet's flagship.

In addition, Hien liked to think that his reputation as a fine line officer made it somewhat easier. Hien had served more than his fair share of time on the wet side of the Navy before promotions took his further and further away from where he always felt his proper place was. He craved the action, the sweat and stank of a bridge working under wartime condition, the lack of sleep and the cravings of nicotine and caffeine stimulants. He allowed Banner to maintain command of the ship, but nobody questioned who really was in charge. Everyone already knew, Hien was certain.

Hien looked over the sensor readouts and sighed. The number of Darian ships that had turned up so far to join them was pitiful in comparison to the tonnage that the Republic was investing into the operation. Three Darian carrier ships, with a cluster of four heavy cruisers and three destroyers accompanying them for support, was not what he had in mind when he had pleaded the Republic's case to the Darian representative. Ambassador Xarn, apparently, had been telling the truth in just how little the Emperor of the Darian Empire was willing to risk in eliminating the Darian's long-time blood enemy. It annoyed Hien to no end about the lack of fight in the Darians, but that was tempered by just how dangerous even that small number of Darian ships could be, and the options that having the Darian carriers offered to the enterprising admiral.

Unlike the other galactic powers, the Darians were firm believers in personal combat, and how they fought reflected that. They had taken the use of the one-man fighters to an art form not seen since the heady days before the Republic's unification of Earth, and were very deadly when attacking larger ships. The small fighters were nimble and quick, able to slip inside the point-defenses of a capital ship to wreak havoc. They also could swarm a larger ship and tear it apart, something Hien had seen personally in action long before. The drawbacks to the fighters, however, was the lack of armor and their limited time in space.

The fighters did carry CKs, however. The capital killers, combined with the swarming attacks of the fighters, could take out something even as large as the *Behemoth*. Hien didn't doubt the added fury and skill that the Darian pilots would bring to the battle, their honor and society demanding the death of as many Rocks as they could. There was no greater glory for a cat than to die in battle, taking as many of the enemy with them as they could.

Hien knew that, worst-case scenario, the Republic super dreadnaughts could more than make up for the lack of Darian capital ships. Over a dozen battleships alone were in his fleet, as well as three more super dreadnaughts. A healthy mixture of thirty heavy cruisers and destroyers were escorting them, establishing a solid picket line that even the Coalition would hesitate to engage. He nodded. His fleet was ready. Their final destination, Ra'tid Prime, was set into the navigator's sensor bank. They were ready, awaiting for him to give the word.

Hien checked the time. He wasn't nervous, merely eager for the operation to get started. His own plan called for the fleet to wait for three more hours before heading through the Terminus, so that any extra Republic or Darian ships could join the fleet. Knowing that it was *his* plan did not ease the tension or eagerness, though. Hien's gut told him that those who were going to arrive already had. He spotted a yeoman bringing coffee for Captain Banner and flagged her down. She nearly tripped over her own feet as she brought him some coffee as well.

Hien accepted the coffee from her trembling hands. "Thank you," he said, and shooed her away as he moved closer to the captain's chair, where Banner sat.

The wormhole flashed beyond the Hector II station, but Hien could not see a ship. He glanced at the captain.

"What was that?" Hien asked.

"Damaged freighter near the junction triggers the wormhole accidentally at random intervals, Admiral," Banner explained as he eyed the coffee in the admiral's hands. "Station says that the company's rep is wringing his hands at the lost revenue, and they're trying to get a replacement ship out tomorrow. Annoying the station commander as well, but there's little they can do about it besides tasking a cutter to tow it away from the junction." He shrugged. "He's got bigger fish to fry, I suppose."

"That's one hell of an assumption, Captain," Hien warned. Banner looked up at the admiral.

"I've had weapons and sensors running tactical simulated attacks on it for the past two hours, including adding in the new difficulty we've had in targeting the Ra'tid ships," Banner explained. "I'm well aware of the security risk, Admiral, and my crew is well-prepared."

"Captain Banner," Hien leaned over, looking down at the seated man. "I want the fleet ready to move inside the hour. I'm tired of waiting around. We need to have an element of surprise, and the more time we waste here, the less likely we are to retain the surprise."

"But sir, your orders–"

"Are my orders, Captain. Do I make myself clear?"

"Aye aye, Admiral," Captain Banner answered with a reluctant nod. He started barking orders to his crew, who passed on the orders to the rest of the combined fleet. Movements began, and the fleet began to prepare for departure from Hector II.

****

Korl was having a very bad day.

First, every single one of his human contacts in the capitol of the Republic had been unable or unwilling to talk to him. Not even a friendly "hello", which was odd in itself. Korl was used to such behavior from his fellow Darians, since being a *darlessar* brought shame and dishonor in a society where combat and personal honor abounded. An intelligence officer had little honor to offer, since they typically skulked about in the shadows, relying on trickery and bribery to attain their goals. A necessary job but a distasteful one, since only the outcasts and non-Initiates ever became a *darlessar*.

Humans, Korl knew, were more open to the idea of *darlessars*. *Spies*, he thought, rolling the word over in his mind once more. It was a more elegant word than its Darian equivalent and much simpler to explain. They were usually more accepting to the position, even admiring the position. He had heard stories that books had been written about them, and were very popular with the humans. That still did not mean his contacts would talk, though, no matter how hard he pushed. And his orders, he recalled clearly, were to push *hard*.

To make his day even worse, some of his contacts had reported his attempt at communication to *their* superiors, which led to his current predicament. Two human spies were following him. Both men were trying to be discrete as they moved through the throngs of humanity behind him, but Korl had been at this a lot longer than most. Earth was rebuilding, albeit slowly and there were plenty of humans and Darians alike assisting with the effort. It made losing his followers ridiculously simple, except that he could not find a place to lay low until they had given up.

He spotted a small pub near the Earth Republic Army Headquarters completely by chance, having stopped to admire the rebuilding process of the Republic's Spire, their symbol for hope and unity for all mankind. He had also stopped to take advantage of an open area between him and his pursuers, who were suddenly caught out in the open and exposed. Korl smiled slightly as he recognized the miniscule discomfort in their bodies as they realized that they had been made. They continued past Korl, chatting amiably, purposefully ignoring the cat as they made their way around the block.

That is how the game is played, Korl thought. He watched them for a moment before setting eyes on the small, dark sign offering cheap beer. His smile grew.

He sauntered past the pub, his eyes focused on the Spire still as he admired the construction efforts. He kept a peripheral lookout for his pursuers, or anyone else he could recall seeing since he had left the small gyro vendor six blocks before. He didn't see the two men who had been following him reappear, so he used the opening to slip inside the pub. He was not disappointed.

Darian and Human alike frequented this pub, he recognized immediately. There was a rudimentary bathroom for Darians, though it had been hastily constructed. Korl was pleased and walked over to the bar, where a diminutive human with facial hair greeted him.

"What'll it be?" the man asked. "I've got stouts, ales, some bourbons and spirits you can handle."

"Pale Ale," Korl replied, surprising the bartender. The cat offered an apologetic shrug of his shoulders. "I enjoy the taste."

"Well, we have a bathroom for your kind if it doesn't sit well with you," the bartender offered as he reached under the counter. He pulled out a small bottle and popped the top. He slid the bottle across the bar to the cat, who twitched an ear in thanks. Korl took a pull from the bottle as the door to the pub opened, allowing the bright daylight outside to spill in. He watched for any sign of the human spies, but only a human in uniform came in. He pulled his hat off and walked over to the bar, taking a chair near to where Korl was standing.

"Jesus, Chris," the bartender said as he pulled down a bottle of bourbon. "You look like hell."

"I *feel* like hell," the man in the uniform replied. Korl feigned disinterest but listened, his training taking over as he continued to nurse his beer. "You know how hard it is to get anything done when they take your best people from you at a moment's notice?"

The bartender clucked his tongue sympathetically before looking back over at Korl. "You going to want another one of those?"

"Please," Korl replied. He flicked a claw towards the newcomer. "And one for your friend there, too. He sounds as if his day has been as rough as mine."

"Thanks!" the man said, pleased. He slid closer to Korl and offered his hand. "Lieutenant Chris Kelsey."

"Grang," Korl lied, accepting the human's proffered hand and shaking it accordingly. He even offered a very human-like smile. "Junior Aide to Ambassador Xarn of the Darian Empire. Pleased to meet you."

"Junior aide, huh? Should we even be talking?" the human joked. Korl smirked.

"Not if I want to keep my job and not be deemed outcast," he lied again, but made no move to leave.

"Well then, it'll be our little secret," the lieutenant said and leaned closer, conspiratorially. "Besides, us being allies and all, we should be able to talk without fear of losing our jobs."

"You are my kind of thinker, Lieutenant Chris Kelsey," Korl said and took another pull from his beer. He allowed a little to dribble down his chin, to hopefully give the impression of being tipsy. "Oops. Haha."

"I've done that too, once on my dress whites," the lieutenant said, laughing. "Please, call me Chris. All my friends do."

"I shall, Chris," Korl shook his head a little. "Human alcohol is... tasty. I have acquired a liking for all of your ales. The hops... make a Darian's skin tingle."

"Bourbon does the same for me, Grang," Chris admitted as he started in on the beer that Korl had bought for him. "So why is your day as bad as mine, if I may?"

"The Ambassador is pushy, meeting with human admirals, demanding that I spend more and more time working on meaningless dispatches home instead of focusing on organizing the historical documents that your government has provided us, to learn," Korl said, which was almost true. He *had* gone over the documents provided by the Republic, albeit briefly, looking for interesting nuggets of information that could help the Ambassador delve into the complex human mind and psyche. "I prefer your historical texts. Very fascinating, your growth as a species."

"Admirals, huh? Try working for a general who steals your best soldiers for some mission, which completely screws up your own missions that you had planned," Chris sighed. Korl's ears perked up at this.

"That must be difficult," he allowed. "Until you've worked with someone like Xarn, however, you never truly appreciate the freedom you used to have. I'm glad I do not have a mate yet, or a litter at home. She would certainly find someone else to satisfy her during the hot months."

Chris slapped the bar top, laughing. "You cats are more like us than you realize!"

Korl smiled again. "I am complimented."

"Right, right," Chris nodded again. "I admire Darian honor. Answer me this, then, my newfound friend. Would your emperor steal troops from the front line to try to infiltrate an enemy when there's a massive fleet bearing down on the target, which could lead to those troop deaths? All for a little bit of technology that the enemy may have?"

By the Emperor! Korl was floored. *That's what they're really doing!*

The Ambassador had suspected that Human motivation had run deeper than they suspected with regards to the Ra'tids, but nobody had suspected this. Korl suddenly realized just why the Admiral had been so eager to have Darian ships involved. If Humans wanted enemy tech, who was to say that they wouldn't want *allied* tech as well?

The Ambassador needs to be told, Korl thought. *Darian tech must not fall into human hands. We'll need more ships to help with the attack on Ra'tid Prime to prevent this from happening, though.* The lieutenant suddenly excused himself, citing a weak bladder, and left for the restroom, leaving Korl alone. He smiled, paid the tab for him and his human "friend", and walked out of the pub.

Korl's day suddenly began to look a little brighter.

*****

Captain Chris Kelsey, Earth Republic Naval Intelligence Service, popped his head out of the restroom the moment the cat had left. He fished in his pocket for his comm and dialed.

"They take the bait?" General Soltus asked on the other end as soon as the connection was secure.

"Hook, line and sinker," Chris said.

"Alright. Good work." The line went dead.

The nice thing about having a paranoid ally, he thought as he walked back to the bar to finish his beer. *Their buttons are pretty easy to push, if you know which buttons to push.* He then had another thought. *Damn. I owe my brother ten dollars.*

*****

"The Darian Empire has sent some ships to assist with your current strike against the Ra'tids, General," Ambassador Xarn said as he eyed the man seated across from his desk. "At the time I spoke with Admiral Hien, unfortunately, I was unable to fully convey to the Emperor the necessity of assisting our allies.

However, I believe that, after careful consideration, the Emperor has come to agree with the Republic's argument, and is offering the assistance of an additional two fleets in ridding the universe of the Ra'tid menace..."

Chapter Six

Lieutenant Commander Paige stepped onto the Weligo's Central Command Deck. He was shaken by how much his life had changed in such a short period of time. Two days before he had been another lieutenant amongst the Terminus' operating crew, passed over for promotion due to an accident, which he could not be faulted for with bleak prospects. Now, though, he was aware of a dark secret on board the station, one that had led to his field promotion and a sudden new fear of the station State Security Officer.

He had stopped by the captain's quarters to drop off the latest SITREP the night before as his shift was ending. Since the destruction of the Task Force, he had been working almost nonstop, readying the station for the inevitable Ra'tid attack. He had almost forgotten all of it, however, when he saw the captain lying naked in her bed – with Manny Herrera in her arms.

He had apologized profusely, leaving as quickly as he could, SITREP forgotten. An hour later, he was promoted, and had relieved the former XO of his command.

He shook his head. The Terminus' crew had welcomed the sudden promotion. He knew them, knew their capabilities, and had worked well with almost all of them in the past. While lacking Berkman's charms and good-humor, he was far more competent and experienced when it came to tactical operations for the Terminus. In a time of war, that mattered far more to the crew than meaningless pats on the back and cheerful smiles, all of which had been part of Berkman's repertoire.

He had avoided Captain Stoko since the incident, though. He could not look her in the face, not after seeing her as he had. It was mildly embarrassing for him to admit that he had actually enjoyed the view, and wished, for the briefest of moments, that it had been him atop his captain. Even now, his cheeks burned with shame at the thought of her dark skin on the white sheets of her bunk.

There would be no avoiding the captain today, however. The Republic fleet destined for Ra'tid Prime would be coming through the Terminus today and both of them needed to be present when that happened. He sighed and wished that he could disappear back to one of the smaller command nodules scattered across the station, as Ensign Dotson did when he was not actually on watch. Nobody ever seemed to notice the man, and for a moment, Paige mentally kicked himself. If only he had been twenty minutes later.

The captain hadn't ordered him to keep quiet about what he had seen. There had been no need. He was a very intelligent man, and knew what would happen if he talked about it, besides which, Paige was almost certain that he'd end up with a bullet to the back of his brain if he even dared suggest that the SSO was involved in some way. With the Ra'tid fleet remaining in the Retina system for now, and being merely one void hop from coming into the station, guns blazing, the crew needed continuity. Captain Stoko could provide that, and Paige wanted the station to survive. So he stayed silent.

He looked around the Central Command Deck. Each and every person was doing their job quickly and efficiently. The Republic fleet was due to arrive in an hour, which would allow everyone to breathe easier. That much firepower hanging around the Terminus was going to be a good thing for as long as it lasted. He assumed that the fleet would regroup at the Terminus and finalize the Order of Battle before heading out into Ra'tid space. He bet that the fleet would deal with the Ra'tid ships in the Retina system too, rather than leaving them alone and risk opening up their flanks to an attack. With the Ra'tid fleet in Retina destroyed, the threat to the station would be gone with it and thing would finally start returning to normal.

Where that would leave him, his captain, the SSO, or his field promotion, he didn't have a clue.

Captain Stoko nodded at him as he moved past her to take his place at the sensor console. Trying hard not to let his cheek flush red in embarrassment, he hurried by her, hoping no one would notice how uncomfortable he was whenever they were in close proximity to one another. He relieved the sensor tech who had been on duty and sat down at his station, bringing up display as he did so. He needed to know what was going on, and it was much quicker this way than to have the man he was relieving go over every little nuance occurring around the Terminus.

Lieutenant Michelle Bernstein, the senior comm officer on the station, spoke up. "The fleet reports that they are ready to begin transit, ma'am. Requesting permission to enter Weligo traffic pattern."

The gathered Republic fleet and its Darian add-ons couldn't move through the Terminus all at once. The wormhole simply was unable to support that many vessels moving through without some of them being damaged or destroyed. In order to compensate for this, regular traffic through the Terminus had been halted by Stoko's orders, and the fleet would arrive in normal space around the Weligo station in waves of three. Paige checked his console.

"Everything says green on our end of things, Captain," he added.

"Begin transit," Captain Stoko ordered. Paige nodded, entered a few commands on his console, and promptly cursed like the sailor he was as everything suddenly went to Hell.

"Transient! Transient! I have five unidentified vessels coming through the Terminus!" Paige called out as he stared at the readings on his screen. The Ra'tid ships, which had been content to stay parked in the Retina system, had finally come calling. "Range indeterminate. Isolating vector now."

"Inform the *Poe* that we have inbound," Stoko instructed the comm officer, her voice shaky for an instant before settling down. "Guns, do we have a go for station defenses?"

"Aye Captain," the gunnery officer called out from behind her. "Guns are go."

"Switch to Condition One-Alpha," Stoko ordered.

"All hands, all hands! Maintain Condition One through the station. Set Condition One-Alpha," a monotone voice echoed through the expansive halls of the massive station. "Repeat, set Condition One-Alpha throughout the station."

The facade around the station began to change as gun ports slid open, the massive batteries of the Weligo Terminus emerging from their protective covers. Missile silos opened, and dome guns – used for point defense against missiles that broke through the electronic countermeasures – swiveled to point outwards toward the growing event horizon.

The station had over thirteen kilometers of surface area, with a tonnage of over fourteen trillion. An ingenious individual could do much with that amount of space to store weapons and ammo, tucking missile batteries away in places where nobody would even think to look. The Earth Republic Navy was *filled* with devious minds, and most of them had helped design the defenses of every station in the Republic.

"Point defenses are a go, Captain," Paige called out. He looked back at Stoko. "Shall we prepare the Snapdragon?"

"No need, XO," she replied. "It's just us and the *Poe* out here, and I doubt that the little destroyer is going to help much. How long until Admiral Hien's fleet arrives?"

"ETA is eight minutes, ma'am," Paige replied instantly.

"Ra'tid translation in ten seconds!" one of the sensor techs barked.

"So it begins," Paige whispered. He wondered just how much longer he had to enjoy his promotion. He might – *might* – have a chance, if they could live for eight more minutes. The white sandy beaches of Senga had never seemed so far away.

"Engage as soon as they come through, Guns," Stoko ordered. "Don't wait for me to give the word."

"Aye, Captain," the gunnery officer replied.

"Holy Mother of God!" Paige blurted out as all five Ra'tid ships appeared on the screen. He glanced down at his sensors and blinked. There they were, as was the norm with all Ra'tid vessels. He couldn't believe their luck. "Captain, we got them on sensors!"

The weapons officer and his team began to open fire the instant the alien ships appeared, launching the first salvo of missiles at the lead Ra'tid ship. With all the little silos hidden around the station, the tactical screens for the weapons station soon filled up as little rods of death hurtled through space. The crew was good, and had been training for such an exercise almost nonstop for three days. Five thousand missiles were launched at the Ra'tid ships in less than fifteen seconds.

"First salvo away! Autoloaders engaged. Second salvo away in one minute, Captain!" the weapons officer called out.

Paige watched as the *Poe* valiantly raced forward to interpose herself between the Ra'tid super dreadnaughts and the station. It was brave, but foolish, he knew as he watched the little destroyer's missiles exit the forward area of the ship and tear through space for the Ra'tid ships. Behind it, the five thousand missiles from the station followed suit.

"They've got lock on the station!" Paige cried. "Engaging ECM measures now!"

"Do we have their missiles?" Stoko asked, concern in her tone.

"Checking... yes! I'm not sure why, ma'am, but we do!" Paige exclaimed.

"Make them earn it, Lieutenant Commander."

"Aye, Captain," Paige nodded. He looked back at his display, as the massive Ra'tid fleet seemed to launch every missile in the universe at them. He felt his sphincter tighten in fear. "Vampire! Vampire! I have seventeen thousand missiles inbound! Repeat, one-seven-zero-zero-zero missiles headed our way. ETA, six point five minutes."

"Countermeasures!" Stoko shouted, standing up from the command chair.

"Engaging!" Paige acknowledged loudly before turning his full attention to the display board before him.

The screen was clouded, something he had only seen in simulations. That many missiles on sensors at once tended to cloud the screen, saturating the feedback and causing the computer programs to complain as they lagged behind, struggling to create a three dimensional picture of the tactical situation. Paige cracked his neck and began to go to work.

He skillfully dedicated the railguns to point defense only as he powered up the ECMs of the station, blasting electronic white noise across the space between the missiles and their targets. Missile-killers – tiny, fast little missiles with small, nuclear tips – began to thread their way through the railgun fire towards the incoming cloud of missiles. While a scoring direct hit was next to impossible, Paige knew that a near nuclear event could cause the missiles to break apart or, better still, fry their electronics due to the electromagnetic pulse that an explosion created. Combined with the ECM that the station was already employing, he doubted that the Rocks would be able to see anything after he was done with them.

His fingers flying, Paige began to see the fruits of his efforts. Missile after missile was veering away from the station, blowing up en route, or simply disintegrating under the constant barrage of the railguns. He grinned savagely as the thick cloud on the screen began to thin itself out. Ra'tid missiles, no matter how good they were, still were outclassed by the Republic's ECMs.

"Second salvo away!" Paige heard a voice shout.

"The *Poe* is gone!" another tech cried out. Paige, so caught up in his efforts at protecting the station, had forgotten about the destroyer. He scanned his readouts and saw, to his horror, that almost four hundred Ra'tid missiles had targeted the Poe. Somehow, almost all of them had struck the ship, blasting it to atoms. The ECM on the *Poe* had absolutely failed. He shook his head.

"How come the *Poe* couldn't see those missiles?" he asked aloud, trying to run the problem through his head. He glanced back at his own readouts and saw that less than eight percent of the Ra'tid missiles were still locked onto the station. A godly high number to be sure, but still much better than the *Poe* had fared. *But the* Poe *had up-to-date systems that* we *don't have!*

"Forty-two missiles have broken ECM!" he shouted. His fingers flew frantically across the board, desperately trying to whittle the number down some more. He knew that he couldn't get them all, but at least he could–

Wham! The missiles struck the station. Despite the massive size and weight of the station, the kinetic energy of the combined fury of all the impacting Ra'tid missiles was more than enough to cause it to move slightly. The slight movement, to the naked eye, was nothing. The amount of energy needed to move anything that size, though, was enough to shatter every bone in the human body into liquid, and reorganize the internal organs into a finely ground powder. Human ingenuity, and a little bit of stolen alien technology, saved everyone on board the Terminus.

The inertial compensators absorbed most of the energy from the blast, keeping the crew alive. The impact temporarily overloaded the compensators, however, as the energy rushed through the bastardized human/alien hybrid technology. This caused the artificial gravity to flicker for a brief instance. Personnel who had been caught on their feet and not seated were tossed about, which included the poor Captain Stoko. She rolled towards the main view screen, cursing every second of the trip. She crashed painfully against one of the standing consoles and struggled to her feet, blood trickling from a small cut near her scalp.

"XO!" Stoko cried out as she stumbled woozily back to her chair. "Report!"

"Structural integrity is sound," he replied as he looked over the status of the station. He had been unaffected by the station's sudden movement, clinging to the console and trying to keep his butt in his seat. His technique, however awkward it appeared, had worked. He counted his blessings. "I have minor hull breaches in cargo bay one, and losing atmo on deck seventeen. Damage control en route now, ma'am. Lost four missile batteries, eighteen railguns and sixty pods. Damn. Sickbay reports four KIA, fifteen wounded and two missing in action. All stations report clear."

"ECM?"

"Still up and running, ma'am," he replied. He grinned as he looked over the sensor screen. "Point defenses took a beating, but structurally, we're good to go. Our missiles are running true, ma'am. The Rocks are trying to evade."

"They're throwing up a hell of a lot of white noise, Captain!" another sensor tech announced, her voice excited. "It's weak but it's there. We've got them! ETA on our missiles, fifteen seconds."

"Keep cycling those missiles through the tubes," Stoko ordered.

"Third salvo away!"

"Five-one-zero-eight missiles inbound, ETA seven minutes," Paige said, nodding. "They're closing the distance on us, ma'am."

"They want a knife fight, do they?" Stoko grinned ferociously.

"Transient! Transient! I count twelve, repeat, twelve, inbound signatures! Translating in ten seconds!"

"*Yes!*" Lieutenant Dera shouted from nearby. Paige glanced over his tactical screen and couldn't keep a bloodthirsty smile from his lips.

The lead Ra'tid ship had taken a beating from the first salvo of missiles, and the second was now closing the distance. The ship, despite the rocky and ungainly appearance, was relatively agile for something so large and it was trying to make a break for it. The other four Ra'tid ships were desperately launching everything they had now at the massive station, and it appeared that there were far more missiles in the blackness of space than stars.

"Second salvo impact in five!"

"They're here!" Stoko screamed in an ecstatic voice.

The Terminus flashed as the *Behemoth* came bursting through, with a ring of eleven heavy cruisers and destroyers around it. The Ra'tid vessels saw them and turned, angling toward the new ships. The destroyers charged forward, interposing their small frames and massive ECM systems between the Ra'tid ships and the *Behemoth*. The fleet began to move towards the station at top speed.

"Thank God..." Paige breathed as he watched the Republic ships arrive. He looked over at Captain Stoko. "Orders, ma'am?"

"Direct hit! She's running now, ma'am!" a tech whooped. Paige looked back and saw, to his delight, that the lead Ra'tid ship was spewing flames into space, the vacuum of space sucking whatever the Rocks used for oxygen out of their ships. His sensors told him that the ship was out of commission, perhaps out of the fight completely.

"Activate the Snapdragon," Stoko said, her face full of relief. "Transfer all data we have to their flagship, the *Behemoth*. Give them my most heartfelt greetings."

"Aye, ma'am," Paige grunted. He typed in a few commands. "Snapdragon activated."

"ERV *Behemoth*, this is the Weligo Terminus," Lieutenant

Bernstein said into the comm. "We have you on scanners. Stand by for the Captain, over."

"Roger that, Weligo. Glad to see that we got here before the attack began, over," came the reply.

"Come again, *Behemoth*?"

"What the hell?" Paige breathed. His tactical screen, which had been cluttered with thousands of missiles on course for the station, had suddenly gone blank. He tapped it with his finger, and then pounded on it. He turned and looked at the captain, panic creeping into his voice. "Captain! I've lost the Rocks! I don't have any, I repeat, any of the Ra'tid vessels on my scanners! We have five thousand missiles inbound, and *I can't see them!*"

"What the hell are you talking about, XO?" Stoko called back. She swiveled her head to glare at the comm officer. "And what did the *Behemoth* mean, Michelle? The battle's been joined!"

"Captain Stoko, this is High Fleet Admiral Hien. How are you this fine afternoon?"

Stoko stared at the comm link on her chair, dumbfounded. She sat back in her chair, her eyes unfocused. Seconds passed, precious seconds that Paige knew that they might never get back.

"Admiral Hien, sir, this is the XO, Lieutenant Commander Robert Paige," Paige took over, his eyes frantically searching for any sign of the Ra'tid fleet on his screens. "We are under attack by Ra'tid vessels, sir. Five of them, and we have inbound. Confirm transmission, over."

"We read you, Weligo. What do you mean, you're under attack? There's nothing out there," the admiral replied.

"Negative, sir. We have five thousand missiles incoming. Somewhere," Paige countered, thinking fast. "We were engaged with the enemy, sir, until you got here. Then they just... disappeared."

"Ships don't just disappear, Lieutenant Commander," a cold voice scolded him.

"These ones did, sir," Paige said. He looked back at the captain, who was shaking her head and trying to come out of her fugue state. "Captain? Orders?"

"I... I don't know," Stoko admitted helplessly.

*****

"Someone over there better not be yanking my chain," Admiral Hien growled as he paced the bridge of the *Behemoth*.

The transit through the Terminus had gone smoothly, with the first wave coming out in near-perfect unison. The Darians, escorted by a few of his heavy cruisers, would be arriving eight minutes later, followed by the third flight. Everything had been in perfect working order until the frantic message from the Weligo Terminus.

Hien scowled. He looked over at the *Behemoth's* sensor officer, who shook his head.

"Admiral," Captain Banner said from his command chair. Hien swiveled his head. "I do believe that the reports of the Ra'tids being stealthy are accurate."

Hien could have slapped himself. He had given that briefing to the President himself! How had he forgotten that so soon?

"Bring up the area around the station on the overhead view screen," he ordered, silently cursing himself. "Warn the other ships."

"Sound General Quarters, Commander," Captain Banner ordered.

"We'll show these bastards," Hien growled as the alert went throughout the fleet. "Let's move us in, Captain."

*****

The missile salvo had ruined the central command deck, as well as most of the beleaguered space station.

Smoke was being pumped out of the room by filters, but it was not enough to keep pace with the burning electrical fires, which had sprouted up when almost five hundred missiles had slammed into the thick, layered hulls that protected the command deck from space. More had struck the outer hulls of the station, ruining sensor pods and point defense weapons, destroying missile tubes outright. One lucky missile had even ruptured a weapons bay, which while thankfully almost empty, had still created a big enough explosion that damage control had yet to fix. Oxygen and debris still exited the hole, though at a slower pace. The airlocks between compartments, while compromised from the shock of the kinetic energies of the missiles, still worked. To a degree.

Paige worked frantically on the central command deck. He and Lieutenant Dera were the only ones still standing after the last salvo had struck, with the junior officer struggling to maintain tactical control while he stayed on the sensors and took over weapons. He could no longer hear the fleet: comm had been destroyed. He also no longer had a good track on the rest of the fleet. The Snapdragon had shut down when comm went, leaving the station in the dark as to the tactical plotting of Admiral Hien's fleet.

Captain Stoko was dead. He wasn't sure what had killed her, though he could easily determine the cause of death: decapitation left little doubt to the unimaginative. He couldn't remove her body, or the others, from the command deck. He didn't have the manpower, nor the time. They would rest there until the battle was over. One way or the other.

"But now, we see the Rocks again," Paige muttered as he wiped sweat and grime from his face with the back of his uniform sleeve. For reasons he couldn't determine, the older systems of the station could see the Rocks just fine, while the newer, updated systems that had been implemented five years before failed. With Dera on tactical and over half of a million missiles still at his disposal, Lieutenant Commander Paige was in a particularly vengeful mood.

"Keep firing as fast as those launchers can reload, Lieutenant," Paige barked, working at a frenzied pace. The Ra'tids had slacked off on their missile salvos, their attention diverted by the arrival of the makeshift fleet commanded by Admiral Hien. Instead of thousands of missiles inbound, he face a mere two hundred. He could easily handle those numbers, even in his disheveled state.

"Yes sir," she replied. "I'm not getting anything from sick bay, sir. That last salvo... I think it got taken out."

Paige closed his eyes for an instant. "Let's hurt them. Hurt them *bad*."

Dera didn't reply, focusing her energies instead on rerouting command nodules within the programming of the station. Removing fail-safes in the autoloaders, she was able to decrease the time it took between missile salvos. She smiled wolfishly as the time between launches dwindled from one minute to thirty seconds. Her smile turned to a confused frown, however, when one of the display terminals shaded red. She looked up from the display.

"Sir, I–" she never finished.

The terminal she stood at exploded, the power surging through the station she had been using to speed up the autoloaders for the missiles. It ripped through the breakers and overloaded the circuitry, melting plastic and metal together. The explosion cast more smoke and debris onto the central command deck.

Paige felt as if he'd been kicked in the side. He glanced down, spotted the jagged piece of metal jutting out from his side, and went back to work for a few seconds before his brain actually recognized the wound. He gasped as pain suddenly flooded though him, then nausea. Burning, icy pain reached up and threatened to render him unconscious.

He fought it off. "Lieutenant, I think..." his voice trailed off as he saw that Lieutenant Dera was lying on the ground, the top half of her head sheared neatly off. A large puddle of blood pooled around her cooling corpse. Her vacant eyes stared into his – *brains are a strange color, when compared to the metal deck of the station* – and he closed his eyes.

He hobbled over to the deceased lieutenant's console – *when did I stub my toe? Why does my toe hurt worse than this piece of metal in my side?* – and looked for something salvageable. The console was thoroughly wrecked. There would be no salvaging anything from the console, he realized. With a heavy sigh and a gasp of sudden pain, he limped back.

He looked at his console. The fleet had managed to work around whatever stealth technology the Rocks were using, and were now pounding them ruthlessly. The Darians, he noted, were having an especially good time of it – their one-man fighters were mincing the Ra'tid super dreadnaughts to pieces. One of them, he watched, broke off from attacking the fleet and it was making a run for it. Paige grinned humorlessly. The ship would be forced to come dangerously close to the station, which would give him a chance to strike back one final time.

He keyed in a command at his console. The computer asked if he was certain. Paige confirmed that he was, indeed, certain, and typed in his passcode. It asked for verification. He typed in Captain Stoko's, and then looked at the speed of the oncoming super dreadnaught. He programmed the timer to coincide with the ship's closest approach.

Confirmed, it said. **Self-destruct sequence activated.**

Ten

Nine

Eight

Seven

Paige closed his eyes, the pain getting the better of him for a moment. He sighed, wistfully thinking back to his plans before the Ra'tids jumped the recon ships, before everything in his calm and structured life had all gone to hell. The white, sandy beaches of Senga called. He smiled as he pictured half-naked women in thongs parading around in the crystal-blue waters.

String bikinis are always fash–

*****

"Jesus!" Hien swore as the Weligo station spectacularly exploded, blinding the view screens momentarily.

"Brace for shockwave!" Captain Banner called out to his bridge crew. Admiral Hien, not hearing Banner's order, tumbled slightly as the *Behemoth* shook violently as the expanding shockwave from the station washed over them. He cursed as his dress whites, which had been neatly pressed and starched, tore where his knee struck the deck. Blood began to seep through the material. Hien swore again.

"Whatever happened at the station, sir, that's one less Ra'tid ship to worry about," a sensor tech called out from her console. Hien looked at the view screen and recognized the skeletal structure of the station for what it was. Or rather, had been. Most of the station was destroyed completely, though the structural core remained. Of the Ra'tid ship that had blown up with it, there was no sign.

"Fleet status?" Hien barked, angry that his uniform was damaged and bloodied.

"Light casualties, Admiral," the sensor tech replied. "The *Minnesota* is damaged and has withdrawn, and the Darians report a few lost fighters. The *Ovezkyn* has two tubes down, nothing more. Our foredecks took a pounding, with some missile tubes down and more beam weaponry destroyed. We took the brunt of the damage, sir, but we're designed for that. We caught the Ra'tids with their pants down, sir."

"It's about time we surprised *them* for a change," Hien spat. His head swiveled towards Banner. "Captain, let's finish these last three ships off."

Banner grunted. "To all ships, this is the *Behemoth*. Let's chase these bastards home."

Missiles poured out of the ships of the fleet, millions upon millions of pounds of explosives screaming towards the Ra'tids. The ships were turning, struggling to escape and make it back through the wormhole and into void space. Controlled by hand and eye, the missiles were still fast enough to close on the Ra'tids. If they would be enough to stop the Rocks from escaping, though, Hien could only hope.

"That's it!" a sensor tech cried out suddenly. "We've got a lock! Once we get in close, the missiles can see the electromagnetic fields around them!"

"So they can't completely hide, eh?" Banner smiled, a thin, tight-lipped gesture. "That's a pity for them."

"Impact in six seconds," another tech said. "Lead missile is relaying the data to the others. Hit!"

On the screen, a bright light blossomed on the distant Ra'tid vessel. Half a second later, more explosions erupted on the other two. Missiles continued to dig into the rocky hulls of the Ra'tid ships and explode, obscuring the image slightly as the nuclear explosions ripped through the super dreadnaughts. The ships began to break up, their engines failing as the missiles did their jobs.

"Yes!" Hien shouted triumphantly. He pumped his fist in the air, forgetting he was no longer a snot-nosed Lieutenant Junior Grade in combat for the first time.

The bridge crew grinned knowingly. It was becoming obvious, despite the beatings they took at Mars and on Earth itself. No matter what the enemies of the Republic threw at them, they all knew at that moment that Earth Republic would always have an answer.

Chapter Seven

"I got nothing, ma'am," Lieutenant Khandry muttered as she dug beneath her comm console. She shined a light around the dark compartment. "Everything looks brand new, fresh out of the box even. We've been out of the dry dock for, what, nine weeks now?"

"Something like that," Captain Hikia acknowledged.

The Helix system was pounding the shielding of the *Potemkin* with vast amounts of radiation as the mighty battleship orbited the bright G-class star. Dancing a dangerous dance with the star, the *Potemkin* held her course, hiding from the armada that had so thoroughly decimated the task force she had previously been assigned to. Even her SSO, crass as he was, stated that they stood little to no chance against the combined fury of stealthy Ra'tid super dreadnaughts. The radiation from the star, because it was so deadly and dangerous to humans, would be the last place anybody – human or otherwise – would think to look.

Captain Hikia also knew that the shielding would hold up against the intense radiation for a few days at most, which made her current endeavor all the more important.

"Then there's no reason why our sensors weren't working back there, Captain," Khandry determined. "All couplings look good. Nothing got screwed in upside down. Comms are solid, ma'am."

Hikia grunted. All around her, the bridge of the *Potemkin* was a bustling beehive of activity as men and women tore apart their consoles, looking for any sign of malfunction or irregularities. So far, the only thing they had discovered was the Admiralty and the dry dock workers really loved their new toys. The bridge of the *Potemkin* was loaded with the latest Republic tech, and much of it was making Hikia's head spin.

She had known at an intellectual level that some of the newest technology in the retrofitted *Potemkin* would be beyond her comprehension. That's what technicians were for, after all. She still had expected to have a base understanding of something on the bridge, however. Even still, she couldn't shake the feeling that the problem with the new Ra'tid ships lay partly in the newest systems that the fleet had foisted onto her ship. She frowned as another tech, one of her comm technicians, slipped by with a bundle of wiring and microchip boards in his arms.

"PO, what is that?" she asked as he passed.

"Ma'am, excess parts for the sensor consoles," the petty officer replied instantly, bracing to attention as best he could. "When the retrofit came through, they just sort of tucked the extra pieces into the undercarriage of the consoles, ma'am. Typical yard dog laziness, if you ask me."

Hikia pursed her lips in a thoughtful manner. "Did the comm consoles have spare parts tucked away like that as well?"

"Uh, no ma'am, I don't think so," the PO flushed slightly. "I'll have to look into that for you."

"Carry on, PO," Hikia waved him off. "I'll take care of it."

She walked over to where Khandry was tearing apart a new console, her acting-lieutenant doing a far better job than the captain could have hoped for. She knelt down to the swearing woman and looked under the console.

"No spare parts tucked away anywhere, Lieutenant?" she asked Khandry.

"Ma'am?"

"Sensor Techies are complaining about spare parts stashed in the undercarriage," she informed her comm officer. "I want to know if comms had anything like that as well."

"No ma'am, we don't," Khandry informed her. "I don't think that the yard dogs are as bad as some people think."

"How well do you know sensor consoles?"

"Not very, ma'am," Khandry answered. She shrugged her shoulders apologetically. "I'm qualified on them, sure. But nuts and bolts? That's the Techies job."

"That's fine, Lieutenant," Hikia said. "Oh, and this field promotion is going to be a permanent one. I filed the paperwork. Congrats."

"Thank you, ma'am!" Khandry beamed. Her face sobered after a second. "Hope we get back to Earth so I can enjoy it properly."

"Me too, Lieutenant. Me too. Carry on."

"Aye, ma'am."

Hikia stood and looked around her bridge. She pinched her nose and sighed. The entire ship was laced with new computer equipment, which she had been thrilled to receive when the *Potemkin* had been in dry dock. Now, though, she was tearing it all out in the off chance that the older equipment might be of better use. She glanced at her clock and frowned. They only had three days left before the radiation of Helix's star overpowered their shielding. With her comm blocked by the immense radiation as well, she had no way of letting the Republic know that their greatest enemy was helping the Rocks.

She was running out of time.

*****

Saul stood on the small bridge of the *Caliban*, hands clasped behind his back. He was the only member of the special operations team allowed up there, and that had almost taken an act of God to get Hunter to agree to it. The rest of the team, more than willing to stay away from the grumpy captain, hadn't made even a token effort in coming forward. He glanced at the erstwhile captain and took stock of the man.

The captain had turned the cloak down as soon as they hit void space after passing through the Terminus hours before, ostensibly to conserve power. Saul wondered about that, and asked the captain, who reminded him that smaller ships like the *Caliban* didn't carry the same energy capacity as the bigger ships. It made sense to the former Templar, given that the design of the small, deadly ship was more focused on stealth and hit-and-run tactics than a stand-up brawl.

The men and women of the black ops team were adjusting to his command. He had thought that there might be some tension or issues once they discovered that he had been in the Order, but a couple of sparring sessions with them in the cargo hold had helped establish his credentials. That and the team was filled with consummate professionals who followed orders and completed their mission. A team that he would have been proud to command back when he was still in the Order.

The mission, however, was still dangerous enough that he only half-expected to survive.

"I still don't understand why we can't make a solid run through to Ra Prime," Saul grumbled. He had expected a fast transit directly to Ra Prime, with no alternate routes along the way. After all, he and his fellow Templars had struck the same way at the Ra'tids years before.

"I wouldn't expect you to," Hunter replied. He looked at the former Templar with grudging respect. "Only someone insanely suicidal would attempt something like that."

"Or someone with God on their side," Saul smiled. "God favors fools, drunkards and children, after all."

Hunter laughed. "That's for damn sure."

After their rocky start, it became quickly apparent to Saul that the captain of the *Caliban* had no love for the Republic. After some effort, he was able to convince Hunter that he was not part of the Republic, and disliked and distrusted them even more. Hunter had warmed up to him after that. They had even shared a few war stories, which always tended to bring men like them closer.

"So tell me why we shouldn't infiltrate the same way as we did before?" Saul asked.

"Because the Rocks have better tech than they used to," Hunter said. "They're probably able to pick up our echoes when we're in void space now, where before they couldn't see nothing. The longer we're in void space, the bigger the echo, right? Easier to pick up."

Saul nodded. He had suspected that was the case, but hearing the captain say it made it official.

"So we're stopping... here?" Saul looked at the chart that was laid out before Mizi, the ship's co-pilot. He looked back at the captain. "That looks pretty dangerous."

"It's *extremely* dangerous," Hunter agreed. "But it's also the best way to get a peek at Ra Prime before we enter their space. Geners don't come here because of how dangerous it is, and there aren't any potentially habitable planets in the system, just gas giants, so the Rocks ignore it. It's a perfect little out-of-the-way place for us to do some reconnaissance."

"Good smuggling location, you mean," Saul guessed.

"I'm not even going to acknowledge that insult," Hunter sniffed. "Me? An honorable businessman insulted by the likes of you."

Saul chuckled. "From here, it's a short hop to Ra Prime, correct?"

"Yeah."

"Okay, I'm going to go check on the others," Saul said and exited the bridge. He ducked past the narrow airlock and into the cargo hold, where the majority of the Republic operatives were snoozing. Zombie and Gunter were awake, which was fine with him. The two had quickly become his seconds on this mission, his trust and understanding of what drove them better than any of the others. He made eye contact with Gunter, who grabbed Zombie.

"What's the news?" Gunter asked without preamble.

"Quick stop before we head in," Saul explained.

"Echo's too big," Zombie said with a quick, jerky nod of his head. "Need to keep it down, so we're doing a short-hop infiltration."

"Oh, like we did at Titan," Gunter realized. She rolled her eyes and looked at Saul. "Forget I said that."

Saul smiled. There had been no reference of Titan or any operation at the moon in her files. "Forget what?"

"How long until we get to Ra Prime?" Zombie asked.

"The captain says about three hours, since we're going to hit the edge of the system and then go in real space the rest of the way," Saul answered.

"In the meantime, we're going to stop in–"

"Yeah," Saul said. Zombie smirked.

"Nothing like a little danger in an otherwise boring mission," Zombie declared.

"It's extremely dangerous there. Doesn't the captain know how bad it is there?" Gunter asked.

Saul scoffed. "It's why he likes it so much. God willing, the plan will go smoothly. According to the captain, almost nobody ever goes to the Helix system."

*****

"Transient! Transient!" the watch officer called out suddenly, her fear-filled voice cutting through the din of the bridge. Multiple heads across the bridge turned to stare at the captain.

"Source?" Captain Hikia barked as she settled into her command chair.

"From the size of the echo, ma'am, I'd guess that this was from the Weligo Terminus."

"So they've come to finish the job, have they?" Hikia growled and leaned back in her chair. "Then we'll give them something to fret about. All the old systems up and running, Lieutenant?"

"Yes ma'am," Khandry replied. "All show green."

"Let's see if the old is better than the new," Hikia murmured. "Prepare starboard missile tubes. Beam weaponry on standby. ECM?"

"Hot and bothered, Captain," came the reply.

"Comms are good, ma'am," Khandry added.

"Weapons are online," her weapons officer confirmed.

"Captain? I'm only showing one ship coming through. Smallish vessel, no cloak. Not recognizing the engine signature at all, though it's definitely not Ra'tid. Designating Sierra-One," a sensor tech said.

Hikia frowned and leaned forward in her chair. "Coalition?"

"Not from the point of origin, ma'am."

"Geners?" her frown deepened.

"They'd be cloaked, ma'am."

"Commander?" Hikia said as she punched up her XO, still cooped up in the auxiliary bridge near the belly of the *Potemkin*. He was more familiar with the sector than she was, having been the weapons officer onboard the *Hornet* previously, which had been attached to the Weligo Terminus once upon a time. The rugged little destroyer had been part of the task force that died trying to protect Mars from the Coalition.

"Smuggler," Commander Nassed replied almost instantly. "We used to make runs out here to keep them from getting too cocky, but when the war kicked up we had to focus on more pressing matters. But I'll give them their due. They're the reason that Mars got food during the Coalition's occupation."

Hikia nodded. Even the most problematic pest could be worth something on the rare occasion.

"Whoever's out there," she said with a small, savage smile. "They're not going to be happy to see us here."

*****

"I never thought I'd see the day when I was happy to have a Republic battleship in my little smuggling hole," Hunter muttered as the massive battleship came into view.

Mizi had picked up the battleship on sensors minutes earlier, her normally cool facade shattered at the ship's surprise appearance. She had nearly overpowered Alves at the helm with her frantic reaction. Only the pilot's cool head and steady hands had kept Hunter's second in command from turning the ship around and running back to Earth.

"So what's the game, Hunter?" Alves asked as he reoriented the *Caliban's* nose around. He punched in the numbers and grunted with satisfaction as the plotted course came online. "I can have us out of here in three minutes."

Hunter pursed his lips. "They think we're a smuggler, probably."

"We *are* a smuggler," Mizi reminded him.

"Yeah, but not this time," Hunter said. "This mission is classified, though. Even admitting it to the captain could potentially damage whatever it is that Saul needs to accomplish."

"I still like the running option," Mizi said.

"Seconded," Alves added his vote.

"No," Hunter said and tapped his data pad. "We need to be

remembered but not as an enemy. We might need them later, actually, if we're running for our lives. No, we gotta play this cool. This is what we're going to do..."

*****

"What do you mean, a courier ship?" Captain Hikia frowned.

"All data I have on this ship's class is designating it as a courier," Lieutenant Khandry said.

"I can *see* this ship with my eyes, Khandry," Hikia said as she motioned towards the view screen. The small ship was bristling with weaponry. "Have you seen a courier ship armed like that?"

"Well, there is a war going on..." Khandry's voice faded as the captain turned her basilisk gaze upon her.

"Lieutenant, I have a request for a voice-only transmission coming through," a comm technician reported, saving Khandry from her captain's anger. She flipped it over to the command chair, where Hikia accessed it.

"Still don't believe that this thing is a courier ship," she grunted and cleared her throat. "Attention unidentified vessel. This is the Earth Republic Vessel *Potemkin*, Captain Mai-ling Hikia commanding. Please declare your intentions, over."

She leaned back and waited.

*****

"How's your poker face, Saul?" Hunter said as the former Templar entered the *Caliban's* bridge.

"Probably better than yours," Saul said. "So you need me to...?"

"Follow my lead," Hunter finished. He flipped on the comm. "Ahoy there, *Potemkin*. This is the courier vessel *Hermes* en route to Ra Prime, under diplomatic colors. Please confirm our registry number... now."

Hunter sent the false data.

"They have no way of checking those codes without leaving the system," Alves informed Saul. "They know that a smuggler would run the moment he had the chance, which we would if they left the system to do the check. So they'll stay right there and do a check on us, hoping to spook us into running, while wanting to speak to our diplomatic courier. Which is you, actually."

"That takes some chutzpah," Saul nodded, impressed. Hunter grunted.

"Welcome to the life of the independent business consultant, illegally acquired goods division."

*****

"This guy has some balls, ma'am," Khandry said as soon as the message came through. "Piloting a courier ship into a potential war zone."

"Damn, he's good," Commander Nassed admitted through the comm. "He might know we can't check his codes without leaving the system. If we leave, he runs. If we hold him there, he could get all antsy and demand preferential treatment, if he's really a courier vessel."

"So a real diplomatic vessel would just stay there and wait for some sort of response?" Khandry asked.

"All right, let's pretend we're running a check on them. See if they spook," Hikia said. She accessed the comm. "Courier vessel *Hermes*, please stand by as we double-check your codes. Also, if your State Department official is on board, we'd really like to speak with them. Over."

"They're going to run, Captain," Khandry predicted. "They've gotta be up to no good."

Hikia grunted. She wondered what she would do if the ship did decide to run.

*****

"They probably expected us to run," Mizi grunted. She looked at Hunter. "So far, so good."

"You're up," Hunter said and patted Saul on the back. "Make papa proud."

Saul took a deep breath and nodded. The comm went live. "This is Saul Derring of the State Department. Is this the captain?

Hello? Hello, Captain? Why are you harassing a courier vessel, captain? This is most unusual. I was told I would have clearance through this region. Hello? Answer me!"

"Mister Derring, you're speaking with Captain Mai-ling Hikia–"

"Yes yes, I heard you the first time," Saul interrupted, his voice nasally and grating. He rubbed his throat and wondered if it was going to be raw from his performance. "I was on a most important mission before you interfered. This will go down on your permanent record, captain. I have a letter guaranteeing safe passage from the Undersecretary of the State Department herself! I'll have you know that I am personal friends with the undersecretary."

"Our apologies, Mister Derring. Protocol demands that we double-check these things, to prevent smugglers and so forth. It will only take another minute."

"Fine, captain. If you must. Make it snappy."

Hunter killed the comm and whistled. "Officious, snotty, demanding... yes sir, that settles it. I am *never* playing poker with you, Mister Derring."

*****

"Dear God, is that how all State Department weenies are?" Khandry's eyes widened as the high-pitched, petulant voice finally stopped talking.

"Most of them, yeah," Hikia shook her head. "That actually sounded legit. Nobody can fake being that big of an ass. XO?"

"Concur, ma'am. That's someone from State, all right."

Hikia sighed. "Typical State. Sending some underling out into the middle of a war zone to die in the name of peace. All right. Attention *Hermes*, this is Captain Hikia. Your codes check out. We're sorry to interfere. Good luck and Godspeed on your mission, *Hermes. Potemkin*, out."

Khandry ended the transmission and watched as the small courier ship powered up its engines. It began to accelerate towards Ra Prime, which was just a short hop away. She looked back at the captain.

"Orders, ma'am?"

"We'll keep our workups going here," she frowned and watched the *Hermes* disappear from system. "I have a feeling we're going to see that ship again."

*****

"I can't believe they bought it," Alves blinked hard, a smile on his usually dour face. Behind him, Hunter was grinning.

"I would have bought it," he said. "All right, when we get out of sensor range of the *Potemkin*, go ahead and bring our cloak up. Full power. Next stop? Ra Prime."

*****

Repairs aboard the *Behemoth* were proceeding well ahead of schedule. Fleet Admiral Hien paced around the captain's ready room as he listened to Captain Banner brief him on the fleet status. Of the fleet, only the *Behemoth* and the *Minnesota* sustained enough damage to slow down the rest of the fleet in order to enact repairs. The staggering death toll at the destruction of the Weligo station, however, offset any joy that Captain Banner might have felt upon the performance of the fleet. The Weligo station was now nothing more than a scant shadow of its former glory, the debris cloud surrounding the core testament at how hard the space station had fought for its life.

So many lives lost, one way or another, and the real battle was yet to come.

"Captain Banner," Hien said, interjecting when Banner had taken a break from his briefing of the fleet's status. The captain looked up, his bloodshot eyes betraying his exhaustion. "I have decided that the *Behemoth* will be staying here to take over the station's duties. I'll be transferring my flag to the *Juggernaut*. Please inform Captain Connor at once, and have my shuttle prepared for departure within the hour."

Without another word, Hien walked to the door, leaving a stunned Captain banner staring after him. Hien had little time to waste, and the time spent repairing his flagship would narrow the window of opportunity that the fleet had available. They had struck a huge blow against the Ra'tids, and now he had to pounce upon that advantage before they could recover. He knew that they had very little time before the Ra'tids realized that their task force had been destroyed. If that meant leaving behind the *Behemoth* and the *Minnesota* in order to achieve total surprise, then so be it.

Captain Banner rose to his feet, his hands shaking as anger coursed through him. "Admiral!"

Hien paused. "You have your orders, Captain. Or did I not make myself clear enough? My shuttle, prepared, within the hour."

"I understood them perfectly, sir. But..."

"You may get your chance yet to engage the Ra'tids again, Captain. It won't be with the fleet at Ra Prime, however," Hien explained. "Someone has to stay here and keep the Rocks from using the Terminus against Earth. That person is you and the *Behemoth*, as well as the *Minnesota*. The sooner you accept your new tasking, Captain, the sooner we can get on with what needs doing. Precisely, destroying Ra Prime."

"With all due respect, sir, the *Behemoth* will be combat ready in only a few hours," Banner continued, trying to plead his case. "With the *Behemoth's* guns and firepower added to the mix, victory is all but assured!"

"And those hours are ones I would rather not waste, Captain. For what it's worth, I am sorry." Hien left the ready room, stepping onto the bridge.

"Attention on deck!" someone called loudly.

"As you were," Hien smiled at the *Behemoth's* crew. "This ship will be taking over the duties of the Weligo Terminus. I expect each and every one of you to perform to the best of your abilities in my absence."

"Yes sir!" the *Behemoth's* XO said, saluting the fleet admiral.

Hien nodded at the XO and proceeded onto the lift. His shuttle should be ready by the time he reached the hangar bay, and he was eager to meet the captain of the *Juggernaut* in person. He was eager to finish this fight with the Ra'tids. The sooner that the fleet was underway, the better.

Behind him, Captain Banner watched him go. His scowl grew darker. "Bastard."

Commander Nick Pasukis entered the ready room, his face a mixture of confusion and anger. He plopped unceremoniously into one of the chairs in the room and threw his feet up on to the table. Normal protocol would have had the XO cast out of the room and possibly in the brig for such an action, but the two men had been working in close proximity for almost four standard years. Their working relationship was solid.

"So what was that all about?" Pasukis asked. "He just up and left. Didn't he know that repairs are going to be finished in a few hours, tops?"

"He knew," Captain Benner growled.

"So he just decided to leave us here in the lurch then? He's that eager to hog all the glory in his one man quest to save the Republic, damn the cost?"

"Apparently."

"Bastard," Pasukis agreed with his boss.

Chapter Eight

The Ra system was one of the stranger anomalies in the explored universe. With a large, primary blue giant and a smaller, secondary white dwarf in orbit, the binary star system had confused the early human explorers, who had thought that such a star formation was impossible. Their meeting of the race, which dwelt on the solitary habitable planet, came as a bigger surprise, since the planet was devoid of oxygen, nitrogen and hydrogen, and nobody suspected it could even begin to harbor life.

The stars played havoc on standard Republic sensors. Thankfully, for Saul and his team, the *Caliban* was anything but standard, and they were able to see the Ra'tid picket line well before they entered the outer system.

With her cloak operating at peak efficiency, the *Caliban* slipped past the picket line with ease, leaving the dozen smaller Ra'tid destroyers behind with little problem. Alves, whose forehead was slick with sweat, guided the deadly little ship into the system. Hunter and Mizi both watched and waited, with the tension thick in the recycled air. The co-pilot stared at her console, watching the sensor sweeps of the Ra'tid ships pass over them, but never getting any sort of return, while Hunter squirmed in his command chair.

"Another patrol coming up," Mizi murmured as the sensors came alive, the passive scans relaying the information to her console, using the active sensors of the Ra'tids themselves to pinpoint their position. "Looks like a pair of destroyers."

"Not taking any chances today, are they?" Saul asked rhetorically. He looked at the course correction Alves had silently inputted and nodded. "Good idea. Let's use that gas giant to gain some speed and conserve fuel."

The *Caliban* shifted course and slid away from the approaching patrol ships. The cloak was good, everyone on the bridge knew, but the unasked question weighed heavily on each of their minds. How good were the Ra'tid scanners? Hunter knew that eventually that the question would be answered, one way or the other.

Using the gas giant's gravity to gain speed, Alves swung around the planet. He checked their speed and grunted in satisfaction. Their energy consumption had dipped due to their course change, which made the pilot as happy as he could be. "Five minutes from Ra Prime."

"Another patrol," Mizi warned. "Doesn't look like we can dodge this one, either."

"Go beneath them," Hunter said. "What type of ships?"

"Uh... light cruisers, looks like," Mizi answered after a moment. "Three of them. Coming right at us."

"Okay. They have weaker sensors than their destroyers," Hunter nodded. "Go low, Alves."

The pilot wiped his sweaty hands on his trousers and nodded. "We should be in passive scanner range of Ra Prime in a few moments."

The bridge fell silent as the cruisers swept above them, their scanners causing the passive sensors of the *Caliban* to glow yellow in warning. The ships weren't large, but compared to the diminutive *Caliban*, their tonnage was more than enough to hurt the small ship. Mizi winced as a particularly close scan hit their engines and bounced off, but the Ra'tids ships did not change course. Hunter exhaled.

"That was nerve-wracking," Hunter admitted. He leaned over and poked his head out the door. "Saul? You mind coming up here? Ra Prime will be on our sensors in a few moments."

Saul came forward and entered the bridge. "Everything seems to be going smoothly on your end of things."

"It was pretty easy," Hunter said. Alves shot him a dirty look. Hunter smiled. "I have a great crew."

"Okay, my team and I need to get on Ra Prime, or as close as you can get us without risking detection," Saul instructed. He jabbed at the sensors. "The moon's too far. Anything closer?"

"Holy..." Alves hissed as the *Caliban* swung around Ra Prime's moon and the planet came fully into scanner range. Hunter brought up the view screen. Mizi gasped as an array of a half dozen shipyards came into view. Fifteen massive ships, each of which looked more of a mountain than a vessel with a Void drive, sat parked in the near-space of the shipyards. A cluster of frigates and destroyers swarmed amongst the giants, pilot fish to the sharks.

Inside the shipyards were six more of the monstrous super dreadnaughts that Saul had seen during his briefing with General Soltus. His eyes tracked their progress and saw that the ships were near completion. Those, combined with whatever the larger ships in orbit around the planet happened to be, were more than enough to destroy almost any Republic fleet in existence. Saul swallowed hard and thought of a quick prayer.

"What in the hell are those things?" Mizi asked.

"Those are the reason that we're here," Saul said.

"Give me a reason why I shouldn't turn us around right now and head back to Helix before we're spotted," Hunter demanded as he glared at Saul. "If one of those things gets lucky and detects our presence here, we're dead. The *Caliban's* as tough as they come, but there's no way I'm risking her by fighting an entire Rock armada by herself."

"A lot of money," Saul smiled. "Have faith. If it were the Lord's will for us to be spotted, it would have happened already. Your job, my friend, is to merely get us on the planet, and should we live, get us off. We'll take care of things."

"Mizi?" Hunter shifted his eyes to his second in command.

She shook her head. "Sorry. Planet has a defense grid like Earth had before the Coalition attack. I can't even promise that the cloak is going to get us close enough to do anything for you, priest."

"You heard the lady," Hunter frowned. "It's not happening.

Got another plan?"

Saul stared at the sensors and knew that Mizi was correct. Seeing that there was little reason to press the issue, he asked, "Can you get us onto one of those space docks then, perhaps?"

Hunter was opening his mouth to retort angrily when Mizi interjected. "I think we can do that, yeah. Those sensors don't seem to be as advanced at the activity I'm picking up from the grid around the planet. Hunter?"

The commander of the *Caliban* exhaled noisily. "You're insane," he said to Saul. "You know that, right?"

Saul didn't answer.

"Cutting engines now," Alves said as he flipped a switch. The steady hum of the engines faded, leaving the ship eerily silent.

"Alves, pick a space dock," Hunter grunted.

"Why'd you shut off the engines?" Saul asked, a bit surprised.

"We're in the shadow of the planet right now," Alves said. "It's −200 degrees Celsius out there. The Rocks would easily see our heat signature. If we were out in the direct light of the suns, then I wouldn't care."

"Ah," Saul nodded.

"Science," Alves said as he targeted the nearest space dock with air boosters. "It's the second religion of being a pilot."

"What's the first?" Saul asked, genuinely curious.

Alves eyed him. "Lady Luck."

Hunter grunted and rubbed his temples with his fingertips. The *Caliban's* air thrusters fired again, adjusting their course and correcting the yaw of the ship as the pilot lined up his approach. Alves' face was dripping with sweat now, his eyes locked on his instrument panel as he gauged the speed of the *Caliban* in correlation to the space docks orbital speed. The pilot finally exhaled as the *Caliban* matched the speed and position of the space dock. He glanced back at Hunter.

"ETA, twelve minutes."

Saul nodded in acknowledgement.

"All right, priest. Off my bridge," Hunter ordered. "You and your people better get suited up. Our window of opportunity is small here, and if your troops are slow then we're all waking up tomorrow in hell."

Mizi looked at Hunter in surprise as Saul headed for the cargo hold. He paused at the door and looked back at the captain. "We'll shoot you the code for extraction when we're ready. Try to be ready for us."

"I'll be ready," Hunter promised. "I said I would. My word is good. You can count on that."

*****

"Transient! Transient!" came the call over the comm. Hikia scrambled out of her bunk and threw on her blouse. She hurriedly tucked it in, straightened her belt, and checked herself in the mirror. She decided she was presentable and headed for the bridge.

"Three unidentified echoes, bearing three-two-two, ETA is thirty minutes," the voice announced overhead. Hikia slowed down, smoothed her blouse once more, and stepped onto her bridge.

"Captain on the bridge!" a yeoman called out.

"As you were," Hikia said as she walked calmly walked over to her chair. She looked over at her sensor techs. "What do you have, Ensign?"

"Just picked up their echoes five minutes ago, ma'am," the ensign on duty said, his voice nervous despite his best efforts. "I double-checked to make sure I wasn't seeing ghosts, and then sounded the alert. Distinct footprints, and from the looks of things, I'm guessing that someone is sneaking a raid on Weligo."

"Well, that'd be pretty stupid," she muttered. "The Terminus is protected by the Weligo station. Wait." She pinched the bridge of her nose, bringing up the galactic borders to mind. "That's coming from Coalition space, isn't it?"

"Yes ma'am."

"I don't have time for their games," she grumbled. "They're going to try to slip past Weligo, strike Earth? That means they're going to use Helix as a jumping point. Damn them!"

"Isn't there some kind of peace treaty out there, ma'am?"

"No, Ensign. It's a proposal for a cease-fire, which could eventually lead to a peace treaty," Hikia corrected the junior officer though her tone made it clear she didn't trust the Coalition offering a cease fire any more than she trusted a Darian to endure an insult to his honor. "You said thirty minutes from now?"

"Yes ma'am."

"So we have about twenty minutes before we need to decide if we're staying here to greet them, or running back to Weligo station."

"That would mean running back through Retina and *that* meat grinder, ma'am," the ensign reminded her. Hikia nodded slowly.

"We can stay in system for another ten hours, tops, before the radiation beats down our shielding," Hikia thought aloud, her mind doing some quick equations. "We can *probably* handle the three Coalition ships on our own. Any indication to their size, Ensign?"

"Mid-sized at best guess, ma'am," the ensign shrugged his shoulders. "The sensors see them, but haven't made up their mind yet as to what they are."

"Stay on it, Ensign," Hikia dismissed the officer and sat in her command chair. A second later, it chimed. She frowned. "This is the Captain."

"Captain, this is Ensign Tomo Katsumoto, down in Engineering," a bright, cheerful voice came through. Hikia rolled her eyes and cursed young people, and more specifically, their seemingly boundless energy.

"Go ahead, Ensign."

"Ma'am, I've been running some diagnostics on the new hardware the sensor techs have been bringing to me. You're going to want to come down here."

"Care to enlighten me further, Ensign?"

"Ma'am, the intra ship comms aren't secure, and well..." the ensign's voice trailed off. Hikia cocked her eyebrow, interest peaked.

"Be there in three minutes, Ensign," Hikia killed the comm. She stood and looked over at Lieutenant Khandry. "Lieutenant Khandry, you have the bridge. Bring the ship fully online for general quarters, prepare for possible enemy action."

"Aye ma'am," Khandry nodded and took over the vacated command chair. "I have the bridge."

Hikia hopped into the lift and rode it down, deeper into the underbelly of the battleship. She chewed her bottom lip as she contemplated just what the ensign wanted to show her.

Just how badly screwed up is my ship, she silently wondered as the lift slowed, then stopped. She stepped out past the yellow safety line and walked down the corridor, enlisted personnel moving to one side or the other to let the captain pass. "Make a hole" was heard further down, and more men and women stepped aside for the ranking officer on board the ship.

She stopped at the Engineering workshop and buzzed the door. It opened a second later, recognizing her by biorhythmic sensor. Two engineers looked up together, and then braced themselves.

"Attention on deck!"

"As you were," Hikia said. She spotted Ensign Katsumoto off to the side near a workbench and approached. "Evening, Ensign. What's so important that you pulled me out of an imminent attack to show me?"

"Attack, ma'am?" Katsumoto's face paled. "I didn't know we were under attack!"

"Not under attack, Ensign," she corrected him. "About to *be* attacked."

"Oh," Katsumoto signed, relieved. "So we have time."

"Time for what, Ensign?"

"Ma'am, take a look at this component right here," the officer said, pointing down at his workbench.

"What am I looking at, Ensign?" Hikia looked at the scattered remnants of the *Potemkin's* upgraded sensor systems, which was spread across the young officer's workbench. She couldn't tell one chipboard from another, though the message from Katsumoto five minutes before had indicated that whatever she was looking at, it had to be important.

"It's not what you're looking for, Captain," Katsumoto said, his voice eager. "It's what you're *not* looking at."

Hikia scowled. "We do not have time for this, Ensign. Get to the point."

"Right. Sorry ma'am," Katsumoto's head bobbed. He grabbed a small chipboard from his workbench and held it up. "This is a Navy standard-issue relay circuit board. We have them in all our consoles. It has breakers built in; circuitry components fused here and here, and has been the source of solid Republic computer engineering for thirty years. With me so far, Captain?"

"I remember those from when I was an ensign," she nodded. "I didn't come out of the Academy as a captain, you know. Go on."

'Okay, perfect," Katsomoto's tone changed to excitement. "Then you'll understand this next part." He lifted another chipboard up. "This is one of the boards we got when the ship went into the docks for the retrofit. Notice anything peculiar?"

"No. I don't... wait," Hikia grabbed the board from the ensign's hand and studied it. She frowned. "What is this? There isn't any noticeable circuitry."

"Precisely my point, Captain," Katsumoto said. "This isn't any Earth Republic tech I'm familiar with, and I design this crap in my free time. It's spliced tech, it's gotta be. There aren't any heat reductors, circuit relays or processor units. This is one microprocessor board with a solid state drive design, and it serves as a processor *and* a conductor platform to support other boards like it."

"Jesus," Hikia's eyes widened. "I've never heard of anything like that before."

"Oh, it gets better, Captain," Katsumoto said. He picked up another piece of equipment of similar design, but much smaller. "This is from one of our missile heads of the new Mark Five's. Same design as the sensor controls, you'll notice. Now, watch this." He pulled up his data pad and linked it to the missile's chipboard. He punched in a command and turned it towards his captain. "The missile is seeking a target, ma'am. At least, the chip thinks it is. Now watch this." He brought the original chipboard online, as well as the old Republic tech. He punched in a new command. "Check it out, ma'am."

Hikia's face shifted from shock to confusion as she read the data. "You're telling me that it only sees the old tech, and not the new? I don't understand."

"Don't worry ma'am, nobody did at first," Katsumoto allowed. "The new missiles don't see our new sensors. Both of which, I'll add, have been spliced from someone else's tech. The programming in here, somewhere buried deep, has it ignoring all tech similar. We had problems before when trying to splice this technology with ours in the past."

"What are you suggesting, Ensign?"

"I'm suggesting that someone with similar tech has been manipulating our own tech to spoof our systems," Katsumoto supplied. "I'm willing to go so far as to say that this tech is the reason we got spoofed by the Rocks."

"The Rocks can't do this sort of thing," Hikia protested.

"I know that, ma'am," Katsumoto nodded in agreement. "We're leaps and bounds beyond them. This isn't even Coalition tech. But someone sure as hell sold them this."

"Whose tech is it?" Hikia asked, though she had a sinking suspicion she already knew. She hoped she was wrong.

Ensign Katsumoto dashed her hopes with a single word.

"Gener."

*****

The *Caliban* drifted up to the Ra'tid space dock, its exterior cargo doors opened. Momentum from the earlier engine thrusts had put the *Caliban* at near-matching speed with the space dock, with just enough of a difference for the small ship to drift by slow enough for Saul and his team to exit and be perfectly lined up with the alien station. With the lights of the cargo hold turned off and the cloak activated, the ship was nigh invisible to the rest of the universe.

Inside the cargo hold, was Saul and his squad, each one of them suited up in sealed combat armor. The magnets in their boots held them in place, and all exterior lights that their armor usually had were either taped over or extinguished completely. There were no insignias, ranks, or any other identifying features on their armor. The Articles of War did not apply to special operations groups, and everyone knew what the punishment was if one was caught behind enemy lines. Saul looked around the darkness and nodded. He felt as ready as he ever would. He activated his encrypted comm link.

"This is Saul. Give me a comm check."

"Zombie here."

"Gunter."

"Rabbit."

"Evil Penguin."

"Jones."

"Rodriguez."

"Ling."

Saul smiled. "All right team. Turn off your magnetics and give me a leap of faith."

One by one, the men and women from the special operations team leapt from the cargo hold and into deep space, their momentum carrying them up and away from the *Caliban*. Saul looked up and saw that the massive station was drawing close and he reached out with his hand. He closed his eyes and offered him and the rest of the team one final prayer before he felt his hand brush against the hull of the space dock. His gloved hand grabbed the metal and the magnets inside activated, securing his grip on the dock. He looked around and saw that the others were securing their holds on the hull as well. He glanced down at the *Caliban*, but it was no longer there. Saul looked around for it, but the small smuggling ship was nowhere to be seen. He hoped it stayed invisible as it made its way back to the outer part of the system.

Zombie came to rest next to him. "Everyone accounted for."

Saul gave Zombie a thumbs up and the squad began to pick its way up the side of the space dock, searching for an entrance into the interior. Since the Ra'tids didn't need to breathe like carbon-based life forms, the shipyards weren't as tightly sealed as a Republic one would have been. Saul reflected back to the first time he had done something similar, though it had been on one of the older Ra'tid ships. Those, like the space docks and shipyards, weren't nearly as well protected from space either.

An hour passed. The team continued to move up – *or was it down*, Saul wondered – the hull of the space dock, progress slow as they inspected any exterior holes as they progressed. Rocky outcroppings slowed their progress, since the rocks contained less metals than the framework of the dock. Saul did his best to avoid the outcroppings, even if it did slow them down. He knew just how dangerous they could be.

He felt the entrance before he actually saw it. His hand fell through a spot where he expected to find more metal, and he jerked back. He lifted his body a little more and peered inside the hole. He could see a light at the far end of it, and judging by the shape of the entrance, he guessed that it was either an exhaust vent for the engines, or a Ra'tid equivalent of a docking hatch.

Praying it was the latter he checked the opening size. It was big enough for the team to fit in, if they proceeded single file. However, he could see a faint shimmer midway through the hatch. Saul recognized it as an energy shield. He paused.

They couldn't cut the shielding from the outside. Even if they could figure out how to cut it, doing so would probably trigger all sorts of alarms. Which would bring Ra'tid soldiers, something that Saul did not even want to get a whiff of while they were infiltrating the space dock.

"Any ideas?" he asked Zombie. When the big man didn't immediately answer, he posed the question to the rest of the team.

"I've got one," Gunter answered. "It might work." Saul swung around to face her, several feet below his position, clinging to the hull. She continued. "We might be able to phase shift through the shield using the suit's—" she banged her fist against the chest plate of the armor she wore "—shield generator. We can match the harmonics of the shield, maybe. Slide right through it without anyone ever knowing. If we do it right."

"How do you find the right frequency?" Saul asked, worried.

"Here, let me get closer," she said and worked her way past him. She held out her hand towards the shielding. Saul waited for a moment before she wiggled backwards to their position. "I think I can do it. I'll match harmonics using the cloak."

Saul was impressed. The suits the squad wore weren't like the standard-issue combat armor that the Republic army wore. The suits contained tech stolen from the Geners, and then spliced to match Republic specifications. Each suit had its own personal cloak, which ran off a secondary power supply that could allow for up to six hours of stealth. In theory, what Gunter was suggesting was possible, since their cloaks acted as a pseudo-shield around the armored combat suits.

It was also extremely risky. If the harmonics of the suits didn't match up to the shield, the alarms could trigger, or worse still, fry them all. They would only get one shot at it, and the procedure would drain a godly amount of their power supply from the cloaks. Still, it was better than anything Saul could come up with.

"Do it," he ordered. "Everyone pass control of your armor's systems to Gunter."

He watched as the data streamed across the left side of his faceplate, her adjustments changing the harmonics of his cloak. New numbers scrolled down, which he guessed were her doing. After a few moments, she grunted.

"It's done. Who wants to go first?"

"Your idea. You get the honor," Saul answered.

"Ladies first," Zombie added. Gunter snorted.

"I'm as much of a lady as you're a gentleman, Zombie," she said as she slipped through the shield. It flickered briefly as she passed, but held. She stopped and stood upright, her boots holding her in place.

"I'm in," she said over the comm. "No sign of detection."

Gunter moved deeper into the corridor as the others entered the shield behind her. Saul went first, followed closely by Zombie. He stood and let the magnets grab the floor as he helped Zombie out of the hatch. Saul counted the rest of the team as they passed through.

"Wait. I only counted six," Saul said, stopping the progression. He looked around. "Who's missing?"

"Where's Ling?" Zombie asked.

"He was right behind me," Rabbit said. He turned around and looked back down the hatch. "He was coming last."

Saul pushed past the diminutive operative and looked down the hatch. He quickly looked away from the charred and twisted corpse.

"He's not coming," Saul said. He turned to look at Gunter. "You said that we all were on the same harmonics."

"We were!" she protested. "I had us all on the same frequency."

"Then what the hell happened, Gunter?" Zombie asked.

"I don't know what happened!"

"Okay, enough," Saul ordered. "Casualties were to be expected on this mission. He's with God now, and that's all we can hope for."

"Still no sign of detection," Gunter said, her tone gloom.

Saul wiped away his faceplate. The air was thick with sulphuric ash and carbon monoxide, which cut his visibility down greatly. He looked down the corridor both ways and frowned. Stalagmites hung from the corridor ceilings, and some even came up from the ground. It reminded Saul of caverns he had explored on Earth a long time before. A lifetime ago.

"What now?" Zombie asked.

"I guess we go find what we came here to find," Saul said, shaking the last vestiges of memories off.

"Which is...?" Gunter asked.

"No idea," Saul admitted.

*****

"We have two options here," Captain Hikia said as she paced around her ready room's conference table. Gathered in the room were her senior officers, which – much to the newly promoted officer's surprise – included Lieutenant Khandry. Hikia looked around. "We can either run the gauntlet back through Retina, hope we survive long enough to toss off a Final Dispatch containing our news of the Gener tech, or we can stay here and hold off the Coalition raid. I'm open for opinions."

"Run and send the message, ma'am," her XO said immediately.

"Explain, Harun."

"We are at war with both the Rocks and the Coalition," he said. "If the Rocks have new tech, and it spoofs our sensors, then the rest of the Republic needs to know that everything we've retrofitted over the past few years is worthless. Something like this can alter the entire war."

"Good idea, Commander Nassem, except you're forgetting one thing," the ship's engineer cut in, his ruddy face bright with anger. "If Earth falls, the Republic is finished. The Rocks seemed content on staying in the Retina system, which is pretty worthless except for the tactical position it offers. These three Coalition ships present a clear and obvious danger to Earth. They are the real threat."

"Real threat or not, Eng, the Rocks can spoof our tech. That means they can strike us anywhere at any time," Commander Nassem exclaimed. "We have to ensure that the Admiralty gets word of this."

"The Coalition's about to attack and you want to run home to Momma?" the Eng retorted.

The room exploded in noise as the XO rose to his feet, pounding the table angrily as he shouted at the engineer. More voices started yelling their opinions, and for a moment, the room descended into bedlam.

"That will be *enough!*" Hikia shouted, slamming an open palm onto the tabletop. The sound went off like a gunshot. The room quieted down as her steely gaze shifted to her chief engineer. "Your point is a valid one, Eng, but so is the XO's. We have ten minutes to make a decision, and I do not want to waste what precious time we have bickering. Now, does anyone have anything *constructive* to add?"

"Ma'am?" Khandry raised her hand timidly. Hikia nodded, giving her permission to speak. Khandry cleared her throat, gathered her courage, and began. "Captain, our duty is to the Republic. While the Ra'tids are a danger in the Retina system, technically the system is neutral territory. Our sworn duty is to protect, defend and preserve the Articles of the Republic. The Coalition seeks to destroy this. I would suggest that we do our duty, which is to stop the Coalition ships from striking Earth. That would be our duty, not to tell the Admiralty about Gener tech being used by the Rocks. We can always include that in our Final Dispatch, should lose the fight against the incoming Coalition ships."

Hikia nodded. "Well said, Lieutenant. Anyone else?"

Silence answered her.

"Okay then," Hikia said with finality. "We stay and we fight. Let's go to General Quarters."

*****

The *Potemkin's* warning klaxons blared as the ship emerged

from hiding, catching the three Coalition ships completely off guard. The Coalition ships, all destroyers, had not anticipated any trouble, from what Hikia could see, and were tightly packed together. She had little problem drawing up a solid tactical firing solution on them within moments of their appearance on the nearside of Helix's star.

"Target the two lead ships," she ordered, knowing that her first action had to be to reduce the number of the enemy she faced.

"Yes ma'am," her weapons officer answered. "We have a solution. Bearings matched and tubes are hot. Birds away, ETA three minutes."

Hikia could envision the panic that the Coalition CO must be experiencing, and it was evidenced by how her opposing commander reacted to her nasty surprise for them. She couldn't fault them too much for it, however, as no rationally acting captain would consider a ship to be hiding out where the *Potemkin* had been positioned. If it had been her, she would never have expected to find a Coalition ship of the line hiding out in the Helix Cluster.

The Coalition formation broke into evasive maneuvers as the *Potemkin's* first volley bore down on them. The *Potemkin's* weapons officer put two more volleys of missiles into space in their wake, recalibrating the new firing solutions as the Coalition vessels changed course. The *Potemkin's* engines burnt at full military speed, chasing her own missiles towards the Coalition ships. She had the superior speed and firepower; the Coalition ships only had maneuverability, and once upon a time, luck.

The *Potemkin's* initial volley reduced the lead Coalition ship to pieces of spinning debris, its hastily brought-up ECM and point defenses unable to cope with the sheer number of missiles it was up against. While the Coalition destroyers were capable ships in their own right, they had nothing on the firepower of a fully armed capitol ship. The second destroyer bucked under the impacts of more missiles from the *Potemkin*, the spine shattering as the concussive blasts wrecked the superstructure of the once-proud ship.

Missiles flew from the tubes of the remaining uninjured enemy vessel, just as she had expected.

"Override drive safety protocols," she ordered her engineering staff. "Increase our speed until the engines are redlined. I want to end this as quickly as possible."

Several of the bridge staff turned to stare at her with mixed expressions of shock and horror. It was a calculated risk and one she was more than willing to take if it won this engagement.

The *Potemkin* blazed forward, the incoming enemy missiles losing their lock on her as she rocketed into beam weapons range. The already panicked Coalition ships barely had time return fire as spears of crackling energy erupted from the *Potemkin*. The beams sliced the remaining Coalition vessel completely in half along its center, shattering her spine and rupturing her Void drive. The ensuing explosion was both spectacular and costly. Shards of the Coalition vessel's ripped-apart corpse hammered into the *Potemkin*, triggering multiple impact alarms as debris bounced along her hull.

Her XO was screaming about hull breaches and the loss of some key systems but Hikia ignored the reports. Beyond making sure that weapons were still online and functional, she could care less about the immediate costs. The other Coalition ship had taken damage from the Potemkin's risky move as well, but not enough. Fires burned along its hull where its atmosphere leaked into space, and the spine was ruined, but it was still trying desperately to fight. There was no doubt of that as it unleashed a point blank volley at the *Potemkin* as she hurtled passed, the beams and missiles gutting the top deck of the *Potemkin*. Even her insane rate of speed wasn't enough to escape the entire volley.

"Impact! Impact!" someone with a talent for stating the obvious wailed as several of the Coalition missiles detonated, their laser warheads ripping through the shielding and wrecking systems. More concussive missiles impacted, shaking the core of the mighty battleship and tossing men and women about as though they were rag dolls.

"Return fire! Everything we got!" Hikia shouted.

New lances of energy streaked from the *Potemkin* into the last enemy ship as she continued to streak forward, leaving beam weapons' range. Her parting shot did its job. The Coalition ship erupted in a flash of orange and red as the Potemkin's fire raked its main engines.

Hikia lurched forward but managed to keep her balance as she felt the Potemkin's own engines flicker and die. Her stunt had pushed them too far and she would paying the price for that now, but she would be doing so gladly. Despite the failure of the ship's main drive they'd made through the battle alive and with no major damage bad enough to beyond field repair, given time. Best of all, the surprise attack on Earth had been stopped.

"Ma'am, all engines are offline," Khandry reported, her face ashen, confirming what Hikia already knew her in her gut. "We're completely dead in the water."

"How long to exact repairs," Hikia asked, exhaustion creeping into her tone.

"Captain..." Khandry swallowed. "Captain, without a dry dock, the Void drive isn't going to be repaired. We're not going anywhere."

So it's worse than I thought, Hikia thought, then shrugged. *Still they had survived three to one odds. That was something to be grateful for.*

"Our shields won't last another two hours against that radiation if we resume our previous hiding location, Lieutenant," Hikia warned, her tone steely. "I suggest we come up with a solution to get out of here before we die."

Chapter Nine

With Evil Penguin on point, the squad moved through the wide corridors of the space dock, weapons ready against their armored shoulders. Light was dim, with fluorescents casting a pale glow and causing their suits to appear darker than normal. Not for the first time did Saul wish he could breathe real oxygen and not recycled gasses. What passed for air in the corridors was clogging their intake filters, and several times the squad was forced to stop and clear out their systems before pressing onwards.

"Hold up," Evil Penguin suddenly said. The each one of them dropped into a crouch, their weapons pointing in different firing angles to cover all possible attack points. After a moment, their point man continued. "Sorry. Needed to clean off my faceplate."

A few nervous chuckles broke out on the encrypted comm that the squad shared. Even Saul smiled a bit. He glanced around and spotted a small data port across the corridor from his position. He slid over to the port and checked to see if it was functional.

"Wait one," Saul ordered as he looked at the port. It was almost identical to the ones he had seen years before, though with a few cosmetic differences. He tapped on the screen but nothing happened. He frowned and tried again. This time is flickered awake, awaiting a command. "Gunter? Come here and take a look at this."

Gunter appeared at his elbow and looked down at the data port. "What am I looking at?"

"A data port," Saul answered. "Do you think you can use this to hack into the space dock's systems? Or, better yet, the entire shipyard?"

"Uh, maybe?" she guessed and looked at the port. "Their tech is a bit different, you know. If I did, my access would be limited at best. I mean, I couldn't take control of anything from here. But monitoring transmissions inside the space dock? I might even be able to stop us from tripping any kind of alarms. Assuming I can even access the port."

"Go ahead and see if you can hack it," Saul said. Gunter nodded and moved past him.

"What about a central database?" Zombie asked. "The Rocks should have something like that, and it might contain information about what we're looking for without us having to risk our necks any more than we already are."

"Give me a moment," Gunter said. Saul watched quietly as Gunter's twisted into an expression of intense concentration as she studied the data port. After a few moments, she shrugged and looked over her shoulder at Saul. "If their security has gotten the same sort of upgrades as their ships, there's no way. If they haven't, then I might get lucky, but it's going to take some time."

"How long?"

"Half an hour, maybe more. Ra'tid firewalls aren't the best ones out there, but they're still decent enough... unless you know your way around them," she explained, flashing a grin at Saul.

Saul wiped his grimy faceplate off and checked the power supply of his suit's cloak. "We should have about two hours' worth of power left for our cloaks. That shield-phase shift you came up with took a lot out of them."

"And they still didn't work completely," she said, reminding him that not all of the team had made it past the insertion point.

"It happens, Gunter," Zombie said. "I've lost more than my fair share of team members over the years. This isn't your first rodeo. You just need to get back on the bull."

"Thanks, Zombie," Gunter said. "Uh... what's a rodeo?"

"Forget it," Saul chuckled. "Gunter, see what you can do with this thing. Zombie, with me. Everyone else, establish a perimeter so she can work. Try to avoid a firefight if you can help it."

Zombie laughed and checked the chamber of the large rifle he was carrying. "Excellent. I get to go play a little."

"If we're not back by the time you get whatever data you can, go ahead and signal the *Caliban* for extraction. You have the extraction codes, right?" Saul asked. "Good. We should be back before it arrives."

"Yes sir," Gunter nodded, and then laughed softly. She shook her head. "Sorry, Saul."

"Wait. You're going off, just the two of you, leaving the rest of us here?" Evil Penguin whistled softly. "I have a bad feeling about this."

"Let's go, Zombie," Saul said and the two of them moved past the point man. Looking down the corridor, Sal lead the way, the big man hot on his heels.

"What are we looking for, anyways?" Zombie asked as they moved deeper into the space dock. Saul swung around a corner, his weapon angled slightly downward as he dropped to one knee. Zombie moved quickly past him, taking up a position further down the hall.

"I'm looking for some way to leave a present for the Rocks without actually getting to the planet's surface," Saul explained as he raced forward and passed Zombie. He pressed against one of the rocky outcroppings in the corridor and looked around before motioning Zombie to follow. "I don't think I'm going to manage it, though."

"What makes you think that?" Zombie asked as he sprinted past.

"Well, part of the problem is that the scientist who gave me the device said that in no uncertain terms would it work anywhere but on a planetary surface," Saul said. "But... I'm starting to wonder if they meant a planetary surface, or something with enough mass to start the reaction."

The two froze as their filters picked up a faint rumbling noise, like an avalanche falling in the distance. Saul recognized it instantly and motioned for Zombie to back up a few steps. The sergeant, confused, quickly followed Saul's lead. They hurriedly ducked inside a small, darkened alcove and waited. They did not have to wait long.

A couple of Ra'tids emerged from a wall across the corridor and set out in the same direction that the two men had been heading moments before, their odd gait distinctive. Saul watched them go, a slight frown on his face. The markings on the back of their cranial hollow indicated that they were diplomats, and were not dockworkers.

"Tell me I didn't just see that," Zombie whispered. Saul remembered that he was with men and women who had never seen Ra'tids in their home environment before. "Those two Rocks just came out of the rock."

"You did see it," Saul replied, his voice hushed. "The Ra'tids can merge with non-organic rock. You know, without carbon organisms in them. They sleep that way, and heal themselves too."

Zombie looked around, nervous. "So they could be anywhere right now, watching us, and we couldn't see them?"

"In theory, yes," Saul checked the power of his suit's cloak. "But thanks to the cloak in these suits, we can too to a degree. The Rocks see in a completely different visual spectrum, and they don't benefit from any sort of ultraviolet spectrums in their sight. They see like our ship sensors do, and the cloak masks that spectrum. There's an excellent chance they could be staring right at us, and not even know we're there."

Zombie grunted in acknowledgement, though it was clear he didn't trust the technology that powered the cloak as much as Saul. Given what had happened to Ling earlier, Saul could hardly fault him for that.

"But what I want to know is why there are Ra'tid diplomats running around a simple dockyard," Saul whispered, more to himself than anything.

The two men picked up their pace, hurrying deeper into the bowels of the dock. Saul detached a hand-held sensor from his tactical holster on his thigh and powered it up. It was a risky move, given that there was always the chance that the Ra'tids may pick up an energy reading. However, Saul knew that being deep within the dock might mask the signal and origin. It was a chance he was willing to take. He did not want to waste any more time wandering around blindly, and he didn't want to stumble upon a random patrol of dock workers.

He adjusted the sensor unit to scan for Ra'tids and clusters of high-energy consumption. It stood to reason that any area where actual construction was taking place would be using more energy, and Saul knew, judging by what he could remember of their insertion aboard the *Caliban*, that super dreadnaughts were being built at this dock in particular. He looked at the screen. Several large blips appeared on the screen, with two indicating that he and Zombie were very close to a manufacturing center of some sort. One was higher than the other was, but slightly further away. Saul picked the closer one and directed Zombie down a separate corridor.

Their visibility grew better as they moved toward the power source, and Saul noted that the air was growing heavier as well. It made sense, since the bonding process of building a Ra'tid ship usually involved fusing silicone with cadmium and graphene. This created an odd mixture, which did not sit well with the usual methane air the Rocks preferred. The solution, Saul recalled as he watched the sensor unit in hand, was to pump in a lot of oxygen and flood the area, forcing the noxious fumes out into space.

"Damned Rocks know how to build themselves a dock, I'll give them that," Zombie said as they turned another corner and looked around. Saul checked his scanner and nodded.

"About thirty meters up, then right about a couple hundred and we're good," he said.

"How big is this place anyway?" Zombie asked.

"Best guess? I'd say about fifteen square kilometers," Saul said. He motioned to the right. "Down here."

Heavy footfalls ahead of them brought the two men to a hard stop. Looking around, Saul spotted a small, dark crevice that looked big enough for the two of them to hide in. He grabbed Zombie by the back of his suit and pulled him along.

"Hey!"

"Quiet," Saul hissed as he shoved the bigger man into the dark crevice. He pressed his body against the sharp rock, wincing a little as a small piece dug uncomfortably into his knee. He looked down and saw that part of his leg was exposed. "Stay here. I'm going to find a different spot."

Saul quickly darted across the corridor and grabbed one of the low-hanging stalagmites from the tunnel ceiling. He twisted his body upward and pulled himself up off the ground, his muscular arms straining as he held himself upside down for a moment. He dug his heels into two nearby stalagmites and used them to help support his weight. He slowly walked the rest of his body up to the ceiling, hand over hand as he gripped the stalagmite. He slowed his breathing as the footfalls came closer and mentally willed himself to be nothing more than a part of the ceiling.

"Holy shit..." he heard Zombie whisper.

"Super dreadnaughts... come well... wish faster," a Ra'tid spoke, the sound devoid of all humanity. Saul felt a chill run down the length of his spine. While the Darians easily reminded humanity of domesticated cats, the Ra'tids were truly alien in every meaning of the word. Even their translators, which converted the rumbling, avalanche-like sound of their speech patterns, sounded empty and alien.

Saul blinked. *Why do the Ra'tids need translators on their own dock?*

"I am pleased that you find things are going well, Great One," another voice said in reply. It was human, but one that sounded like the singing of an angel and the beauty of a Greek god. It caused tears to appear in the corner of Saul's eyes and wrenched at his heart, the pitch one of perfection. The melodious voice continued. "I am hopeful that we can continue to achieve amazing things while working together."

As the group rounded the corner and came into view, Saul spotted a tall, thin man walking alongside a mobile, bipedal jumble of rock. Behind them were three more Ra'tids carrying long, rifle-like weapons that were covered in jagged hooks of diamond that glowed. Their elaborate weapons told Saul far more about the Ra'tid in front of the group than any markings on the back could. He looked back at the man he had mistaken at first glance as a human. Saul recognized the wardrobe of an ambassador and realized just where the Ra'tids had gotten their new technology. He was not looking at a human, not in the strictest of terms. He was looking at a Gener.

Perfection. Geners were all about perfection, with their entire society revolving around the quest for it. The Gener walking down the hall towards Saul reflected that ideology. He was strikingly handsome, with cold, ice blue eyes that sparkled like raindrops. His chin was perfectly chiseled, and his high cheekbones offset his smooth, unwrinkled forehead. Beneath his exposed skin, beads of light moved rhythmically through his arteries and vein, flashing like distant stars in the night sky. His movements were graceful, elegant, appearing even more so with the accompanying Ra'tid escort.

Saul knew that many of the Republic's finest theologians and philosophers were at odds over why the Geners appeared to look more and more like biblical angels with each passing generating. Some insisted that it was merely a sign of Gener arrogance, and another way to show humanity that they were less than the Geners, putting their full stock on display, as their genetic manipulations were far superior to humanity's. Others believed it was mere chance, wherein natural selection after birth – much like the ancient Spartans did on their own male babies soon after birth – weeded out the ugliest and only allowed the beautiful to continue onwards.

Saul had a theory of his own, but it followed what the dogma of the Order thought on the subject. Or had, at least, once upon a time that no amount of genetic manipulation could achieve what God had intended, and knowing this, the Geners had tried instead to attain the closest thing to perfection that they could – angels. But in doing so, they had changed from men and women born upon Earth a long time ago to become alien-like, distant from their Earthen cousins, different, lost. They had given up so much of what it truly mean to be human in trade for becoming perfect, with unparalleled beauty and intelligence, that they were a mockery of what humanity strived for.

The ambassador's presence, however, also confirmed that another of the galactic empires was helping the Ra'tids. Given that the general consensus regarding thus had been the Coalition, Saul was just a bit surprised to find the truth. Saul reorganized his priorities, now that the proof was before them. The Gener had to be taken alive and returned to Republic space.

Saul dropped down from the ceiling in the midst of the group and swung his carbine around, depressing the trigger and sending a fusillade of rounds into the closest Ra'tid. The Rock jerked in shock and surprise, as the rounds tore through his silicone membranes, and he toppled over, dead before he hit the ground. He twisted his body and slammed his foot into what passed for the ankle of a second Ra'tid as Zombie stepped out of the shadows, his massive rifle up and ready.

Using non-standard issue ammunition, Zombie fired two quick shots into the leader of the Ra'tid group, one to the cranial region and one directly in the center of his mass. The lead Ra'tid fell heavily to the deck, body crumbling as death took hold. Zombie shifted his angle and fired one shot into the chest of the Ra'tid Saul had tried to kick. Rock blasted off the impact wound and the Ra'tid fell with a grunt, the massive caliber round tearing a huge chunk out of his center.

The Gener froze for a split second, unsure, before he gracefully pivoted and started to run back down the corridor. Zombie's gun came up and the big man took aim at the fleeing Gener.

"No!" Saul cried out and shoved the barrel of the rifle aside. The round exploded from the rifle and slammed into the wall of the corridor. Zombie looked at Saul, annoyed. "We need him alive!"

Saul set out after the Gener, desperation loaning him more speed. The thin Gener was beginning to outdistance the former Templar, though, and Saul saw that the Gener was going to get away. However, the Gener slipped as it tried to round a corner, pirouetting elegantly in a remarkable display of agility to stay upright. The maneuver kept him on his feet, but slowed him down enough to allow Saul to close the distance.

Saul grabbed the Geners arm and twisted, surprising the man. The Gener struck at Saul with the edge of his hand, the strike nearly a blur as the enhanced speed of the genetically enhanced being sliced through the air. Saul ducked, narrowly avoiding the blow, and grabbed the other arm of the Gener. Pinning them together, he dropped the Gener to the floor of the corridor.

"Name!" Saul shouted as he shoved the barrel of carbine into the face of the Gener. The beautiful being's features filled with horror. Saul pulled back the charge handle on his weapon. "I said name!"

"Kratos-3-A," the Gener answered, his perfect ice-blue eyes wide with terror. "I am–"

"I know what you are, messenger," Saul growled. "Not even a Hermes? Seriously? Why would the Geners send a lowly Kratos, and not a normal ambassador? I don't care how high your batch number may be either. Where's the Demeter? Why no Artemis?"

"I am the ranking member of my race here, human," Kratos answered instead. "You do not fully grasp the concepts of our society."

"I grasp enough, Plastic Man," Saul retorted. "How many of you are here?"

"Too few to be of a threat to our friends, the Ra'tids," the Gener replied, his voice smug. "But more than you could ever guess. Our beauty, our perfection, knows no bounds, and soon we shall sweep all the lesser races–"

Saul smashed the butt of his carbine into the Gener's perfect nose with a satisfying crunch, breaking it. Kratos stumbled back and fell down, his face bloodied and swollen. Tears ran freely down his eyes as his hands flew up to feel the damaged area. Red blood, twinkling in the dim lighting, seeped from between his fingers. Saul grunted.

"I didn't know what we were supposed to find when we got here," he admitted to Zombie. "But this is as good as it gets. Let's get back to the rest of the group. We've got evidence that the Admiralty is going to want, and our ride is waiting for us. I hope."

Saul saw that the Gener was looking intently at him, studying him. Saul frowned and cracked the Gener across the temple with the butt of his carbine, knocking him unconscious.

"Great," Zombie groused as he looked at the drooling Gener. "I get to carry him, don't I?"

"Only because I have one more thing to do on our way back," Saul stated. "I hope that Gunter was able to crack their database somehow."

The walls of the corridor began to vibrate, the Ra'tid equivalent of an alarm echoing throughout the entire space dock. Zombie reached down and hoisted the think Gener effortlessly over his shoulder as Saul contemplated the secondary aspect of his mission. More than likely, he would not be able to leave behind the "package" that Earth Republic scientists had cooked up, unless he somehow managed to take over a Ra'tid vessel or something with similar mass before they were forced to leave.

However, capturing the Gener was good enough for him. Up until that point, it had been everyone's assumptions that the Ra'tids were being helped by the Coalition. Now, with proof that the Geners were assisting the Rocks, the game had changed. Saul needed to get the unconscious Gener back to the *Caliban*, back to Earth itself.

Besides, he thought as he patted his hip, where the package was stored in a small vial. *I didn't really want to go down in the books as one of the worst war criminals in history anyway.*

*****

The *Juggernaut* sat in Void Space with the rest of the combined Republic and Darian fleet, every system running at full power. Captain Jack Connor was more than a bit put out to find Fleet Admiral Hien on his bridge, and a bit more annoyed to have him looking over his shoulder. He didn't care for the attitude that Hien had showed since transferring his flag to the *Juggernaut*, and wondered just how Captain Banner over on the *Behemoth* had tolerated it.

The *Juggernaut* was Connor's ship, and had been for the better part of two years. He had carefully guided the massive dreadnaught through multiple engagements with the Coalition, and he would be damned if he let some high and mighty admiral dictate tactics to him on his ship. Let the fleet admiral command the fleet; Connor's ship was *his*, and in the heat of battle, his crew would only follow his orders. Nobody on the bridge would trust the commands of an unfamiliar man during shipboard maneuvers, and the lack of trust could get them all killed.

"All systems show green," the *Juggernaut's* primary helmsman informed the captain. "We're ready to drop out of the Void on your mark, sir."

"Good," Connor answered before Hien had even opened his

mouth. The Admiral glared at him. Connor ignored him. "I want all weapon systems up and running, and the ship ready for evasive maneuvers. I want all ECMs up and running before we drop out of the Void and comms ready to be linked with the Snapdragon."

Connor spun his chair sideways and he stood. "A word in my ready room, Admiral?"

"I don't want to leave the bridge this close to combat," Hien said in a steely tone. Connor shrugged his shoulders.

"Fine by me, then," the captain said. "This is *my* ship, Admiral. While your flag is here, this ship itself is under my command. You are responsible for the *fleet*. I am responsible for the *Juggernaut*. You will do well to remember that, sir."

"I could have your command for your words, Captain," Hien warned.

"With all due respect, Admiral, even the most brilliant tactician would be unable to command both a ship and an entire fleet at the same time. We are mortal men, sir. I will retain command of the *Juggernaut*. You will retain command of the fleet," Connor said. He let Hien mull over his words for a few moments before he continued. "The *Juggernaut* and her crew are yours, sir, as is every crew in this fleet. I'm merely pointing out that *your* attention needs to be focused on the fleet."

Hien glared at him, his face sullen and angry. "I understand what you mean, Captain."

"Excellent news, sir," Connor said, giving him the biggest, most insincere smile he could manage without being completely insubordinate. "Glad we understand each other, sir. Now, if you be so kind as to give us your orders."

"Take the fleet out of the Void, Captain," Hien said, his voice colder than ice.

Connor sat back down in his command chair and opened a fleet-wide channel. "All ships, this is Captain Connor of the *Juggernaut*. The order is given. Let's show these Ra'tid bastards how a real war is fought. Do not, I repeat, do *not* release towed sensor arrays. They'll be worthless in this fight. Stand by... Execute!"

The *Juggernaut* dropped into real space, followed immediately by the rest of the combined Republic/Darian fleet. Ra

Prime was in their view screen, large and imposing. In front of it was a massive collection of space docks, a shipyard that the Republic would have been envious to have. Fifteen of the new Ra'tid super dreadnaughts were exiting the docks, with several of the older Ra'tid battleships interposing themselves between the arriving fleet and the massive ships.

For a few seconds, both fleets stared at one another, unblinking, before one of the Darian carriers began to launch fighters. The Ra'tid fleet exploded into activity, missiles pouring forth in a massive tsunami as the Republic and Darian ships responded in kind. Small, nimble fighters darted out from their carriers, their Darian pilots fearlessly guiding their small craft into the maelstrom. Still more Ra'tid missiles, with diamond-tipped explosive heads, volleyed out in reply.

"Vampire! Two-seven-zero missiles inbound! ETA is forty seconds!"

"Evasive maneuvers!" Connor shouted. The crew of the *Juggernaut* worked feverishly as missiles from the mountainous Ra'tid dreadnaughts rushed towards them.

The *Juggernaut's* electronic countermeasures were stretched thin as the sensor techs worked against the Ra'tid volley, which was closing in on the ship. The techs called out to one another as they worked seamlessly together, the team forcing missile after missile to lose track and veer away, or to cause a missile to prematurely detonate. The Republic destroyers, flying in a triangle pattern, interposed themselves between the deadly swarm of incoming missiles and the *Juggernaut*, struggling to protect the flagship. Their ECM, combined with the massive amount of white noise that the techs about the *Juggernaut* were pumping out, caused many of the missiles to lose lock. Their railguns fired into the midst of the missiles, trying to kill any interlopers that made it through.

Two of the destroyers exploded as missiles, which had diverted from the *Juggernaut*, had reassigned themselves to the smaller vessels. The debris from the dead destroyers caused the ECM aboard the *Juggernaut* to become confused for a moment. This moment, a narrow opportunity at most, proved to be enough, though, as a half dozen missiles slipped through the point-defense system of the *Juggernaut* and impacted near the port side of her bow.

The massive dreadnaught shuddered from the missiles detonating along the hull, causing more than a few discerning glances back at the captain. Connor looked at the data scrolling down his personal screen, his eyes narrowing as he assessed the damage. He recognized it as minimal, with a hull breach that had already been contained and the loss of a solitary missile tube.

The *Juggernaut* had gotten lucky. Connor smiled grimly. He wanted to make the Ra'tids pay for their misfortune.

"No problems with seeing them on sensors yet?" Connor asked.

"None, sir," a tech responded back immediately. "Snapdragon is up and running with no problems."

"So whatever hit us at Weligo was a prototype of some sort," he mused.

One of the Ra'tid super dreadnaughts erupted in flames, the ship breaking apart as it attempted to turn away from the continuous barrage of Republic missiles that had targeted it. Several other of the Ra'tid ships too damaged to continue included three battleships, most of which had suffered the same fate as the downed super dreadnaught. Connor noticed smaller shapes darting amongst the Ra'tid vessels and recognized the knife-fighting tactics of the Darians as the small fighters ripped apart another battleship as close range.

A second wave of Darian fighters launched from their carriers. Connor allowed himself a small smile as he watched the tiny, one man – or in this case, Darian – fighters blaze across the short distance that separated the two opposing fleets. The fighters interposed themselves between the incoming missiles and the larger ships, their flechette rounds cutting through the missiles easily. The number of incoming Ra'tid missiles dwindled considerably as the crack Darian pilots did their job.

"Helm to port, course three-one-five, and increase speed," Connor ordered. "I want to shove our missiles right down their throats!"

"Order the fleet to follow suit," Hien added.

"Aye, sir, new course three-one-five. Course laid in!" the

helmsman responded immediately.

With the Darian fighters clearing a path, the Republic fleet began to close the distance. Every Republic and Darian ship in the fleet was firing missiles continuously as their engines burned at maximum power. As large and slow as the Republic super dreadnaughts were, they were still an order of magnitude faster than their newer Ra'tid counterparts were. They used this difference to their advantage, pressing the issue as they drew within range of their powerful beam weaponry.

The Ra'tids emptied their missile tubes in a concerted display of firepower that was too much for the Darian fighters to handle on their own. It was a desperate move on the part of the Rocks, Connor recognized even as the missiles closed the small distance rapidly. It would take the Ra'tids longer to reload, and in that time, the Republic fleet would be amongst them. He briefly wondered if he would have taken such a risk, had the situation called for it.

The Ra'tid missiles began to overwhelm the highly trained crew of the *Juggernaut*. The ECMs, already thin from the immense barrage it had been facing, was unable to cope with the sheer magnitude of missiles, which had begun to flood the system as the Ra'tids gave them everything they had. Ship after ship began to explode as the missiles struck true, the Republic ships being damaged or outright killed. Their deaths filled the view screen of the *Juggernaut*, enraging the crew, causing them to work harder, faster.

With the speed the fleet was bearing down on the shipyard, there simply wasn't enough time for maneuvering of the larger vessels. Missiles found the large capitol ships to be fat, easy targets and began to hone in on the Republic super dreadnaughts. Seconds passed as the ECM tried, and failed, to kill their would-be assassins. The closest cluster of Ra'tid missiles tracked the *Juggernaut* and drew close, and then exploded.

The ship shuddered again from impacts, though this time, it was a violent reaction as dozens of diamond-tipped warheads dug into the thick plated hull of the *Juggernaut* before detonating. Explosions ripped through the decks, unceremoniously killing all in its path. Crewmembers, caught completely unaware, hadn't even had a chance to realize what had happened before their corpses had been flung out into space, the vacuum finishing what the exploding Ra'tid missiles had begun. Lights flickered throughout the ship as explosions cut power and damaged fuel cells.

Alarm klaxons blared throughout the *Juggernaut*. Casualty reports came flooding in on Connor's chair. The lighting on the bridge flickered once before power was restored, but that was enough to tell Connor that his ship had been badly damaged. He glanced at his screen and saw that his presumption had been correct.

"Heavy damage, sir!" one of the *Juggernaut's* junior officers screamed nearby. "Main power is at sixty percent, but holding for now."

"Connor!" Hien snarled angrily at him. The captain ignored the admiral as best he could.

"Beam weapons range!" one of the weapons officers cried out.

"Give 'em hell!" Connor ordered, pounding his fist onto the arm of his chair emphatically. "Unload everything we got into them!"

The *Juggernaut* danced through the Ra'tid formation, beam weapons lancing out in flickers of light that looked harmless to the naked eye. Moving at the speed of light, the energy beams tore into the thick armor of the Ra'tid super dreadnaughts, superheating the rocky armor and creating stress fractures. The armor cooled just as rapidly as it had heated, with the metal contracting where it was exposed to the cold of space. Large cracks appeared as the metal became brittle, then exploded outward as the stress became too much.

The *Juggernaut*, while massive in scale to typical Republic ships, was still dwarfed by the mountainous super dreadnaughts of the Ra'tids. The damage caused by the *Juggernaut* on a human ship would have disabled it completely, even destroying it. However, the Ra'tid ships were able to shrug off the intense firepower of the beam weaponry and punch back.

Staggering under the intense onslaught of the Ra'tid beams, the *Juggernaut* slipped out past the shipyard and accelerated back towards the moon, with Ra'tid super dreadnaughts in hot pursuit. Missiles from the Rocks pursued them, doggedly ignoring all

ECM and countermeasures as they sought to kill the massive Republic ship. The *Juggernaut* had one other trick up its sleeve, however, one that it had never used in battle before.

Connor had been watching the pursuit closely. He looked over at his weapons officer and nodded.

"Laying mines now," the woman said as she punched in a new command into her console.

Behind the *Juggernaut*, thousands of small, miniature tactical nukes surrounded by metallic orbs dropped out of the stern of the ship. Momentum dragged them along behind the ship for a few moments before the continued thrust of the super dreadnaught left the mines behind. Drifting there, the mines went active at the command of the ship's weapons officer. They would wait until the next target came along.

They did not have to wait long. Eager to pursue the *Juggernaut*, the two Ra'tid ships pursuing her plunged into the minefield, oblivious to the danger they were in. The mines, built to withstand high velocity impacts, burrowed into the tough surface of both ships before detonating, the nuclear fire cracking the skin of the ships. In a brilliant flash of light, the two ships crumbled as the thousands of small mines did their job the near perfection.

Connor sighed with relief. "That's one trick we're not going to get away with again."

The *Juggernaut* disengaged from the battle briefly, allowing the crew to receive some first aid. Connor's eyes scanned his bridge crew and recognized one sensor tech lying on the ground, her arm clutched to her chest. Bright bone poked through the uniform, the jagged edge obscene and covered in blood. The young woman's face was pale and sweaty, though she gritted her teeth and barely whimpered as the corpsmen helped her from the bridge. He shifted his scrutiny from his bridge to the rest of the fleet. He did not like what he saw.

Nearly half of the combined fleet was destroyed, including one of the Darian carrier ships. Multiple ships had been mauled, with differing reports ranging from structural damage to containment failures cropping up on his screen. He spotted a Republic ship floating in space, completely dark except for the random firing of her engines, spiral in close to the moon. He ran an analysis and saw that, if left uninterrupted, the ship would crash into Ra Prime's moon in a month. There would be no recovering of the deceased.

Of the Ra'tids, he saw that they had suffered almost as much as they had. While their losses were not as high, their smaller ship count made their losses more palpable. Four Ra'tid super dreadnaughts had been destroyed, and two more were drifting helplessly in space, severely damaged and out of the fight. Dozens smaller destroyers and corvettes had been shredded by the Darian fighters, while only a few Darian fighters had been lost in return. The biggest loss, Connor recognized, had been the loss of the *Prideful Hunter*, the Darian carrier. Once the small fighters were out of ordnance and fuel, they would slowly suffocate and die in space unless a spot opened up in one of the other carriers.

"My God," Hien muttered as he stepped past Connor and took over at the console of the fallen sensor technician. The admiral, who had been tossed from his feet during the furious exchange of fire during the *Juggernaut's* run into the heart of the Ra'tid fleet, was shaking and sweating profusely. Connor glanced back to his personal screen, eyes tracking the information as fast as it came in. He drew a mental image in his head of the battlefield and imagined different scenarios. In the blink of an eye, he decided on the *Juggernaut's* next move.

"Helm, come to starboard fifteen degrees, slow engines to two-thirds, raise our angle up five degrees," he ordered. "Let's focus on the remaining super dreadnaughts."

He knew that if the fleet tried to close on the planet, the super dreadnaughts would pincer them in, combining their own firepower with that of the planet's defenses. They had to be dealt with first to prevent the fleet from fighting in too many directions at once. He counted eight still fully fighting, though he could have sworn there had been nine moments before. He smiled, a thin, dangerous smile that would have scared anyone looking at him, as he saw the latest fleet update.

The Darians had used almost all of their fighters in an attempt to bring down one of the Ra'tid super dreadnaughts, and while it had worked, had cost the Cats far too many pilots. Connor commended their bravery while cursing their recklessness as well.

With the majority of the Darian fighters gone, the picket screen that the Ra'tids had would be able to protect the super dreadnaughts better.

"Order the fleet to aim for the super dreadnaughts," Conner said, ignoring the dangerous glare he received from Hien. "Try to thin them out."

"Vampires! I have eighty – repeat, eight-zero – missiles inbound on inbound tracks!" the tactical officer barked. "ETA is two minutes!"

Connor glanced at the missile track in disbelief. The Ra'tids had somehow managed to come about a full one hundred eighty degrees instead of having to veer sharply to port as the Republic ships went the opposite direction, and saved time in doing so. It had given the Rocks the opportunity to fire with their unused missile tubes instead of being forced to reload them. The mountainous ships had simply pivoted and continued firing.

Squadrons of Darian fighters, who had survived the onslaught earlier and the hell of flying into the battle formation of the Ra'tids, streaked towards the inbound wave of death. The fighters tried to destroy as many of the missiles as they could, but they were overwhelmed and found themselves quickly in pursuit. Ra'tid interceptor missiles, designed to kill Darian fighter craft, began to launch from the smaller destroyers. The Darian fighters, struggling to kill the larger missiles while dodging the interceptors, began to be whittled down by the anti-craft weaponry of the Ra'tid ships.

"ECM?" Connor asked.

"White noise at maximum, Captain. Chaff screen deployed and point defenses are engaging," the tactical officer replied immediately. Connor grunted.

"We can't take a knife into a gun fight a second time, Captain," Hien warned him. "Don't let those super dreadnaughts engage us in beam weapon range again."

Sanctimonious ass, Connor thought. He gritted his teeth. "Of course, Admiral."

He knew that he would never risk beam range again, not against the new Ra'tid ships. Not only were their hulls thicker and better designed against beam weapons, they boasted many more missile tubes that the *Juggernaut* could ever hope to achieve. The

Rocks could take more damage and still engage with beams, as they had so aptly proven minutes before. The fleet was outgunned, he knew, and that was including the Darian carriers. While he still outnumbered the Ra'tids, he knew that it would be suicide to risk another close engagement with the Rocks. He needed to use his numbers and his range. He needed to think tactically.

"Snapdragon still up?" he asked the comm officer. Seeing her nod, he activated his comm link. "This is Captain Connor of the *Juggernaut*. I want all remaining ships to close in on the *Juggernaut*. I want an overlapping screen of ECM from both Darian and Republic ships. We need to make those Rocks blind before their next volley arrives. Transferring coordinates now." He wiped sweat, born of stress and battle, from his brow with the backside of his hand. "All ships, pick your next targets carefully. I want concentrated fire on the lead super dreadnaughts, then the support vessels."

Every Ra'tid mountain destroyed is that much less firepower they can bring against my ships, Connor thought as he looked over the tactical display again. *Any of the older Rock ships that come to support the original force here we can deal with once the big boys are gone.*

"All incoming missiles are targeting us, sir!" his tactical officer shouted. Connor looked up sharply.

"*All* of them?"

"Yes sir!" the man's face was sweaty and pale. "ETA is thirty seconds."

"Evasive actions!" Hien cried out, his eyes wide. Connor shook his head.

"Too close," he told the admiral. "Their engines haven't cut off. They'll just follow us. No sir, we need to take this one on the chin and punch back, just as hard."

"Are you out of your mind?" Hien asked.

"With all due respect, sir, you've been behind a desk way too long," Connor said. He looked back at his bridge crew. "Keep the ECMs up and running. We're going to get hit, but maybe we can get lucky and divert some of those missiles elsewhere."

"Sir, the *Macedon* is engaging with counter-missiles," the tactical officer said. "Brave bastards. They're trying to run a screen for us."

"Tin can captains are always undervalued and unappreciated," Connor murmured. He glanced at his screen and activated his comm. "Crew, this is the captain. Brace for impact."

The *Juggernaut* shuddered as the first Ra'tid missile arrived, the explosive little killer digging deep into the thick armor of the capitol ship before detonating. More missiles slammed into the rear of the ship, killing indiscriminately as explosions vented the sealed decks into space. Damage control immediately sealed the new holes as quickly as they could, but the sheer number of impacts made their job difficult. They worked tirelessly to keep their ship alive and in the fight.

A smaller cluster of missiles slipped through the ECM screen and slammed into the spine of the ship, causing a more violent reaction. The spine, which kept the structurally integrity of the ship in one piece, also boasted the thickest armor. The ship barely budged, though the impact had a secondary and far more deadly result.

The spine, because it was so heavily armored, also housed the compartment that allowed for the combination of theoretical physics and practical engineering to collide and allow the ship to enter Void space. The small device, barely the size of a soccer ball, traversed the spine, keeping the ship intact when it entered Void space. The device was heavily armored, but physics once more reared its ugly head.

The violent momentum of the missile impact jerked the device off kilter for the briefest of moments. However, the reflex action bent the box back *towards* the explosion, damaging the delicate internal mechanisms inside the well-protected spine. This sent another shudder along the spine, one that set every alarm klaxon in the ship screaming in warning as the entire Void drive of the massive super dreadnaught suddenly went offline.

Connor heard the high-pitched alarm and looked around, slightly confused. Structural integrity aside, he could not figure out what was causing the new alarm. The last wave of missiles had hurt the super dreadnaught, but he was well aware that the ship could take quite a bit more of a beating before he would really begin to worry.

"Captain! We've lost our Void drive!"

"Dear God in Heaven..." Connor whispered. Even if they won the fight against the Ra'tids – and that was a big *if* at this point, there would be no escape for the *Juggernaut*. He swallowed his pride and looked over at the admiral. "Sir! We need to consider retreat as an option for all ships capable of doing so."

"No," Hien growled, his hand tightly clenching the edge of the console. "We can still win this fight."

Connor checked his urge to punch the arrogant officer in the face. The *Juggernaut* jerked sideways as another missile snuck through, opening a massive hole in her armor. He looked at his screen and immediately knew that there would be no repair of that hole, not without a space dock and six weeks' worth of repairs. Another missile snuck through and exploded, which made the hole even bigger and the damage irreparable. Connor began to doubt that they were going to survive the next five minutes, much less the battle itself.

Off to their port side, a massive Darian carrier suddenly buckled under the immense firepower of another Ra'tid super dreadnaught. The engines went offline, and then back as power surged through the Darian ship. Engines blazing at maximum, it accelerated towards a super dreadnaught, which had been closing on the fleet. The Ra'tid super dreadnaught tried to turn away but, with merely five hundred kilometers separating the ship and the Darian, there wasn't enough time. The Darian rammed the ship, the angled bow piercing through the heart of the super dreadnaught. They hung in space for a split second, dark and silent, before the engine plant of the Darian carrier went critical and exploded.

The shockwaves of the explosion shook the already-damaged *Juggernaut*, pushing the flagship to the brink. More alarms screamed as the *Juggernaut's* life support systems began to fail. Damage control raced to the environmental control section, but never made it as another missile snuck through the point defenses of the wounded flagship and tore another hole in the armor. The team was sucked out into space before they knew what had happened, and were dead before they had a chance to be afraid.

"Structural integrity failure imminent!" someone on the bridge shouted into the chaos swirling around Connor. Hien's face went white. Connor keyed in his comm link, surprised and thankful that it had survived the battle thus far. He coughed slightly and steeled himself.

"This is the captain. All hands, all hands... abandon ship. I repeat, abandon ship. Make ready the rescue pods and prepare to crack the spine."

Hien was already hightailing it for the lift but Connor stayed seated. He glared at his tactical officer, who had been halfway to the lift before looking back at his captain. He stopped, sheepishly grinned, and returned to his station as the rest of the bridge crew vacated. Connor nodded approvingly.

"I want one more volley, Tac, before we abandon ship."

The tactical officer typed in commands at his console, then looked up at his commanding officer. "What few birds we could put into the air, sir, are away. I recommended that we follow them, post-haste."

"Well, what are you waiting for, man?" Connor said as he pulled himself out of his seat and looked around his ruined bridge. He had given up so much for command of the *Juggernaut*. He shook his head. Recriminations would come later. "Let's go."

*****

Algorithms flew across the screen, the patterns delving into newer ones as a pair of brown eyes tracked the progress of the worm. Fingers flew across the small, alien console as subroutines were uploaded as quickly as the firewalls tried to defeat them. Systems crashed, came back online, only to be attacked more thoroughly a second time. The firewall fought against her, valiant in its effort, but ultimately was no match for the aggressive specialist. The screen flickered for a moment, and the walls began to shake softly, a gentle hum, which began to grow in pitch.

Gunter was so lost in her work that she didn't realize that the walls of the corridor were vibrating like a tiny earthquake until Evil Penguin nudged her with his elbow.

"Yo, Gunter?" he said. "I think something bad has happened."

"*Waidmanns heil*," she whispered, a triumphant gleam in her eye as the worm began attacking the subsystems of the Ra'tid space dock. She looked at the short black ops man and grinned. "I should hope so. I just hacked their propulsion system."

Her original attempts had been a bust. As a whole, the firewalls of the Ra'tid shipyard had been substantially upgraded over the last time she had attempted a hard hack. Tech upgrades aside, she had been able to recognize Gener fingerprints all over the crucial data stored in the mainframes. That information alone would be interesting to the Admiralty, she had recognized instantly. The fact that the Geners were selling their tech to both the Coalition and to the Ra'tids meant... something. Exactly what it meant, however, was beyond her.

After recognizing the Gener firewalls all over the mainframe, she tried various subroutine attacks, looking for a way into non-classified – yet still crucial – systems. Those had not been built with the typical elaborate webs of the Gener cryptography. Instead, they had been protected by the best that the Ra'tid engineers could provide. The best had been laughably easy for Gunter to break through and plant the worm she was now guiding through the system, devouring memory as it went and slowing down all of the dock's systems.

She also had control of what passed for a surveillance system, but she had yet to fully take that over yet, since she had no idea how the Ra'tids were actually monitoring the system. She was pretty certain they used seismographic scanners, and that they could see the shapes of carbon-based life forms this way by determining their biological vibrations. Everything that would be seen was not Ra'tid, which would make it easy for the Rocks to find any and all non-Ra'tid life forms in the dock. Other than that, however, she was a bit lost. That didn't mean that the worm couldn't devour everything in that system, though, so she had directed it to feast on the memory within the surveillance system. She hoped it would be enough to slow down whatever was going on, and allow for Saul and Zombie to make it back to the rendezvous point.

"Gunter!" Gunter, come in! Are you there?" Saul's voice came over the commlink of her helmet.

"Yes sir," she answered. "I may have found some information

that the Admiralty might find interesting."

"We did, too," Saul replied with a dark chuckle. "Zombie and I are headed back with a prisoner in tow. Get on the horn with Captain Hunter and tell him we need extraction ASAP. ETA in three minutes, unless we run into more trouble."

"On it, sir," she said as he cut the link. Gunter reset the parameters of the worm and unplugged herself from the Ra'tid system. She looked over at Evil Penguin. "We're going to do a breach exit. Saul and Zombie are coming in hot. Make the call for extraction. Jones, prepare a shaped charge for an airlock. I saw one when we were coming in."

"Isn't that going to help the Rocks find us?" Jones asked, surprised.

"By the time they get to where we're at, we'll be long gone," she said. She didn't mention that she was pretty certain that the Ra'tids already knew where they were at. She tapped her comm and switched frequencies. "Hunter? Hunter, do you read, over?"

"Loud and clear," the smuggler replied instantly. "Did you know that there's a–"

"No time!" she cut him off. "We need extraction, now. Feeding you coordinates to the extraction point. Meet us there in five minutes."

"It's going to be a little longer than that," he said. "Lots going on right now."

"Your problems don't concern me, Hunter," Gunter said, her tone sharp. "Meet us at the coordinates I'm sending you."

"Uh, you might want to reconsider your opinion about my problems," Hunter said. "A Republic fleet just dropped into the system and everybody is shooting at each other. A Darian fighter blew past me, and I swear I thought I saw his face. The *Caliban's* going to be coming in hard and fast. If you're not at the coordinates you sent when we get there, we're making a run for it, and you're going to need another ride home."

"Oh, that's just *perfect*!" she snarled and cut the commlink, switching back over to the squad's link. "Can't wait on Saul and Zombie. Jones, take point. We've gotta get going, now!"

"On it," Jones said and began to move down the corridor.

"Let's go," she ordered the rest of them after Jones had turned the corner.

Two by two, they hurried down the corridor, never quite running but quick enough to suit Gunter's needs. No Ra'tids met them on the way, which she found odd, considering that she was nearly certain that the Rocks had their precise location. She counted her blessings and checked the chamber of her rifle, just to be sure.

They arrived at the designated extraction point with time to spare. Next to the airlock was another Ra'tid console, one that she had missed earlier when they first came aboard the dock. It was partially hidden behind a large stalagmite, which hung from the ceiling. She plugged into the system and checked the progress of her uploaded worm.

""Two minutes until the *Caliban* arrives, Gunter," Evil Penguin said as he sidled up to her. "How's the worm doing?"

"Absolutely *feasting* on their security systems," she answered. "I think I know why we haven't run into anyone yet."

"Hey, could you hack the airlock, so we don't have to blow it?" the shorter man asked. Gunter blinked as she lifted her eyes from the data stream she had been tracking.

"Yeah, Jeez, why didn't I think of that?"

"Because you like to blow things up?"

"Point," she conceded. She dug back into the mainframe and within moments had the airlock door accessed and ready. She activated her comm. "Hunter, let me know when you have a positive lock."

A minute passed, then "Green light."

"Let's move," she said and opened the airlock. Standing on the other side was Mizi, a short rifle in her hands. Her eyes were bright behind the rebreather apparatus she wore over her mouth and nose. She glanced past the team and motioned for them to come aboard. The team piled into the small craft ahead of Gunter, who turned and looked down the long corridor.

"You coming or what?" Mizi asked, her hand hovering near the airlock lever. Gunter cursed.

"One minute!"

"We don't have one minute," Mizi snapped back. "In or out!"

"I said, one minute!"

"I need to seal this lock, now!"

Gunter jerked back the charge lever of her rifle and stuck the barrel of it under Mizi's chin. "I said, one minute."

"And I said, I need to seal this lock," Mizi growled and pushed the rifle barrel away. "I don't know who you think you are, but this is *my* ship as much as it's Hunter's. I'll be damned if I'm going to have her damaged just for your precious Templar."

"My name is Specialist Hera Shan Gunter, Earth Republic Marines, Special Operations Team Four, and we *will* wait for the rest of the team," Gunter replied, her tone icy. "Marines do not leave any man or woman behind. You get me?"

"Shoot me if you have to," Mizi retorted, "but we're leaving. Now."

"Hold it!" Saul screamed into the comm link. Mizi and Gunter looked back down the corridor and spotted Saul and Zombie moving as fast as they could. Draped over Zombie's shoulder was an unconscious Gener. Gunter's eyes went wide and she whistled.

"Definitely better than what I found," she said as Zombie pushed past Mizi, the Gener's head flopping loosely against his back. Saul stopped and looked at the console terminal nearby.

"You said you accessed their mainframe?" he asked her.

"In a way," she allowed.

"There is a damned *space battle* going on out there, Templar!" Mizi practically screamed. "Now get your holier than thou ass onto this ship!"

"Can you access their propulsion?" Saul asked.

"Access their... what? Why? This dock moves at a snail's pace!" Gunter protested, ignoring Mizi.

"Can you do it?"

"Well, it's not in their Gener encrypted mainframe, so yeah, I guess," Gunter allowed.

"Okay," Saul nodded. "Point this thing towards Ra Prime and fire the thrusters at maximum."

"What?" Mizi and Gunter asked together.

"Just do it!" Saul urged.

"It'll take an hour to reach the planet," Gunter said. "Other than leaving a small crater on the planet's surface, what good will that do?"

"Don't worry about it," Saul said. "Just do it."

"Okay," she typed in a few more commands. "It's done."

"Good," Saul nodded. "Lock everyone out and let's get out of here."

Gunter nodded and closed her link to the terminal. Mizi rolled her eyes.

"It's about time," she muttered as Saul moved past her. She sealed the airlock from inside the *Caliban.* "Everyone's on, Alves. Punch it!"

Saul moved to the bridge of the *Caliban,* where Hunter was standing behind Alves. The crafty pilot had already begun to plot a course away from the dock and into deep space. Saul tapped the captain on the shoulder.

"I need to buy a missile off you."

"Excuse me?" Hunter asked as he looked back at the former Templar.

"I need one of your missiles," Saul said. "I'll buy it off of you."

"Those missiles cost about a million credits each," Hunter frowned. "What in the seven hells do you need a missile for?"

"Two million," Saul said. "I'll give you two million, no questions asked."

"Seriously, Templar," Hunter's tone was doubtful. "What do you need one of my precious missiles for?"

"To prevent a prolonged war that could destroy the entire Republic."

"I thought you didn't care much for it?"

"It's preferable to the other option."

Hunter nodded. "I understand that feeling. Mizi? Take Saul back to our launch tube."

"What? Why?" Mizi asked as she stuck her head into the cabin.

"Mister Saul just bought himself a missile," Hunter replied. Mizi looked over, her eyebrows arched.

"I need to see that missile right now, if you please," Saul said and allowed Mizi to guide him back to the missile tube. He flipped open the panel she pointed out to him and withdrew a small, clear vial from his pocket. He set it inside the warhead housing and disabled the explosive.

Mizi, watching him work, frowned. "That sort of defeats the entire purpose of a missile, doesn't it?"

"Just wait," Saul murmured as he closed the housing. He glanced around. "Comm to call Hunter?"

"Here," Mizi said and pushed a button.

"Hunter, this is Saul," he said.

"Go ahead."

"Can you target the dock we just left with my new missile?"

"Yes..." Hunter's voice trailed off. "Okay, target locked."

"Fire it, please."

"One missile isn't going to do much to that space dock," Hunter observed. Saul's face was grim.

"I know."

"Okay, firing now," Hunter said as the *Caliban* shuddered slightly. "Missile away."

"Let's get out of here," Saul said. "Take us back to Weligo."

"We'll be stopping in the Helix system first, though," Hunter stated. "Don't want anyone guarding the Weligo Terminus to see us coming from too far. Smaller jumps, while cloaked, is the way to go."

Saul shrugged. "Sounds good to me. Status of the missile?"

"Just impacted on the surface of that space dock," Hunter replied. "No explosion. Looks like I sold you a dud."

"No, I disabled the warhead," Saul said. "I just wanted the missile for the delivery system."

"Delivery system?" Hunter asked as the *Caliban* flickered and jumped into Void space. "What did you deliver?"

"A message."

*****

With the *Juggernaut* breaking apart and in her death throes, command of the fleet passed to Captain Marcus Ryan of the *Arrow*. The *Arrow* was an older battleship, not designed to go toe-to-toe with ships of the line for long amounts of time like a dreadnaught or super dreadnaught. Typically, the ship was not one that anyone would look at for command of a fleet, and without the experience and time in rank that Captain Ryan had, it would never have been considered. The Snapdragon had assessed the capabilities and time in rank of all the remaining ship's captains, however, and had chosen Ryan.

Captain Ryan had last been in command of the *Watkins*, a top-secret research vessel. The same Watkins had been involved in the Republic's attempt to capitalize from the resources on the now-infamous Lancaster's World. The Republic had attempted to recruit him to lead a second expedition to the world, but he had stood firm on his sworn oath never to return to that blood-soaked, cursed planet.

The Admiralty had decided, instead of forcing the issue, to assign Ryan to the *Arrow* and shuttle him off to an unforgotten outpost as far away from anything important as they could manage. Normally, that meant a trip to the Weligo Terminus but, with Ryan actually having not done anything wrong, led to the *Arrow* being tasked with picket duty near the Coalition and Darian borders. He had been recalled when the Ra'tids had attacked Weligo, however, which deepened his suspicions that the universe was completely and utterly out to get him.

Ryan watched on the view screen as the *Juggernaut* disintegrated beneath yet another volley of Ra'tid missiles, launched from a pair of smaller destroyers which had swooped down upon her already-broken corpse. All communications with Fleet Admiral Hien and Captain Connor had been lost minutes before, and both were missing in action, presumed dead. That left Ryan with the problem of commanding not only his ship, but the tattered remnants of the fleet as well.

Of the super dreadnaughts, which had been a part of the original fleet, only one now survived. The Darian contingent was in worse shape, with all of their carriers destroyed or damaged enough to be completely out of the fight. Their fighters still buzzed past, their cannons blazing as they moved to intercept a wave on fresh missiles incoming from the Ra'tid fleet. Out of CK missiles, the Darian fighters were rendered useless against the remaining Ra'tid super dreadnaughts and had begun working as an additional layer of ECM against the incoming missiles.

The dying Darian carrier's engines suddenly flared to life.

Ryan watched on the display as the ship darted forward, crashing into one of the mountain-like Ra'tid super dreadnaughts. Both vanished in a brilliant blast of flame and shrapnel so intense that Ryan felt their deaths from the bridge of the *Arrow*. He whispered a silent prayer for the Darian warriors, who would rather die by taking the enemy with them than turn tail and run.

Ryan frowned. Such sacrifice, no matter how noble and honorific the Darians intended it to be, was wasted here. The battle was all but lost, and there was little anyone could do about it. The *Arrow's* long-range scanners were picking up a new cluster of incoming ships, and from the looks of the size of the echoes, it was a rather large fleet destined for the Ra system. When they arrived, even the Republic's waning numerical advantage would be completely gone.

"ETA on those inbound Ra'tid ships?" Ryan asked his tactical officer as he looked over his own console.

"Estimating ten minutes, sir. Maybe slightly more. Their echo is large enough to mask their arrival time."

"Order the fleet to disengage the enemy," Ryan shook his head. Defeat was at hand, and while he knew that he was not at fault, it still left a black smudge on his soul. Defeat always left a bitter taste on one's mouth. "This battle's over."

"Sir?" his executive officer asked, surprise in his voice. "Admiral Hien's last order was to hold fast."

"The Admiral's missing, probably dead," Ryan pointed out. "Are you that eager to join him?"

"No sir, not really."

Ryan opened a channel to the fleet himself, not wanting anyone else to have to relay the orders he was about to give. It was his responsibility, his burden. "This is Captain Ryan of the *Arrow*. All ships disengage and make ready an escape vector into the Void at best possible speed. Once again, I am giving the order to disengage the enemy and retreat."

"Sir!" one of the sensor techs cried for his attention.

"What is it now?" Ryan growled, his frustration seeping through despite his hard-fought attempt to hide it.

"Did we... shoot at their space docks, sir?"

"I have no idea," Ryan admitted. "We didn't target them. A

few strays might have... why do you ask, PO?"

"Sir, one of them just crashed into Ra Prime."

"And?"

"Sensors are going wild, sir. I... well, sir, I think that something is *eating* the planet!"

"*What?*"

*****

In stasis, a nannite is nothing more than a piece of dust. A microscopic machine, it has the capabilities to do wondrous things. They have been used in medicine, metalworking, machinery and plastics since before the birth of the Republic. They were considered the wonder invention of the late twentieth century, and their potential had seemed limitless.

The first attempt the Republic made to weaponize nanotechnology had ended in a complete disaster. The nannites had broken containment within the laboratory and ravaged every single organism on board the research station. Men and women were devoured as the nannites used the organic fuel helpfully provided by the corpses of the dead to self-replicate and continue to attack everything that came within their range. Eventually, the facility was nuked by the Republic navy as a precautionary effort to contain the nannites and prevent their spreading throughout the star system. As an extra safety measure, the entire Van Maanen system was declared a hazard against any sort of exploration and travel.

During the disaster, though, one of the scientists, before dying, had noted that the nannites were focusing primarily on everything carbon-based, leaving the silica alone. It would be easy, he had surmised, for the nannites to be switched and focus only on devouring anything silica-based. It was all a matter of programming.

Unfortunately, for the doctor, his final transmission had moved at the speed of light, not arriving to Earth until seven years after the station had been destroyed. Scientists, who had almost given up on weaponizing nannites, were suddenly reinvigorated by the stunning message from beyond the grave. In that timeframe, humanity had also stumbled upon two new races in the galaxy – the Darian Empire, and the Ra'tids.

With new information on hand, military scientists quickly were able to reinvest in the nanotechnology weaponization programs. Assistance from the Darians and tech stolen from the Geners pushed the research beyond anything that had ever been achieved before. The sudden uprising by the Coalition of Outer Planets put most of that research on hold as the Earth Republic fought for its very life, but it was restarted soon after, as it became obvious that no traditional means were slowing down the Coalition's inevitable march for Earth. Everything from biological warfare to the reintroduction of nannites was floated. It was fortunately unnecessary, however, after the Darians allied themselves with the Republic and helped to save Earth.

That didn't stop the idea of weaponized nannites, though.

The nannites in the vial awoke from stasis the moment the vial shattered upon the rocky outcropping of the space dock. For a brief instant, the nannites did nothing as their power systems booted, their central programming kicking in. Half of the nannites floated off into space, unable to start their systems in time to grab hold of the dock. More failed in their startup parameters, self-destructing instead of running the risk of another Van Mannen situation.

Still, thousands of microscopic nannites managed to attach themselves to the space dock, their systems active and running as they sought out their fuel source – silica, which according to most of scientific theory available was the basic chemical structure that gave life to the Ra'tids and their ships, buildings, and life in general.

Scouring the surface quickly, the nannites started to replicate as soon as enough fuel had been consumed for separation. More nannites were created as they mimicked cell reproduction, and the feast continued. Boring holes into the harder silica surface, they soon found the softer, more pliable material and began to replicate faster as more refined fuel became available. The nannites soon began to work their way into the innards of the dock, where softer silica lie. Primarily, the Ra'tids themselves.

The first to die was a maintenance technician, who felt a strange sensation and reported into his sleeping berth to rest and recover. Inside the sleeping berth was pure liquid silicone, which helped heal the Ra'tids as well as keep them attuned to the technology around them. The technician didn't even realize he was dying as he rested, waiting for his rest cycle to complete so that he could continue his work. He would never wake from his rest cycle.

As the dock swung towards the planet, other technicians began to realize that something was wrong. The worm that Gunter had uploaded previously was causing their systems to run at such a slow pace that they could not even execute simple commands anymore. Warnings were shared throughout, but not fast enough, as the doomed personnel of the space dock realized that they were on a collision course with their home world, unaware that the real danger was not their falling space dock, but the insidious nanotechnology of the Republic that it carried.

The space dock crashed into the planet before the technicians on board could figure out a way around the blocks and worm that Gunter had uploaded. Two thousand Ra'tids immediately died as they were crushed by the impact of the dock onto the planet's surface. Four hundred *trillion* hungry, self-replicating nannites were released onto the planet's surface simultaneously and immediately began to feast of the rocky surface of the planet.

The war with the Ra'tids was over; nobody knew it just yet.

*****

"Transient! Transient!"

"They're early!" Ryan slammed an open palm down upon his command chair. "Do we have a firm number on them yet?"

"I'm counting twenty-five capitol ships-of-the-line, sir," the sensor tech responded. "They'll be in-system in about fifteen seconds."

"How long until we have enough velocity for Void space?"

"Four minutes, sir."

"Not enough time, not enough time..." Ryan drummed his fingertips. "Helm, push the engines as hard as you can. If we have to go above redline, do it."

"Sir, solution is firming up on the new fleet," the sensor tech announced. "Twenty-five capitol ships, dreadnaught-sized. Forty-six smaller ships of varying... sir! These aren't Ra'tid ships, sir!"

Ryan whirled around. "They're not? Then what are they?"

"Sir, they're Darian!"

"Captain, the Rocks have stopped attacking! They're falling back to Ra Prime, sir!" another sensor tech reported.

"All ships, belay that last order. Come about and target the Ra'tid shipyard with everything you have. Empty your magazines!" Ryan ordered.

The *Arrow* joined the survivors of the crippled Republic fleet as they swept in on a strafing run at the bulk of what remained of the Ra'tid industrial base. Dock after dock dies as the concentrated firepower of the crumbling fleet poured into them. The space docks tried to fight back but the complete and utter confusion, which dominated the entire Ra'tid military structure, prevented them from organizing any cohesive defense. A light cruiser fell to one of the dock's armament, but two more destroyers finished the dock off in return. Ryan grinned savagely.

"Captain? I'm getting a message from the lead Darian ship," his comms officer announced suddenly. Ryan nodded for the young officer to patch it through to his chair.

"This is Captain Marcus Ryan of the *Arrow*," he said in the comm. "To whom do I have the pleasure of thanking?"

"This is Commander Menc of the *Stalker*," the mewling reply came immediately. "There is a saying by a great human military leader that we believe is pertinent in this time. 'Do not interrupt the enemy while he is making a mistake.' Fortunately, the Republic is not our enemy, so we give you this advice. You are making a mistake. Recall your fleet and withdraw. The Darian Empire will finish what you have so admirably started."

"Like hell..." Ryan muttered. "We won this fight! We shed too much blood and sweat to let you waltz in here and steal our victory!"

"Captain, the history books shall state that your ship survived and defeated a vastly superior Ra'tid fleet," Menc replied, his tone amicable. "I would not think to deny you this honor. However, your ships are badly damaged. More loss of life amongst our allies in such dangerous times is unnecessary. Please withdraw so that we may finish this."

"You've got a point," Ryan allowed. "If you find any survivors during your operation...?"

"We shall treat all our allies as we would treat our own littermates," the Darian promised.

"Thank you, Commander," Ryan breathed, his anger evaporating. "*Arrow*, out. Comms, signal the fleet. Let's get to Void Space. Turn our IFF on so that the *Behemoth* doesn't blow us up when we get there."

The survivors of the fleet pulled back from the shipyard, and one by one, jumped into the Void.

Chapter Ten

The *Caliban* lurched into normal space, the entire hull shuddering violently as she did so. The normal humming of circuitry quieted to barely a whisper, and the familiar vibrations of the ship ceased. Off in the distance, the Helix system's star shone dimly beyond the asteroid belt, which circled the entire system. Hunter looked around the cockpit with a frown.

"That sounded bad," he muttered. "Alves, did we hit something? Asteroid?"

"Not that I saw," the pilot replied.

Hunter clicked the comm on. "Saul, did you or any of your troops touch anything?"

"That reentry did feel a little rough," Saul responded a few moments later. "My team is crashed out in their racks, Hunter. I didn't do anything."

"Okay, wait one," Hunter rubbed his forehead. "If we're in Helix, then let's continue onward."

"We are," Alves nodded. The pilot punched in the next set of coordinates, then frowned. "Well, that's strange."

"What's strange?"

"The Void drive isn't responding," Alves said.

"What do you mean, isn't responding?"

"Well, I mean, I sent the coordinates for Retina into it, but it didn't respond."

"So send it again."

"I can't," Alves tried to explain. "It's like the computer doesn't recognize the Void drive at all."

"What do you mean it doesn't recognize the Void drive?" Hunter grunted, frustrated. "It's either working or it's not. Recalibrate the damned thing so we can go home."

"No, I mean that the computer says we don't have a Void drive."

"How is that possible?"

"Beats me, Hunter."

"Great. Now what?"

"I have no idea," Alves admitted with a shrug. "This isn't something I've ever come across before."

"Mizi, get up here," Hunter called out. A few seconds later, she appeared, her forehead creased with worry. "We've got a problem."

"So I gathered," she said as she slid into the co-pilot's chair. "Hey, where's our Void drive?"

"See?"

"Find out what is going on," Hunter growled. "Now."

"I've got something weird on the scanners," Mizi said. "Looks like a ship is decloaking off the starboard bow."

"Ra'tid?" Hunter asked.

"No, too small for them," Mizi responded. "Looks like–"

"Gener," Saul finished for her as he entered the cockpit.

"Oh, hock," Hunter grumbled.

"Republic vessel *Caliban*, we control your Void drive and your systems," a voice from the heavens came through their comms unbidden, melodious and beatific. "Your life support system is in our hands. Stand down and prepare to be boarded. Any resistance and we will cut off your oxygen and wait for you to suffocate."

"Well, now what?" Mizi asked. "If they really did take down our Void drive, then they can hack our entire system. How did they do that?"

"I'm beginning to think that the Geners have the entire Republic wired," Saul muttered. "This is far worse than I thought. I believed that the Geners had only assisted the Ra'tids with technological upgrades. This... this is bigger than any of us."

"So what do we do?" Hunter asked. "We can't fight them, can't run."

"Let them come aboard," Saul commanded, his tone firm and uncompromising. "I have a plan, but I would like to know what they want first. They didn't need to warn us beforehand."

"We have a prisoner," Mizi reminded him. "It's obvious what they want."

"No, he's just a lowly Kratos." Saul shook his head. "They would have just destroyed us if this were about him. No, something else is going on, and I want to know what."

"I hope your plan is better than your last one, Templar," Hunter said. "Because they're already extending an airlock tube."

"Comms up? Short range?" Saul asked. Mizi nodded. "Good, I just need to fire off a quick message."

*****

Seconds turned into minutes. Hunter paced the bridge, waiting for the Geners to make their unwelcome appearance. Their ship had docked with the *Caliban* and they were supposed to be on their way forward, but were moving at a slow enough pace to drive Hunter mad. He checked the ship's chronometer again and cursed under his breath. He shot Saul a venomous look.

The former Templar couldn't blame the man, not really. The *Caliban*, while designed for covert warfare and operations, was most attuned to hiding and striking, much like a rattlesnake. He had been forced to risk his ship and his crew for a strange mission into the heart of Ra'tid territory, had a battle break out in the middle of the op, and then forced to run for their lives. Saul knew that the man was having what the Templars would have called a very bad day.

Zombie and Gunter had joined them on the bridge, crowding into the smallish area with little difficulty. The special operations team in back, led by Evil Penguin, was under orders not the resist the Geners unless Saul gave them a signal. He hoped that it wouldn't come down to it, but he had to be prepared in any case. Zombie was calm, his massive frame leaning against the bulkhead, while Gunter looked as nervous as Mizi did.

Saul's biggest worry wasn't whether the crew of the *Caliban* would hold it together and not try to kill the Geners boarding their vessel, nor was he overly concerned about whether Zombie or Gunter might snap and ignore his orders. He wasn't even disturbed by the idea that all the valuable data Gunter had pilfered from the Ra'tid computer systems would be confiscated by the Geners.

No, his only worry at that moment was whether his message got through.

The lift doors hissed open and three Geners stepped onto the bridge, their beauty and elegance causing all of the men and women to gasp. The two male Geners on either side of their apparent leader were dressed in skin-tight battle armor, glistening gold and silver as rivulets of lights traversed up and down their bodies. Both of their heads were partially covered with gold helmets, though their faces were exposed. Their hands rested near their holstered weapons, an elegant pistol on the right, and a sheathed poniard on the left. They were interesting specimens, as far as Geners went. Saul's attention, however, was on the leader.

She was exquisitely beautiful, with eyes that flashed through different colors like the sunset and full, rose-tinted lips. Her cheekbones were high, and her silvery hair was pulled back, away from her face. Her robe was gathered on her shoulders, and her slender frame barely hinted at her femininity, covered as it was by her armor. The symbol of an owl rested on a gold coil pinned to one shoulder. She ignored the rest of the men and women of the *Caliban* and stared at Saul, as though everything else was beneath her. She approached him.

"Templar Saul Derring, formerly of the Order. I wish I could say that it is pleasing to be meet you at last," she purred softly, her pitch carrying through three different octaves and set Saul's nerves on edge. "I am Athena-2-A."

"Oh, shit," Saul swore for only the second time in his adult life. His previously unanswered questions about the Gener involvement with the Ra'tids and how deeply it went had been suddenly answered by the high-ranking Gener before him. Athena smiled.

"Quite indeed, Templar," she said. "I am here to place you under arrest."

"Under arrest?" Hunter asked, incredulous. "For what?"

"For the crime of genocide, committed against the Ra'tid

peoples."

"Genocide?" Mizi and Hunter said together.

"You did not tell them of what you did, Templar?" she asked, her voice as smooth as silk as she looked about the bridge. "You did not tell them that you committed a crime so heinous that your deeds will rank you with genocidal maniacs of the past like Hitler, Stalin or Pol Pot?"

Saul shook his head. "You're the one who got the Rocks killed, not me. You led them against the Republic, pawns in your little Orwellian scheme. What did you expect?"

Athena ignored his verbal jab and continued. "You will be remitted into Coalition custody, by way of the nearest Coalition vessel, to be tried by proper authorities for your crimes."

"What does she mean, genocide?" Hunter demanded. "What did you do, Templar?"

"Coalition?" Gunter asked. "Since when do Geners recognize the rebellious Coalition government?"

"Come peacefully, Templar, so that you may yet live to see your trial," Athena ordered.

"What does she mean by genocide?" Hunter asked, his hands shaking angrily as he glared at Saul.

"Why don't you tell them, Templar?" Athena purred, her eyes fixed on Saul. "Tell them the horrors they helped you unlock on a now-dying world. Tell them of the billions who just died as a result of what you did. Tell them of the legacy this ship will have for all of time."

"I offer you no resistance and will come with you peacefully," Saul said instead, presenting his wrists to the Gener. "I will stand for my trial."

"*What?*" Hunter raged. "*That's* your miracle plan? To surrender?"

The male Gener on Athena's left moved, his form a blur as he slipped past Mizi and Zombie. He struck Hunter three times, causing the *Caliban's* captain to fall to the ground, gasping. The Gener stood over the downed man, his hand resting easily on the hilt of his poniard. Hunter lay on the ground, gasping for air, his hand clutching his throat, his face a slight bluish tint.

"Pale skinned bastard," Hunter managed to croak after a few

deep breaths.

"That will be quite enough," Athena said, her voice calm. The male Gener returned to her side. "Now then, surrender yourselves to the Law of the Coalition, and return the data you have stolen while inside the Ra'tid dock."

"How did you know about that?" Gunter asked. "I erased all traces of the hack!"

"Sweet child, I am on the road to perfection. You are merely a flawed and simple human, always destined to be lesser than my kind. I will say that how you managed to acquire the data was impressive, but even so, surely you do not believe that we would allow it to reach the Republic, do you? You did not believe that you could... *win?* So amusing. So... refreshing."

'I'm actually surprised you let it get this far," Saul said instead. "Something this valuable? Surely, you would have had a better chance at retrieving it in the Ra Prime system. Why risk us escaping? I think you slipped up, and then had to chase us down when you realized we got more than you thought. I think you made – dare I suggest it – a mistake."

"I grow weary of this discussion," Athena said. "You are stalling. Hand over the data. Now."

Saul cocked his head to the side and glanced at the console next to Alves. His eyes tracked the lines on the screen. He smiled when he finished and looked back at Athena.

"Actually, I think it's you and your guards who had better put down your weapons and surrender peacefully."

Athena laughed. "And why, pray tell, is that?"

One of her guards reached up and touched his ear gently, a frown forming on his handsome face. After a few moments, he leaned close and whispered into her ear. She looked away from Saul for a moment and conferred with her subordinate. It was Saul's turn to smile.

"Our escort, the *Potemkin* – a full battleship, I might add – is coming within range of your vessel now and has been ordered to lock all weapons on your ship. Have your soldiers stand down and surrender peacefully or they will open fire."

Athena smiled sweetly. "Well played, human, but we did not come alone." She touched her wrist and waited.

A minute passed and nothing happened. The Gener's perfect mask slipped a little, displaying the all too human emotion of uncertainty and traces of fear. She touched her wrist again, frowning, her soldiers by her side growing restless. Another minute passed.

"Expecting company?" Saul asked, breaking the uncomfortable silence.

"Yes," Athena admitted.

"I think they're being held up."

"It would appear so."

"Attention Gener vessel," a voice came over the comm, loud and commanding. "This is Captain Mai-ling Hikia of the ERV *Potemkin*. Stand down or you will be fired upon."

"*Potemkin*, I have three Coalition ships en route to take the war criminal Saul Derring into custody," Athena replied, anger tinting her voice. "I would suggest obeying Coalition law and leave this situation to us."

"Three, huh?" the captain replied. "I don't think they're going to be making much of an appearance. At least, they're not going to be much of a threat to us."

"Human arrogance in the face of impending death," Athena said. "How charming.

"It's not arrogance, so much as certainty," Hikia said. "I think you'll find their charred hulls about thirteen thousand kilometers from your position."

Athena's head whipped around. "What?"

"I believe that you've overplayed you hand, Athena," Saul said, his voice calm. "We no longer need the data we stole from the shipyard. We've got you."

"Only if you live," Athena purred, a smile back on her lovely face. "If you die here, all alone, no one will know what has happened."

"But then my secret is safe," Saul replied. "Either way, you don't win."

"Holy crap!" Mizi exclaimed. "Missiles! Dozens of missiles launched by the Gener ship!"

"Please tell me they're targeting someone other than us?" Hunter asked, taking his eyes off Athena.

"The *Potemkin*," Mizi answered after a moment. "The Gener ship just broke off their airlock with us and is closing on the *Potemkin*. A small scout ship against a battleship? What are they, suicidal?"

"No," Saul answered. "They're determined to win."

*****

Captain Hikia killed the commlink and began to cough, a wet, hacking sound, which emanated from deep within her chest. She held the handkerchief over her mouth to catch the blood and prevent a mess. She finished and wiped the corner of her mouth, her eyes yellow and raw. Her skin was just as yellow, jaundiced as the radiation continued to ravage her body. She felt weak, drained. The authoritative voice she had projected had taken a lot out of her.

"Khandry?" Hikia called out weakly as she scanned her bridge. The majority of her crew were gone, too sick to continue. Hikia had let them leave the bridge when it became obvious that they did not want to die in front of their comrades to make it easier for the corpsmen to remove their bodies from their bunks than their duty stations. Only five people remained on the bridge of the *Potemkin* now – Hikia, Khandry, two sensor techs, and one lowly weapons apprentice on his first cruise.

Khandry had taken over at tactical while still running her own sensor platform. She began to draw up targeting solutions, her hands shaking. The intense radiation, which had defeated their shielding two hours before, had pummeled her body mercilessly and caused many of her organs to falter and fail. Her skin, once flawless, was now splotchy with dark lesions. She was mildly glad that her sense of smell was completely destroyed, though, since everyone still on the bridge had voided their pants repeatedly as the radiation continued to assault each and every one of them.

"Multiple tracks, Captain," Khandry managed to gasp after a few dry swallows. "ECMs are up and running."

"Launching our birds now, captain," the weapons apprentice announced tiredly.

"Thank you, Buckley," Hikia said. "Launch everything...

everything we have."

A beam from the small Gener craft cut through the hull of the ship, the energy weapon drilling a perfect hole near the berthing areas, which were filled with men and women who had already succumbed to the radiation. Their corpses were tossed about, burned beyond recognition and sucked out into space. No damage control team came to seal the hole. There was none to be had.

Hikia watched as Buckley launched the last of their missiles before slumping over his console, dead on his feet. Hikia sighed, and with effort, transferred the weapons control to her command chair. She wished she could move Buckley off the bridge and put him somewhere more dignified, but she wasn't sure she could even stand. She carefully tracked the small Gener craft as it drew closer, her older targeting systems tracking the vessel better than she could have hoped. She fired and saw the Gener craft dart away, oxygen spewing from the wounded craft. She grinned.

"Good shot, ma'am," Khandry whispered. She leaned heavily on her console and tried to update the tactical solution. After a few bungled attempts, she finally managed. She glanced over at the sensor techs, but both of them had died sometime during the exchange of fire. She transferred control of the sensor consoles to her own station and hoped that she would stay alive long enough to help keep the *Potemkin* in the fight.

More blasts rocked the ship. Khandry looked over at the captain, who was slouched down in her chair. Khandry felt her own focus slipping as a fresh wave of nausea ripped through her. She leaned over, as far away from her console as she could manage without leaving her station, and threw up. Blood and bile splashed upon the steel deck. She wiped the back of her mouth with her sleeve and spit, trying to clear the bad taste.

"Captain, fuel cells are ruptured," Khandry reported as she struggled to read the numbers through her cloudy vision. "Structural integrity failing on decks five, six, nine and ten. Spine is cracked, ma'am."

Hikia nodded. "Putting the weapons system up on auto-fire. As long as we've got missiles, we'll keep shooting."

"Even... even when we're gone?" Khandry asked.

"That's correct, Lieutenant."

"Good."

Hikia watched as the *Potemkin* continued to battle, taking hit after hit from the smaller Gener craft as she continued to cycle her missiles through. Her superior toughness overmatched the smaller vessel, but the Gener's superior beam weaponry leveled the field. Hikia's eyes drifted to Khandry's console, where she saw the young lieutenant slumped over her station, painfully and obviously dead. She leaned back and closed her eyes, oblivious to the alarms around her as the ship continued to take a beating.

"Just hold together, old girl," Hikia whispered as she drifted away into the darkness. "Just hold together a little bit longer."

*****

"That," Hunter whistled, impressed, as everyone on the bridge of the *Caliban* stood and watched the intense fight between the Gener vessel and the older Republic battleship. "That is one tough old girl."

"Why must you humans always stay so stubbornly stupid and fail to admit when you are beaten?" Athena asked.

Saul lashed out with the heel of his boot, catching one of the Gener guards squarely in the chest. A sickening *crunch* filled the bridge as Saul's foot shattered the breastbone of the delicate Gener. Saul pivoted and kicked the falling Gener a second time, driving the tip of his boot into the temple of the guard.

The rest of the crew of the *Caliban* was slow to react to Saul's sudden and violent maneuver. Gunter moved first, her hand flying towards Athena. The Gener, however, was far faster than the woman was and blocked her attack easily. She twisted Gunter's arm, breaking it at the elbow, and pushed her away. Gunter cried out and cradled her injured arm. Athena whipped her pistol out of its holster in one smooth, easy motion and shot Gunter in the chest. Two more shots and Gunter fell, her mouth open in surprise and pain as she dropped to the floor, dead.

The other Gener male tried to bring his firearm up but Zombie stepped in front of him. Rounds spat from the end of the barrel of the Gener weapon, punching into Zombie. The massive operative grunted and soaked up the fire as his right hand wrapped around the delicate throat of the Gener. He lifted him and slammed the Gener into the bulkhead. Stunned, the Gener released his grip on the gun. Zombie twisted him and grabbed him with his other hand, then slammed him violently down onto his knee. The Gener's spine snapped cleanly upon impact and the male gasped. Zombie pushed him off his knee and slowly rose, his eyes tracking Athena. Saul was already moving, though.

Athena was quick, faster than the human eye could track; a blur in her movements as her lithe form danced away from them. She struck at Saul, who she had deemed to be the biggest threat, and found his arm blocking her blow. She frowned and lashed out, the points of her fingertips thrusting at his exposed and vulnerable throat. Saul countered and snuck a strike in on her solar plexus. She gasped. Her nails raked across his cheek, drawing thin scratches, but he ignored it as he drove his foot into her knee. She cried out in real pain as Saul pressed his advantage, thrusting his forearm into her throat. She gagged as he struck her again, slamming her into the bulkhead. Before she could react any further, Saul had moved close, his own movements as fast as hers were.

The entire sequence between Saul and Athena had taken less than two seconds. Nobody on the bridge had been able to track their movements during their brief but violent fight.

"How?" Athena hissed, her eyes wide in fear and confusion. Saul's face was grim.

"The Order knew that the Geners were tampering with God's plan," Saul explained. Athena struggled but his superior strength kept her at bay. "Devils, disguised as angelic helpers, corrupting the souls of humanity. The Order believed that to combat that sort of evil, a new warrior of God must arise. Barring the second coming, there was only one way to level the playing field."

"You..."

"Genetic manipulation is illegal and a crime against God," Saul continued, his eyes cold and hard as they bored into Athena's. "But the Order believed that one exception to the rule, one case, could be allowed. They tested many men and women, trying to find the most compatible. In the end, they found me. They rescued me, gave me purpose. They gave me... life."

"I don't..." Athena hissed as Saul applied more pressure to her delicate throat.

"They called me the Hand of God," Saul whispered in her ear as he leaned closer. "I was created to smite the usurpers of the Word. But who would try to usurp the Word? Not the Republic or Coalition, nor the Darians or Ra'tids. Can you guess, Gener, who the Order considered the usurpers of the Lord our God to be?" Saul slowly shook his head. "No, I don't think you do. Your arrogance blinds you. O Lord, the God who avenges. Shine forth."

He crushed her windpipe with his forearm and kept her pinned against the bulkhead, his eyes fixated on hers, his other hand holding her lithe frame up. She gasped and tried to draw in a breath but was blocked. Her face, once the picture of perfection became splotchy, as oxygen was unable to reach her brain. Saul continued to apply pressure. He could feel her pulse frantically beating through his paper-thin skin as panic and desperation set in. He stared deep into her eyes, as she died, unblinking.

"Seal the bridge!" Hunter ordered, breaking the silence, which had suddenly descended upon them. "Alves, get us in position to help the *Potemkin*. Saul? What do we do about the Geners in back with your troops?"

Saul released the corpse of the Gener and she fell heavily to the deck. He thought about what to do with the remaining Geners on board for a brief moment before deciding. "Give me the comms."

"Go," Hunter said and pressed a button.

"Attention, Gener soldiers on the ship," Saul announced. "Your Athena is dead. Your guard up here are dead. Your ship has abandoned you. You have nothing left but your lives. I do not wish to take them. Throw down your weapons and surrender before we are forced to kill you as well."

"You're just going to let them go?" Mizi hissed angrily.

"They're probably just lowly Achilles," Saul replied. "Maybe Hectors. They are warriors but not the brightest. They follow orders. Without orders, they do nothing."

"Still," Mizi sniffed. "They killed Gunter!"

"No," Saul shook his head and nudged the dead Athena at his feet. "*She* killed Gunter."

"Uh, not being one to interrupt," Alves called out. "But this is all assuming that we can kill that damned Gener ship. We don't do that, doesn't matter who killed who."

"Right," Hunter nodded and slid into his command chair. "Let's show them just what the *Caliban* is capable of. Open fire!"

Gunfire erupted from the mounts above and below the cockpit, the solid plasma rounds cutting through the Gener ship from behind. The *Caliban* shifted fire, driving the rounds up and through the command nodule of the Gener ship. The Gener ship tried to turn and fire against the new threat, but with her shielding already damaged from the massive wave of missiles that the *Potemkin* had tossed out at her, the combined firepower of the *Caliban* and the *Potemkin* was simply too much and the hull of the Gener ship buckled. Muted flashed erupted near the aft of the ship and the lights dimmed. Moments later, the ship went fully dark as the engines sputtered and died. The ship began to cartwheel slowly in space, no longer under control as it drifted further away from the *Caliban*.

The men and women on the bridge of the *Caliban* remained silent as power returned to their Void drive. Alves laid in a new course for the Weligo Terminus without being told and the *Caliban* began to move through space, the engines pulsing as it prepared to shift into the Void. Everyone else stared at the *Potemkin*. The sensors showed that there was not a single person alive on the ship.

"Saul?" Hunter asked, breaking the silence on the bridge.

"Yes, Hunter?"

"You going to explain why she kept accusing you of genocide?"

"No."

Hunter grunted. "Fair enough."

"What about the *Potemkin*?" Mizi asked.

"Leave her be," Saul suggested. "The Navy will come for her when they're ready. She'll get a proper burial, and that captain will get full honors."

"Hitting Void space now," Alves stated. The *Caliban* twisted into Void space and was gone.

Chapter Eleven

Ambassador Xarn slowly strolled into the meeting room, the long folds of his robes concealing his hands, which were clasped together in front of him. He looked around, saw the open chairs, and let his ears twitch in acknowledgment of the new reality. He was not very troubled by the recent turn of events. In fact, he was certain that the Emperor was extremely pleased, and Xarn's duty was to make his Emperor's desires known to all. It was his duty, after all.

The Ra'tid ambassador had been recalled back to Ra Prime following the destruction of their home world. After the combined attack by the Republic and Darian Empire, the Ra'tid ambassador had been the remaining senior official in their convoluted hierarchy. He was back home now, struggling to put together an interim government and fighting to keep his species alive. Xarn did not envy him the troubles that he would face. The Ra'tids were a broken race now, no longer a threat nor deserving of a seat at the council table.

His eyes slid over to the next vacant chair, where the Gener ambassador had once sat. Their claims of neutrality were gone now, their allegiance clear for all to see. Xarn did not understand why the angelic beings would skip the council meeting, however. He guessed that they were afraid of showing themselves on Earth now that their complicity with the Coalition and Ra'tids was in the open. They would no longer be able to hide in the shadows and be the puppet masters. It was open warfare now, and Xarn was convinced that this terrified the Gener race as a whole.

Only the newly appointed Republic ambassador, a man named Tim Kelsey, and the new Coalition representative were in the room with him. While Kelsey was in a simple business suit with a small decorative flag of the Republic pinned to his lapel, his Coalition counterpart was fully decked out in an admiral's Class "A" uniform, resplendent with ribbons and honors that Xarn could only guess as to their origins. *Perhaps it was before the split between the Republic and Coalition,* he mused as he nodded his head towards the Coalition's representative.

"I don't believe that we've met," Xarn said as he sat across from the Coalition representative.

"Admiral Joseph Langston," the man replied. He stank of hatred and fury. Xarn flicked his whiskers in distaste. He reviled ambassadors who could not play the game, refused to obey the rules of civility, even in a state of war. Honor demanded that one treat their enemy's representative as an equal, even if they weren't.

"Gentlemen," Kelsey began, taking control of the room. "As you can see, the Geners have elected to recall their ambassador and are no longer participating in these meetings. Am I to assume then, Admiral, that you represent them as well?"

"The Gener race are a free people. If they choose not to send a representative to these meetings of the council, then that is their right. They are our allies, not our slaves, and are in search of justice."

"I... see," Kelsey glanced over at Xarn. "And as we all know, the Ra'tids, being in such disarray following the destruction of their home world and the continuation of their species threatened, no longer have a place in these meetings. As thus, we three are all that remain. You called for this meeting, Admiral Langston, so I shall pass the floor to you." Kelsey nodded at the Admiral and took his own seat next to Xarn.

"The Coalition of Outer Planets strongly condemns the Republic's genocidal attack upon the Ra'tid people, and such an act cannot be ignored, in the name of justice. The survivors of the Ra'tid race have asked for the protection of the Coalition against future attacks upon their fragile system, and it has been granted," the Admiral locked eyes with Xarn and smirked. "All Darian incursions into Ra'tid space must stop at once, or face the dire consequences."

Xarn chuckled, a human habit he had picked up during his long stay on Earth as ambassador. "Incursions? Is that what you call them? My people are merely reclaiming systems that the Ra'tids stole from us during the cease-fire talks during our second war, in clear violation of interstellar law."

"Who's law?" Admiral Langston challenged him. "The Republic's law, which derives from oppression and control of any and all?"

"The interstellar law Ambassador Xarn refers to is the same one that was established by the council meetings, such as this meeting, which began long before the Coalition broke away from Earth," Kelsey reminded him.

"The Coalition no longer recognizes the repressive laws of the Republic. No formal declaration of war has been issued against the Darian Empire yet, Ambassador Xarn, despite you aiding the Republic during the Battle of Earth. In a fit of generosity and in the spirit of peace, the Coalition offers your people a chance at neutrality and asks that you stay out of the Coalition and Republic conflict. This is our last offer."

"What a charming way with words you have, Admiral. You will forgive me if I reject your somewhat callous and pathetic attempt at both threatening my Emperor and asking Him to join your side." Xarn showed his teeth in a silent hiss, ears flattened back against his head.

"As for you, Ambassador Kelsey," the admiral turned back to the younger man. "The Coalition hereby demands the Republic's immediate and unconditional surrender. Failure to do so will result in your complete and utter destruction."

"He knows about your new armada, Admiral," Xarn interjected, his tone calm once more.

"And how do you know this, cat?" Langston asked, his lips in a tight smile.

"Because I told him of it," Xarn shrugged. "Allies share information, Admiral."

"You know what we will do to your people next, cat?"

Langston spat out the insulting moniker.

Xarn leaned forward across the table and revealed his claws for the first time during the meeting. "Come what may, the Darians *will* stand or fall at the Republic's side. Send your new armada if you must, and we will meet it with tooth and claw." Xarn extended his claws out fully, the seven centimeter sheathed daggers exposed for all to see. "Tooth and claw, Admiral."

Ambassador Kelsey appeared to be relieved by Xarn's words. With each passing day, the losses on the front lines added up for the Republic, while the Coalition only seemed to grow stronger. With the Geners tossing their hat into the ring, and the remaining Ra'tids offering their full support, it would take a miracle for the Republic to hold onto their core worlds once the Coalition decided to attack a final time. The Coalition's last all-out assault had taken Earth to the very brink of defeat, and the subsequent battle to drive the Coalition from the surface and from the space around had cost more lives than any battle in the history of modern space warfare.

The Emperor had made it very clear to Xarn, however, that he was in no way cowed by the Coalition's demands or threats. From a Darian standpoint, it was better to die on one's feet, claws ready to fight, than to roll over at the feet of a tyrannical master. The Coalition treated the other races as lesser beings, unequal in their pursuit of justice.

Xarn silently scoffed at their use of the word. His primary concern at the moment, however, was just how they had brought the arrogant and self-serving Geners onto their side in the war. Possibilities came to mind, each one being a more disturbing possibility than the last. His people would die, down to the smallest infant, before giving up their independence and culture to the Coalition. His ears perked up as Kelsey's voice dragged him out of his thoughts and back to the meeting at hand.

"You know that the Republic will never surrender to the Coalition, Admiral. If you only came here to demand our surrender, you have wasted your time," Kelsey stared at Langston coldly as he spoke.

"The death of millions of innocents be on your head, then," Admiral Langston said. "You've had your chances. Do not expect mercy the next time we meet, Ambassador Kelsey, while your beloved President Ryan is kneeling before a firing squad of Coalition shock troops." The Admiral stood and stalked from the room, leaving Kelsey and Xarn alone.

"Thank you," Kelsey exhaled as soon as the admiral was gone. "The Republic is blessed to have allies such as you and your people."

Xarn grunted. "I suggest we depart now to put all our affairs in order. His threat will become a reality all too soon, I fear." Xarn stood and started for the door. He paused when he reach it, looking back at Kelsey. "It has been my honor to meet you, Ambassador Kelsey. When the Coalition comes, may our deaths be valiant, and our sacrifices be sung by the children we give our lives to protect."

*****

The massive Coalition armada rested in space, beyond the edge of Republic borders. Thousands upon thousands of ships stretched out in battle formation, billions of miles wide as they awaited the command. Among the vast number of coalition vessels were scattered Gener warcrafts, and a few of the surviving Ra'tid destroyers and battleships moved between them. It was the largest fleet ever assembled by far.

Admiral Langston emerged from the lift, walking onto expansive bridge of the *Scythe*. The *Scythe* was larger than a super dreadnaught, the biggest ship ever created. It was to be the first of its class, nearly the size of a small moon. The bridge was open and wide, bustling with activity as Coalition personnel moved about with resolute purpose. Beyond that, near the rear of the bridge, a massive throne rested. Around it, a web of black energy pulsed and throbbed in rhythm to the ship's propulsion system.

Atop the massive throne sat the Lord of the Coalition. Langston could feel his master's ancient eyes upon him, judging him. Sweat beaded on his skin as his heart quailed under the old man's knowing gaze. He stopped and knelt, head bowed. He waited long moments before his master began to speak.

"They refused, did they not?" the Lord of the Coalition asked, his voice soft. The full weight of power behind it, though, remained in check. For now. Langston swallowed nervously and nodded.

"Yes, milord. They did, as you said they would," Langston replied.

The old man laughed gently. "Such blinded fools. It matters not, though. Soon, they will learn their place. Prepare the fleet for transit, Admiral."

"As you command, Lord Hades," Langston bowed slight before he headed towards the center of the bridge. The *Scythe's* command chair awaited him there. He sat down and surveyed the bridge. There was much to do, and so little time to do it.

*****

It was quiet in the bar. Not many patrons frequented the business during midday hours, something that Willy was none too pleased about. He finished wiping down the old oak countertop for the third time in the hour and sighed. While he made enough money at night to keep his little dive open, he still longed for the days when regulars came in and chatted him up during the day, perhaps having the *con carne chile especiale*, enjoying one another's company over a cold draft of beer. He never thought that he would be lonely, not as a mildly successful businessman.

He heard footsteps near the door. He glanced up and could barely contain his surprise as a ghost walked through the door.

"Hey Willy," Saul greeted the bartender as he took a stool at the counter. "Got that beer you set aside for me?"

For a moment, the old bartender was stunned into silence. He slowly grinned and reached beneath the counter and opened a small cooler. He withdrew two bottles of beer and passed them over to Saul. He then grabbed a third from beneath the counter for himself.

"Of course," Willy said. "I knew you'd be coming back, sooner or later."

"That makes one of us," Saul admitted as he popped the top of the beverage. He took a long pull and sighed appreciatively.

"Where you been, Saul?"

"Around."

"Ah."

"You know what, Willy?"

"What's that, Saul?"

"There are some things that make returning home a wonderful thought," Saul said, his mind drifting back to the memorial service he had attended two months before. The full honors rendered for Specialist Gunter and Sergeant Ling had moved him, and while the mission they had died on was classified, every single human and Darian in attendance knew what had transpired. There had been no tears, only somber reflection. He shook off the thoughts and continued. "Then there are men like me. Men who just want to escape from what is familiar to chase that elusive quest for inner peace."

"Hock, boy," Willy grunted. "Inner peace is only what you make it to be."

"True," Saul allowed. He glanced at the beer in hand. "I just wanted a drink, Willy. Is that so hard to believe?"

The two men drank silently, and for one brief instance, all was right in the universe.

www.ingramcontent.com/pod-product-compliance
Lightning Source LLC
Chambersburg PA
CBHW031340170626
46807CB00002B/777